Tim Pratt

THE ALIEN STARS

And Other Novellas

ANGRY ROBOT
An imprint of Watkins Media Ltd

Unit 11, Shepperton House
89-93 Shepperton Road
London N1 3DF
UK

angryrobotbooks.com
twitter.com/angryrobotbooks
It's never over...

An Angry Robot paperback original, 2021

Cover by Tithi Luadthong
Interior Illustrations by Aislinn Quicksilver Harvey

Set in Meridien

ISBN 978 0 85766 9285
Ebook ISBN 978 0 85766 9292

Printed and bound in the United Kingdom by TJ Books Limited

9 8 7 6 5 4 3 2 1

PRAISE FOR TIM PRATT

"Fun, funny, pacy, thought-provoking and very clever space opera – a breath of fresh air."

Sean Williams, author of *Twinmaker*

"The engaging, inclusive, and entertaining Axiom series, may be his best work yet... witty, heartfelt sci-fi romp."

Tor.com

"Pratt's thoughtful worldbuilding, revealed little by little, continues to impress... This well-imagined universe, populated by original and empathetic characters, has enough energy to power what could become a long-lived series."

Publishers Weekly

"Brilliantly fun space opera that reminds me of *Killjoys* but with more Weird Alien Cool Shit."

Locus

"A really good read that was intelligently written and skilfully put together."

Two Bald Mages

"Expansive world building, great movement coupled with interesting characterization and a story line that is not only intriguing but brings back the grand spacefaring odyssey."

Koeur's Book Reviews

BY THE SAME AUTHOR

THE AXIOM SERIES

The Axiom

The Wrong Stars

The Dreaming Stars

The Strange Adventures of Rangergirl

Briarpatch

Heirs of Grace

The Deep Woods

Blood Engines

Poison Sleep

Dead Reign

Spell Games

Bone Shop

Broken Mirrors

Grim Tides

Bride of Death

Lady of Misrule

Queen of Nothing

Closing Doors

For Elsa,
a saint of the Church of the Ecstatic Divine

INTRODUCTION

From 2017 to 2019 I published three space opera novels: *The Wrong Stars*, *The Dreaming Stars*, and *The Forbidden Stars*, about a group of humans and aliens on a ship called the *White Raven* who fight against an ancient, malevolent galactic menace known as the Axiom. People liked the series! The first book was a Philip K. Dick Award finalist, and the other two were received enthusiastically by critics and readers. The general consensus seems to be that I wrapped up the trilogy pretty well, and I was happy with the shape of the series, too.

But I didn't feel quite *done*. Each of those novels loosely focused on a particular member or members of the *White Raven*'s crew: the first was about the captain, Callie, and her love interest, Elena, who was fresh from centuries of cryo-sleep; the second delved into the character of the ship's XO and doctor, Stephen, nearly perpetual pessimist and member of the Church of the Ecstatic Divine; and the last explored the origins of the pilot-and-navigator odd-couple of Drake and Janice.

I enjoyed organizing the books that way, but the thing is, there were a few characters who never got sufficient time in the spotlight over the course of the trilogy: specifically, the ship's guiding artificial intelligence, Shall; the intrepid and adorable alien truth-teller Lantern; and the cyborg "radical self-improvement" advocate Ashok, who stole every scene he ever appeared in. I was sad about that.

This collection is the solution to my sadness: three novellas, each focusing on one of those unjustly neglected supporting characters. (Captain Callie Machedo, who dominated the trilogy, doesn't even appear in these stories, though of course she's mentioned; she has a way of taking over any story you let her wander into, you see.) "The Augmented Stars" sees Ashok as the captain of his own ship, going on a deep-space mission and encountering assorted disasters. In "The Artificial Stars", Shall receives a mysterious summons and investigates a threat to the universe itself (with the assistance of scientist Uzoma, who also didn't get enough time on stage in the trilogy). And finally, in "The Alien Stars," Lantern confronts a monstrous threat from her past… and works out some matters of the heart (or hearts; she has several) in the process.

I loved writing these, and spending time with the characters again. I'm thrilled I can give you a sense of how everything worked out for the characters after the trilogy ended, too. I hope you enjoy this time in the stars.

Tim Pratt
Berkeley CA
October 2020

THE AUGMENTED STARS

*

Delilah Mears settled into the pod in the Hypnos parlor on New Meditreme. The pod closed over her, and she underwent a moment of swirling disorientation before opening her eyes in a cluttered machine shop that smelled of hot metal and solvents.

This was supposed to be a job interview, but the interviewer wasn't in evidence. "Hello?" she called. No response. Well, she was a couple of minutes early. She hadn't wanted to risk being late. She didn't really *need* this job, not this one in particular… but she wanted it. Doing the interview in a simulation was a little strange, since she'd already come all the way out to Trans-Neptunian space anyway, but maybe the captain was busy preparing for the voyage and this was easier to schedule.

Delilah paced back and forth beside a table cluttered with hand tools, snips of wire, shiny gear wheels, circuit boards, and weird stuff like faintly shining blue crystals and palm-sized cubes of greasy black material. Pegboards on the walls held more tools, coils of cord, and protective equipment. The lights overhead were long strips of steady whiteness, illuminating the space as thoroughly as an operating theater.

She leaned closer to the table and grunted – she could see the wood grain in the top, and when she ran her thumb across the surface, the tiny irregularities and indentations felt completely real. This simulation was far more realistic than the low-res headsets-and-gloves stuff she'd used for training in engineering school;

she'd never been much for recreational interactive immersives, but she hadn't realized they'd come *this* far.

"Pretty nice, huh?"

Delilah looked up into the face – if you could call it that – of a cyborg. Instead of eyes he had complex clusters of lenses, and very little flesh showed through a mask of copper-colored metal, though he had a human smile and chin. He held up his hands– "Didn't mean to startle you" – and one of his arms was artificial too, encased in translucent crystal, gears and pistons visible underneath the casing.

"Dr. Ranganathan?" She looked down at her own avatar, which was just a simple scan of her real body taken when she stepped through the door of the Hypnos parlor, dressed in a plain gray jumpsuit. "I feel underdressed." She knew people sometimes appeared in fanciful avatars, elves and pirates and dragons, but she hadn't expected something like that from a ship's captain in a job interview.

"Call me Ashok. You mean the cyborg thing? Huh. I was about to argue, because this avatar is based on a scan of my body, but to be fair it's a few years out of date, and it's true – I don't look like this anymore."

Delilah blushed and wondered if her avatar would do so too; how responsive *was* this technology? "Oh, I'm sorry, I didn't know you were, ah…"

"Augmented? No problem. You're from Earth, right? New on New Meditreme?"

"Isn't everyone new here?" New Meditreme station had been built only a few years ago, and parts of it were still under construction. She'd walked here through corridors that still smelled of offgassing polymers. The original Meditreme Station had been destroyed in what was either a terrible accident or a more terrible terrorist attack – accounts varied – with all 50,000 of its residents killed. The tiny corporate polity known as the Trans-Neptunian Alliance had nearly perished with its capital, but the TNA had since been reconstituted. Their first order of business was building a new city-station named in honor of the lost one, and they once again ruled inhabited space on the fringes of the solar system. The new TNA had developed a reputation for innovation; they had impressive proprietary tech, and their president was supposedly an artificial intelligence, though back home everyone thought that was a publicity gimmick, and assumed the organization was secretly run by a human board of directors. The TNA's reputation for daring drew the ambitious, the impatient, and the innovative from all over the inhabited galaxy, and Delilah considered herself all three.

"Oh, some of us are newer here than others," Ashok said. "I used to call the *old* Meditreme Station home."

Wow – he must have been one of the few residents who'd been off station when the place exploded. "I'm so sorry. I didn't mean to be insensitive."

His eye lenses spun, and after a moment, he chuckled. "Don't worry about it. I wasn't hurt. My friends tell me I can be insensitive occasionally myself, and even with all my upgrades, I don't always realize it." His lenses shifted again, one lighting up with a golden glow. "So. I've got your résumé here, and you're totally qualified to be my ship's engineer. You went to Mumbai Tech! I got waitlisted there and ended up at Lunar University."

"That's a good school," Delilah said, and it was; it was just that Mumbai Tech was a great school.

"I've got no complaints, but practical experience was my real teacher. You can do simulations all day, but repairing a breached reactor in an immersive isn't the same as doing it in space where, if you mess up, everybody dies, and you die *first*."

"I know I don't have much actual work experience but–"

He shook his armored head. "Oh, whoa, no, wait, that came out wrong. I don't mean, like, 'don't come in here with your fancy book learning.' I mean, you're more qualified than I was when *I* started out, and I ended up being a pretty good engineer, so once you log some time in space, you're going to be better than I ever was, I bet. I am kind of wondering, though... why come all the way out to the edge of the galaxy and try out for a spot on a ship heading to deep space? With your qualifications you could get a job that pays more and is less likely to, uh, well, end up with you irradiated or exposed to vacuum or worse things."

Delilah considered how to answer, and decided honesty was best. "I came out here because I grew up on Earth, and my whole life has been spent learning the skills necessary to get me out of the gravity well and into the unknown. I love engineering, obviously – I'm at my happiest tinkering around inside a ship – but for me, that study was all a means to an end."

"What end?"

"Just… going as far as I can. I turned down jobs on Earth, Mars, and Luna, and I was actually on Ganymede, doing interviews with a few different Jovian Imperative companies, when I saw your listing on the Tangle." She had, in fact, been offered a cushy job on Ganymede, but if this worked out…

"I can't pay as well as the Almajara Corporation can," Ashok said. "I've got a ship, and it's in good shape, but my budget is… basically what I got for this." He knocked on the work table.

"For… what?"

"This tactile texture thing. Feel how real the wood seems? I did that."

"Oh! I didn't know you did software design."

"Me neither. I was always a hardware guy, but for personal reasons, I took an interest in simulation technology a couple years ago, and figured out how to improve tactile detail. My friend Callie said I should have licensed the tech, not sold it outright, but then people would be bugging me to do updates and stuff, and – well, it's like you said. The software was a means to an end. I wanted seed money for deep space explorations, and I got some, but I'm not rolling in lix, and you won't be fixing the light bulbs on a luxury liner if you sign up with me. It's going to be real nuts and bolts and radiation and hard vacuum stuff."

"I understand."

He grinned, which was disconcerting, but also charming. "So you'll take the job?"

"Does that mean I *have* the job?"

"You had the job as soon as you told me why you wanted it. A one-year contract to start, but the penalties if you break it aren't substantial, as long as you don't try to leave during, like, a critical drive failure."

"That works for me."

"Nice. You know, I came out here to Trans-Neptunian space for all the same reasons you did. I wanted to know: what's on the other side of the far side of everything?" His lenses both glowed gold now. "Why don't we go and find out?"

"It feels so *real*." Delilah bounced on the balls of her feet as they walked down the corridor toward their dock.

Her new crewmate – she was on a crew! – looked at her curiously. Winslow had dark skin that contrasted with a fuzz of bright yellow hair and shining blue eyes, and he wore a black jumpsuit that covered every bit of his skin up to the chin. "What does?"

"The gravity!"

Winslow chuckled. He was her new ship's doctor and first officer, and thus technically her superior, but over the course of get-to-know-you drinks at the New Spinward Lounge he'd proven himself informal and affable. They both dragged rolling suitcases behind them. "I did hear artificial gravity is still pretty rare on the other side of the asteroid belt."

Delilah nodded. "Back home they're trying to reverse engineer the tech, but nobody's managed it quite yet, as far as I know." She was itching to get a look at one of the gravity generators herself.

"It's all going open source in five more years," Winslow said. "The TNA is only keeping the tech proprietary long enough to stabilize themselves financially. Rebuilding a nation from ashes is tough." Winslow cocked his head at her. "Our boss invented it, you know."

Delilah looked at him blankly. "He… invented what?"

"Artificial gravity. Well, he *discovered* it, technically – it's ancient alien tech – but Ashok is the one who figured out how to crack open the alien black box and replicate the effects."

"That's… but… why isn't he a trillionaire? He said he was funding this expedition with money from simulation software!"

Winslow nodded. "He's very close with Kalea Machedo and President Shall – he used to be on a crew with them – and he donated his work on artificial gravity to the TNA. He refused all proceeds, and insisted his rightful share be poured back into infrastructure. He won't even let them put his name on any buildings."

Delilah whistled. "Modest guy."

"Not exactly," Winslow said. "It's just… he doesn't care about that stuff. He told his friends they should name buildings after people who care. Money doesn't interest him, either, as long as he has enough to fund things like this expedition. Which, incidentally, the TNA offered to cover, but he said, no, he didn't want to dip into their funds. To him, making money is just another engineering problem. He sketched out how much he needed, did enough work to cover it, and moved on to the next problem."

They reached airlock NMS-18, and Winslow put his eye to a scanner. The door unsealed and they stepped in. "You've known the captain for a long time?" Delilah asked.

"Not really. We spent some time on the same station a while back, and when he started putting a crew together, he thought of me."

They waited a moment for the airlock to match pressure, and then, there it was: the door to the *Golden Spider*, which would be her home for the next few months (or her grave, if things went bad, but they *wouldn't*). They entered through the cargo bay, which was mostly empty, though the walls were lined with supply crates, and she noticed one box that was three meters to a side and held together with fist-sized bolts.

A Liar dropped from above and landed in front of them. The small squidlike alien – the size of a human toddler at most – wore a bright orange suit and had around half a dozen pseudopods, a few holding tools. Its head – which was more of a domelike bulge from its central body – had just a single pair of forward-facing eyes, an unusual configuration in Delilah's admittedly limited experience; Liars usually had lots of eyes scattered all around their heads.

"This is Crowbar," Winslow said. "He's our communications tech and backup pilot. Crow, this is Delilah Mears, our engineer."

"You are shorter than average for a human," the Liar said, a melodious tenor emerging from his artificial voicebox.

"I keep hearing that," Delilah said. "I grew up on Earth, though. The gravity keeps us from stretching out too much."

"My own comparatively small stature does not inhibit my ability to function with excellence," Crowbar said. "Though I have the advantage of more appendages. Have you considered adding some augmentations to your basic form?"

"Okay, Crow," Winslow said. "How about we let Dr. Mears get settled before we interrogate her life choices?"

"You emphasized her title as a subtle rebuke," Crowbar said. "To encourage me to be more respectful. But I have no inherent respect for the standards of higher education in human cultures, so my opinion cannot be shaped by such signifiers. I will form an opinion of Dr. Mears based on direct observation. I will share my determinations once I have gathered more data. I am going to check the aft communications array now." Crowbar scuttled off and disappeared behind a crate.

"He was… very direct," Delilah said.

"Have you spent much time with the Free?"

That's right–"the Free" was what Liars called themselves *among* themselves. At least sometimes. At least some of them. The aliens were hard to generalize about. "Not really. There are only a few of them on Earth."

"As a rule they aren't fond of gravity wells. They like to leave their exit options open. I've known… many of the Free. They're just like people. Some are wonderful, some are awful, and most are a little bit between. Crow comes from a group, or a tribe, whatever, called the truth-tellers. They hate deception, and always tell the truth as they see if. For some truth-tellers, that comes across as refreshing frankness. For others, it's more like rudeness."

"A Liar who tells the truth?" Everyone knew Liars were fundamentally untrustworthy – as a species they were pathological liars, spinning an outlandish array of stories about everything from the mundane to the cosmic. Every group had its own version of reported reality, and none of them were consistent with the others.

"The Free," Winslow said, and this time Delilah noticed the tone of subtle rebuke. "You get used to it. Crow is really… sort of an intern. One of the captain's old friends is a member of the Free from the same sect, and she asked him to give Crowbar some work experience. The captain will be doing most of the actual piloting."

"Do you know where we're going?" Delilah said. "The job listing just said 'long-range research mission.'"

"I'll let the captain tell you about that," Winslow said. "We have an all-hands meeting in three hours. I'll show you to your cabin and you can rest or wander around the ship in the meantime."

The ship was an odd mixture of state-of-the-art and… well, junk, honestly. One of Delilah's uncles back home had hit the lottery and, rather than buying a new house, had chosen to renovate his falling-down old shack, shoring up crumbling foundations and tacking on new rooms and floors, when a complete tear-down would have been more advisable. The *Golden Spider* had a similar aesthetic: shiny new plates alongside patches of epoxy, scuffed corridor floors but top-of-the-line adaptive lighting overhead, old-fashioned vents with metal grates pumping in air cleaned by the finest new scrubbers. The engine room was a similar mishmash, and she shook her head over ancient exposed cooling pipes running alongside gleaming induction coils. The reactor at the heart of the

Tanzer Drive was brand new, at least, and the radiation shielding was way better than spec.

She prowled through the space at the heart of the ship, familiarizing herself with its peculiarities and trying to predict where failures might occur. She paused before a peculiar object – a greasy-looking black cube about the size of her head, stuck into an alcove cut into the wall. Was it some kind of backup power supply, or something related to the artificial gravity? She followed the cables (jammed seemingly arbitrarily into its sides) and found they were hooked into the navigation system. Some kind of emergency distress beacon maybe? What was it *made* of? Liars – no, the Free – had sophisticated material technology, but she'd never seen anything like this.

A bright yellow repair drone the size and approximate shape of a human hand crawled across the wall toward her. "Mears!" Ashok's voice emerged from the machine. "I see you've discovered my secret device of enigmatic mystery! That's why you had to sign all those non-disclosure agreements, you know. This little thing has been my project for the past few years – it's a fully-functional copy of a piece of alien tech my old crew found on an Axiom space station."

"The Axiom. Wow." There was a lot of debate among the people of the Inner Planets Governing Council about whether the so-called Axiom were real, or just a propaganda trick made up by the Jovian Imperative and the Trans-Neptunian Alliance. Both Delilah's mothers thought it was the latter, and that the upstart polities just wanted people to think they were special, saving the galaxy from ancient alien horrors. Delilah was reserving judgment about the whole issue. "What does it do?"

"It's a bridge generator," Ashok said. "It opens wormholes from here to… well, anywhere in the galaxy."

Delilah didn't want to say "That's impossible" to her new captain, but her heart sank, because it *was*. The bridges that linked the colony worlds together weren't generated by anything, let alone a greasy black cube. The bridges were ancient, invisible structures of unknown provenance, activated by streams of radiation pointed at a specific point in space. Those bridgeheads were usually "anchored" near large celestial objects (Jupiter, in the case of this solar system). The Liars had arrived through the Jovian bridge centuries before, and shown humanity the combinations necessary to activate them and reach the twenty-eight other systems that became human colonies. When it came to fast interstellar travel, though, those twenty-eight systems were the whole deal; if you wanted to go anywhere else, you were stuck with Tanzer drives.

Ashok saying he could create wormholes was like saying he had a star in his pocket. "Wow," Delilah said. "That's amazing."

"You don't believe me!" the chipper little bot said in her captain's voice. She wondered where he was transmitting from. "Who can blame you? Personal wormhole generators violate everything we know about physics. But then again, the fixed bridges do that, too – wormholes were predicted for a long time as theoretical objects, but when you enter a bridge, you spend twenty-one seconds in darkness before emerging on the other side, no matter how fast you're going when you enter or where you're coming out, and nobody knows why. 'Weird alien shit' is the best explanation we've got. Same as artificial gravity – it doesn't make sense, it shouldn't work, but there it is. Here's a secret: the Axiom built the bridges. We think of the known bridges as wonders of the universe, but for the Axiom, they were more like toll booths or checkpoints – ways to control where lesser beings were allowed to go. The Axiom's *own* ships were equipped with these smaller bridge generators, and they had the freedom of the galaxy."

"Winslow told me the Axiom invented the gravity generators, too, but that you figure out how to replicate them."

The bot chuckled. "A guy needs a hobby, I guess."

"Winslow also told me you refused all profit from the generators."

"Did he. Well, the TNA needed it more. And anyway, all I did was some reverse engineering. My name's on the patent, but the real inventor is probably called Gorgax the Eviscerator or something and he's been dead for ninety thousand years. We hope. The Axiom invented all *kinds* of things, and their technology was so advanced that, for them, the laws of physics were more like… gentle suggestions. "

This was all just too much. "I don't even know if I believe in the Axiom, captain," Delilah said. "You make them sound like gods, and that… doesn't help."

"Huh. This is why they call Earth the 'Show Me' planet, I guess? The Axiom aren't gods. They're more like demons, or else one of those pantheons where the gods were jealous jerks. We don't know a ton about them, but as a culture they were vicious, controlling, and murderously competitive, and that's why, even with all their tech, their empire fell apart. I welcome your skepticism, Delilah. It's a healthy quality, as long as you're capable of changing your worldview in the face of new evidence."

Delilah nodded toward the bridge generator. "You mean, like seeing that thing in action? If you can actually open a wormhole, like you said… then I'll have to revise my worldview a lot."

"Believe me," Ashok said, "it'll be good practice for the rest of the trip."

Crowbar and Winslow sat on the other side of the pitted white galley table from Delilah, arguing good-naturedly about which additional modules for the ship's Hypnos suite they should download before they moved beyond the reach of the Tangle and other communications. "We need the new update to *An Epicure's Delight,*" Winslow said, "It includes the new restaurants opened in the Vanir system, and that place on Owain where every ingredient is sourced within five klicks of the kitchen. Believe me, after a month of eating *my* cooking, you'll want the variety, even if it's all flavor and no filling."

"*Meditation Challenge Four* is a better use of our recreational budget," Crowbar said. "I have mastered *Meditation Challenge Three,* even the final stage, where one must maintain focus, breath, and calm while space pirates bombard your ship and breach your meditation chamber. The new version promises further challenges, including an invasion by eldritch horrors from beyond the back of the stars–"

"Family meeting!" Ashok crowed over the ship's PA system, startling Delilah. "I know, we aren't quite a family yet, but begin as you mean to go on, right?" Wasn't he going to join them in person? She hadn't actually seen him since – well, ever, really. Their only face-to-faceplate interaction had been in a simulation.

The captain went on. "Now, I've been a little coy about the mission parameters, but before we undock and head to the edge of the solar system, I want to tell you our destination: we're aiming for a spot halfway along the New Outer Arm, just about as far as you can get from here without actually leaving the galaxy."

Winslow whistled. "And I thought the Vanir system was off the beaten path. What's way out there, captain?"

"A mystery," Ashok said. "One we're going to crack open. Winslow and Crowbar, you both know about the Axiom-eradication missions, but it's news to Delilah, so let me fill her in: a while back, my old boss Kalea Machedo got her hands on a list of coordinates for Axiom facilities, scattered all over the galaxy. For the past several years, with the support of the Jovian Imperative military, she's been checking out those facilities, using her own bridge generator – the one I finally replicated successfully here. You're from Earth, right Mears? So you know about wasp nests?"

"I… Sure?"

"Picture Callie Machedo poking a bunch of wasp nests with a big stick and killing everything that comes out of them with fire. They've bombed a whole bunch of weird space stations and hollowed out moons, and this one asteroid they found covered in fungus, and turned them all into radioactive dust."

"You're saying they destroyed alien artifacts?" Delilah said.

"In their defense, most of the artifacts tried to destroy them first," Ashok said. "The Axiom themselves are mostly long dead, with some unpleasant exceptions, but they left lots of nasty security systems behind. A few of the locations they visited seemed harmless – there's a planet with these giant bug-like biomechanical life forms crawling around, but they don't *do* anything, so we just pop in and check on it every once in a while, in lieu of figuring out how to blow up a whole planet. A few other locations were shells, places that once held personnel or tech, but they'd been stripped, and we blew those up, too, for the sake of completion. At this point, every Axiom facility we know about has been dealt with or placed under observation… except for one. They tried to blow that one up, and they couldn't."

"Why not?" Crowbar said.

"Who knows!" Ashok said. "What happened was, they launched nuclear missiles at the thing, and the missiles exploded, or started to, and then they… stopped exploding."

"The nuclear reaction was interrupted?" Delilah said.

"Somehow! We don't know of *anything* that can stop a nuclear reaction in mid-boom. Callie and her team pulled back to a safe distance, expecting retaliation, but nothing happened. The station just sat there. We've never seen a purely defensive reaction from an Axiom facility before – usually they go full-on kill-crazy at anything that wanders close. That station is really far from inhabited space, so they just withdrew and flagged the place for further study."

"Long-range research mission," Delilah said.

"That's right!" Ashok said. "The subject of our research is: why won't it blow up, and can we change that? There are actually two missions though. Not exactly a primary-secondary thing, more like… co-primaries. They sent a miniature fleet through Callie's wormhole, but they didn't all come back. One of the Jovian Imperative scout ships went missing."

Delilah shivered. "Did the thing… station, object… do something to the ship?"

"If I had a head, I'd be shaking it right now. The *Pikeville* was nowhere near our mystery object when they lost contact. It was one of several small scout ships, each with a two-person crew, that spiraled out in a search grid. That's standard procedure, because Axiom facilities sometimes have associated objects and installations nearby, and it's good to know about them before you start poking around for wasps. The *Pikeville* lost contact with the fleet, and when the other scouts went looking for it… nothing. Now, like Shakespeare said, 'space is big,' and in theory it's easy to lose something as small as a rather small ship, but Callie did a search from the *Pikeville*'s last known position, and found traces of the radiation signature from its Tanzer drives. They followed that trail until it just… stopped. Which suggests the *Pikeville* lost its engines at some point. That *should* limit how far they could drift, but even an army – navy? – of probes dispersed in every direction didn't find any sign of them, no debris, nothing. A few of the probes disappeared, too, but you expect a certain amount of breakage, since they're not smart enough to avoid crashing into space rocks and stuff. Eventually the search petered out and everyone went home. They weren't prepared to be out that long anyway."

Delilah considered "So was the *Pikeville*… taken? Picked up by some unknown larger ship?"

"It's a possibility," Ashok said. "Though not the only one. We're supposed to keep our eyes open for either signs of the *Pikeville*, or what *happened* to the *Pikeville*. So. That's the situation. If anyone wants to hop off the ship because what I just outlined sounds like a terrible no fun very bad idea, now's the time. Otherwise, well. We're going to be real far away from anywhere soon, and at that point, there's no turning back for a while. The bridge generator takes time to recharge between uses. Callie's generator, the real original, is ready again after about seven hours, but that's one point where my version isn't so successful – the one on this ship takes just under four days before it's capable of puncturing space-time again. Axiom power sources are so efficient they might as well be perpetual motion machines, but I had to work within the limits of known physics, like some kind of cave person or an animal in a zoo."

This was a *lot* to take in, and Delilah was already feeling supersaturated with impossibilities, so when Ashok said, "What do you all think?" she had no immediate reply.

Winslow snorted right away. "You know I'm going. I figured it was some kind of Axiom shit."

"I was aware of the nature of the mission from the beginning," Crowbar said. "My kindler told me."

"Kindler?" Delilah said.

"My… parent, mentor, teacher, guardian. The one who opened my incubator and taught me the ways of the world."

"That's my friend Lantern," Ashok said. "She knew about the mission, and suggested Crowbar would be a good addition to the crew."

That wasn't quite the "he's an intern" version Winslow had told her, but maybe the truth was in between.

"What do you think, Delilah?" Ashok said. "Is all this too weird? You can still take a job at Almajara Corp. Even if they're annoyed you blew them off, I know a guy, and I could make a call, he's pretty high up, they'd treat you right."

Delilah was slowly getting the sense that Ashok was some kind of legend out here on the edge of the solar system, so she believed him. He could smooth her return to a more predictable sort of life… but he could also offer her access to a *different* sort of life, couldn't he?

She said, "If this is real… if you can really travel that far, to see things created by aliens – aliens *besides* the Free – that's the kind of opportunity I never imagined having. How can I say no?"

Ashok said, "You just put your lips together, and 'no.' But I'm glad you went yes instead. Welcome to the crew. I'll undock, and off we'll go. You can head to the observation port in a few hours, if you want to see the bridge generator in action." His comms clicked off.

"This is all real?" Delilah said to her crewmates. "The Axiom, and everything?"

Winslow nodded. "The Axiom themselves are mostly dead, and any who aren't dead are likely all in hibernation, because even their lifespans aren't infinite… but they were real, and they still have servants, tending their machinery and looking after their ancient agendas. You heard about the Vanir system?"

"Sure. The forbidden system." The Vanir system was accessible through the twenty-ninth gate, and had been cut off from contact with the rest of the colony worlds for decades – until several years ago, when it abruptly rejoined the rest of galactic civilization. It turned out a group of Liars calling themselves the Exalted had seized control of the bridge in that system and performed horrific experiments on the human inhabitants, until a rebellion overthrew them.

"That's where I'm from," Winslow said. "The Exalted were worshippers of the Axiom."

He was *from* the Vanir system? She'd never met *anyone* from there.

"The Axiom ruled over my people for millennia," Crowbar said. "Some sects remain loyal to those old masters, and hope to usher in their return. The rest of us are the Free. The Axiom are very real… but almost extinct now, we think, thanks to the efforts of my kindler and her old crew."

"They're really real..." Delilah said. Or else her crewmates were insane, or tricking her, and neither seemed likely. "And… this business with a bridge generator?"

"You can't rule a galactic empire unless you can pop in and subjugate your subjects at will," Winslow said. "For a long time, there was only one ship with a fully operational bridge generator: Kalea Machedo's. Now there are two. This ship… it's a hell of a first job, Delilah."

"Why did Ashok pick me?" Delilah said.

"You'd have to ask him," Winslow said.

"I will, but it seems like a conversation better had in person." Winslow stared at her without blinking, and Crowbar's two eyes focused on her too. "What?" she said.

"Ashok!" Winslow barked. "You mean you didn't tell her about your situation?"

The captain's voice spoke over the PA. "About my – oh. Right. It didn't come up. Do you think it's important?"

Winslow closed his eyes. "Delilah. Would you please accompany me to the captain's quarters?"

They didn't go to the crew deck, where the cabins (small, but well appointed) were located. Instead, Winslow took her to the center of the ship, down a ladder into an engineering corridor, and then pressed on a piece of bulkhead indistinguishable from the rest.

A section of the wall slid away, revealing a space smaller than her cabin, full of softly blinking lights and kilometers of bundled cable. "Engineer Delilah Mears, meet Captain Ashok Ranganathan."

Delilah understood immediately. "Our captain is an *artificial intelligence*?"

Winslow nodded. "The original Ashok was the engineer on the *White Raven*, serving with Kalea Machedo. Several years ago, he was killed by an agent of the Axiom. But Ashok always had a habit of crawling into dangerous places without worrying overmuch about the danger – that's how he lost an arm and both legs and a chunk of his face – so he'd prepared for the eventuality of sudden death. He designed and implanted a special recording device at the base of his spine. It might have paralyzed or killed him, but instead, it actually worked. The little black box created a template of his mind's structure and a recording of his memories, or most of them, at least."

Delilah gazed at the blinking lights. She knew the breakthrough in creating stable artificial intelligences had hinged on using human brain scans as a basis for the new minds. Earlier versions of artificial intelligence had no more interest in humans than humans did in dust motes, and those alien intellects soon stopped communicating with their creators, vanishing into their own intellectual abstractions. If you built a nascent machine intelligence around the template of a human mind, with their thought patterns and personality and intelligence intact, the resulting AI retained an interest in human affairs, with the benefit of a vastly increased intellectual capacity.

"But... making an AI is ruinously expensive and takes forever! There's only one lab in the Jovian Imperative that even does that work, heavily subsidized by the government, and even the president of the Inner Planets Governing Council has been on a waiting list to get scanned for ten years!"

"When you save the galaxy, you get to jump the line," Winslow said. "Ashok has a powerful and wealthy friend at Almajara Corp. It helped that he'd recorded his own data – usually the scientists have to spend years hooking their subjects up to their systems, building up a working template over hundreds of sessions, but Ashok was recording himself constantly while he went about his life."

"But to have an AI as captain... Oh. The Trans-Neptunian Alliance."

"Right," Winslow said. "AI have citizenship there. They can own property and enter into contracts and everything."

"I knew that, but I never thought much about it, because I thought there was only one AI citizen, President Shall. Back home a lot of people think he's a figurehead, a publicity thing – just the TNA trying to look progressive and advanced."

"I have met Shall," Winslow said. "He's very much his own person. So is the captain. Ashok made a backup of himself before he started this mission, and stored it on Meditreme. If our ship doesn't come back, that will boot up, and he'll continue to live... which is an advantage he has over both of us. For now, though, *The Golden Spider* is Ashok's body. He really should have told you. By all accounts he wasn't very good at understanding people even when he was a person himself." He put a hand on her arm. "Do you want to quit? We're still within shuttle range of New Meditreme."

"No," Delilah said. "If I leave now... I'll feel like a coward. I left Earth because I wanted to see what else the galaxy has to offer. I didn't expect anything like *this*, but that's sort of the point, isn't it?" She glanced at the ceiling. "I did have one question, though... Is he watching us, right now?"

Winslow shook his head. "There are no cameras in here. The captain said, 'It would be like having a camera inside my *brain*.' No cameras in your cabin or other private areas, either. You can talk to the captain over the ship's comms, just like you can talk to me or Crowbar, but he's not constantly listening. In the public areas, he *can* see and hear, but that's no different from being on any ship with a captain who keeps an eye on the security monitors."

She relaxed a little. "Did you know, ah, the real Ashok?"

Winslow winced. "He prefers 'original' to 'real,' though sometimes he says 'meat-brain me,' or at least he did until I begged him to stop. No, the Axiom lasered a hole through his brain before I met him, not long after he helped save the Vanir system. After the system was liberated, I started working in the Jovian Imperative, for Almajara Corp, doing research on biomechanical augmentations." He gave a funny sort of smile. "That's a specialty of mine. As a doctor, I'm honestly better at grafting on a new or artificial limb than I am at saving an old one, but the ship has a smart medical bay. Anyway. Part of bringing a new AI online is social interaction, and Ashok and I knew a few people in common, because I was friendly with some of the resistance people he met back on Vanir. Plus, we share an interest in augments and prosthetics. His doctors brought me in to help with his development, and we ended up becoming friends."

"So you don't know if the new version is the same as the real – the original."

"Not personally, but I've talked to his friends, and I know the science. Artificial intelligences start out as near-copies of their templates, but then… things diverge. They're the same minds running on new equipment, and that alone changes things. Once they start having new experiences, the gap widens. Our captain is not *exactly* Ashok as he was – his old friends tell me he has better impulse control now, and he thinks a lot faster, since he's running on a quantum computer instead of a kilogram and a half of gray matter – but he has continuity of memory with his original self. I don't know. I'm not the same person I was five years ago, either. Are you?"

"Me five years ago could not have predicted that present-day me would be doing something like *this,*" she said.

Three hours later, she joined Winslow in the curved observation deck near the nose of the ship. The walls were opaque when she entered, but gradually grew transparent, except for a bit of "floor" beneath her feet. There were distant stars, but mostly, all Delilah saw was darkness. "It's so strange, being on a ship with steady gravity. I was floating or under thrust gravity on all the ships between Earth and here."

"Want me to turn it off?" Winslow said. "Floating in a room like this is a lot like being in open space, but with less chance of death."

Delilah shook her head. "I'm good. Microgravity makes me a little sick anyway." That was an understatement. She still had anti-nausea pills in her cabin, but she hadn't needed them today. "So what happens now?"

"I've never been on a ship with its own bridge generator," Winslow said. "Only through the big bridges."

"I've never even been through one of *those,*" Delilah said. "I saw the one in the Jovian Imperative, the line of ships waiting to go through, but I didn't use it. This is the farthest I've been from home." That bridge was an immense oval, marked by a perimeter of floating buoys that turned red or green depending on whether the bridge was active or not.

"Are we ready to *venture into the unknown*?" Ashok said over the shipwide comms.

"That's what we're here for," Winslow said.

"Let there be hole," Ashok said.

At first, Delilah didn't see anything, but then she perceived a thickening of the dark – a blot in space that started to spread. This bridgehead looked like a swirl of black ink in water, with irregular tendrils that stretched from an expanding center, reaching out to embrace the ship.

"That's different," Winslow said.

The darkness before them became larger than the ship, and the tendrils streamed by on all sides. Delilah had expected them to fly through a gate, but this was more like a jellyfish reaching out to capture and feed on prey… and they were the prey.

The ship hummed and moved forward, and while Delilah was in the middle of a blink, they transitioned. The *Golden Spider* was suddenly in a cylindrical tunnel, the walls dark and metallic, with bands of light at irregular intervals, stretching as far as they could see. She'd heard the space between bridgeheads was dark, and impenetrable to sight or sensors; apparently the personal bridges were different. Were they in an actual *place*, or was this just her brain's way of making sense of a space outside ordinary space-time?

"It's so weird. I just see darkness." Ashok's voice was wistful. "I had lots of extra lenses back when I was still meat-me, but the eyes underneath were original spec jelly-cameras, so I could see the tunnel, and the lights. They're only visible to organic senses. Another Axiomatic mystery. Now, even with all my sensors, it's like there's nothing there at all. I'm playing myself an overlay based on one of my memories of traversing a bridge, just so I can see *something*, but it's not the same."

After twenty-one seconds, they emerged into a new place, surrounded by tendrils that rapidly withdrew. There were more stars, and different ones, in Delilah's field of view, but overall, the destination wasn't radically different from the place they'd started. "I don't see an alien space station," she said.

"Oh, we're about a day's journey away from the thing," Ashok said. "It's not a good idea to open a bridge in close proximity to an Axiom facility. Some of those stations react badly to unexpected visitors. The place we're going *seems* inert, but Callie would never let me live it down if I lost the *Golden Spider*."

"Plus, if you lost the ship, your crew would die," Winslow said.

"Oh sure, also that. Goes without saying."

"You think so?" Winslow said. "I don't mind hearing you say it."

"I'll protect you all more diligently than I'd protect *myself*,"

Ashok said. "After all, you don't have backups. In the meantime, how about you get some rest, and when you have a minute, familiarize yourself with the data from the last visit to the object of entropic mystery."

"Did you send the info to our terminals?" Winslow said. "I didn't get a notification."

"Where's the fun in that? Nah, I knocked together an immersive experience. It's almost as good as being there!"

"But with less chance of death," Delilah murmured.

"*Considerably* less!" Ashok agreed.

The ship had a fancy Hypnos suite, the kind with full-immersion sensory deprivation tanks to minimize outside interference. She'd never used such advanced simulation tech, not even on New Meditreme. Her understanding was that this experience was almost indistinguishable from real life – an idea that terrified the traditionalists back home. What if people chose to spend their lives in an imaginary world instead of the real one? On Earth there was legislation to slow down the introduction of such advanced simulation tech and curtail its use for public health reasons, but beyond the asteroid belt things were far less regulated.

Delilah checked the connections on her diadem and then opened up the smooth black lozenge of the tank. She climbed inside, settling into the perfectly neutral conducting fluid. She took a breath, then slid the lid closed.

A soothing chime let her know the simulation was about to begin, and then light appeared. Her perspective shifted, and she was no longer horizontal, but vertical, standing on a flat gray plain. Gradually, the environment around her coalesced until she was standing on the bridge of an unfamiliar ship, one with a dozen crew members working at assorted stations. A woman in a dark jumpsuit stood nearby with her arms crossed, gazing at an immense wraparound viewscreen. The screen was dominated by a black sphere inlaid with shining white lines in geometries that seemed to squirm and shift – unless Delilah focused on them, at which point they proved static and unchanging, but continued wriggling in her periphery. The woman had a cloud of curly dark hair, a prominent nose and an annoyed expression. She looked vaguely familiar.

Ashok, or rather his avatar, stepped up beside Delilah, making her jump. "That's Callie, my old captain, and head of the Axiom Extermination Task Force. The Scourge of the Exalted, the Benefactor's Malefactor, She Who Runs Toward the Sound of Explosions." He snorted. "It's a good thing she's just a recording right now, or she'd throw something at me for calling her all that."

Delilah walked around the woman, and yes, now that she had a name to put with the face, that's who it was – the woman who'd reconstituted the Trans-Neptunian Alliance, a big enough event that they'd even paid some slight attention to it back on Earth. Delilah waved a hand in front of her face but Callie didn't react. "So we're ghosts here."

"Pretty much." Ashok picked up a flat cap off a crew member and pulled it down on his head, and when Delilah glanced down, the hat was back on the crew member, but its double stayed on Ashok, too. "We can interact with objects in the simulation, but they'll revert after a moment. They flicker back to baseline when we aren't looking directly at them, to maintain the sense of realism." He took off the crew member's hat again and placed it on top of his first one at a jaunty angle. "Infinite hats. What a world."

Delilah looked at her hands, and they were hers, down to the tiny scar on the back of left one from a bot-welding mishap in college, a detail the Hypnos suite from their interview had overlooked. "This is amazingly realistic."

"It's okay," Ashok said. "It's a pretty good scan of you – the ship made it when you came on board, and it's way more high-def than the one you had on New Meditreme. We even caught that little twitch that happens sometimes in your left eyelid." Delilah instinctively put a hand to her face, but Ashok didn't seem to notice. He was gazing past her, at the viewscreen. "You should see what the Axiom could do with virtual reality, though. They had direct brain interfaces, which helps, but still. They used to have a virtual world so detailed you could count the grains of sand on the beach, and if you looked at them under a microscope, every one would be different."

"Used to?"

"Oh, we had to blow up their computer. That faction of the Axiom was just hanging out in a simulation while they waited for their doomsday program to finish compiling. But I mean… I took some notes. It helped with my software work. Okay, things are about to kick off." He sat down in an unattended crew seat, and Delilah took the one beside him.

"Still nothing from the probes?" Callie said.

A blonde woman standing at a terminal said, "Nothing. The object seems totally inert, except for the twisting lines, and as best we can tell, that's an optical illusion."

"Hmm. We're at double the minimum safe distance?" Callie said.

"Even if that sphere turns out to have a black hole inside, we should be fine," another crewperson said. "Of course, if it's some kind of previously unknown system-destroying bomb, that's a different story."

"At least we're way the hell away from anything else at all," Callie said. "As a rule, the Axiom were keen on destroying everybody else, not themselves, anyhow. Ready the missiles."

"Missiles ready."

"Launch," Callie said.

After a moment, six objects appeared on the viewscreen, lit up an unnatural green to make them stand out, and hurtled toward the sphere. Their view of the object must have been highly magnified, or more likely relayed through probes situated closer in space.

"Ten seconds to impact," a crewperson said. "Nine. Eight. Seven. Six." The objects were so small now they were just green dots, and Delilah realized the sphere must be nearly the size of a small moon. "Five. Four. Three. Two. One. Impact."

The missiles exploded, the light from the detonation expanding from pinpoints to overlapping flashes that entirely obscured their view of the object –

– and then the flashes shrank again, the edges of the light pulling inward, returning to pinpoints, and then to nothingness, and then to the green dots of the missiles, now unmoving, floating against the face of the object.

"What?" Callie and Delilah said simultaneously. "Why did the feed run in reverse?" Callie demanded. That was exactly what it looked like: a recording of an explosion, running backward, showing the bombs un-exploding.

"It didn't!" someone said. "We – this is the real-time view!"

"Are we still getting data from the missiles?"

"We are!" the blonde said. "According to the data, they detonated, but then their systems came back online, and now they're throwing errors, because even the missiles know that doesn't make any sense. Should I… detonate them again?"

"Why not?" Callie said.

This time, the explosions didn't go as far before reversing: a mere blip of light, a slight flash, and then back to baseline green.

"Fuck," Callie said. "Is it… are they fucking with time? Are the Axiom messing with *time* now?"

"The system clocks on the bombs aren't running backward," the blonde said. "They're not quite in synch with our ship clock anymore, they lost a couple of seconds while they were, ah, blowing up, but, no, they didn't rewind."

"So *what* then?" Callie said.

"I have no idea," the blonde said.

Ashok waved a hand, and the screen froze. "Do you drink, Delilah?"

"Not often. Now seems like a good time to make an exception."

"Come with me to Callie's ready room. She's got some real nice bourbon in there. The nice thing about drinking in a simulation is, it tastes great, and you can even get drunk in here if you have the right settings turned on, but you're sober when you come out, and no hangover."

"What if I don't *want* to be sober when I come out?"

"Then I have to be all captainly and say, no drinking on duty."

They walked through the frozen scene, down a short corridor, and into a small, neat room with a desk, a terminal, and a comfortable-looking armchair positioned facing a viewport on to scattered stars. "They had to redecorate this whole ship once we got a gravity generator installed," Ashok said. "You don't need all the loops and straps and rails and velcro when you can have the same part of the ship be the floor for the whole journey. Here, let me glitch you up a seat." Ashok lifted the armchair and moved it a few feet away. "Avert your gaze," he said, and Delilah looked briefly at the ceiling with its warm, indirect lighting. When she looked back, the original armchair was in place, while Ashok sat in its duplicate. Delilah took her place, and Ashok opened a desk drawer and removed a bottle of brown liquor. "Fortunately she has two glasses. No duplication glitch needed."

He poured, and Delilah sniffed hers before taking a sip. She mostly drank cocktails with a high fruit-to-rum ratio, and she was prepared for the bitter burn she associated with taking shots. There *was* an alcohol bite, but mostly the sensation was warmth, and the taste was sort of caramel-apple-y. "This is delicious. Is it this good in real life?"

"I was never much of a drinker when I had a body," Ashok said. "In here, I can tweak my virtual taste buds. To be a hundred percent honest, this tastes like a mango lassi to me right now. But *yours* is probably a pretty accurate simulacrum, yeah."

Delilah settled back and thought about what she'd seen. It made no more sense in retrospect. "What happens next?"

"We head for the inscrutable object, and bring our unique perspectives to bear on the problem of what the heck it is and how it does the things it does."

"I don't know if I have a unique perspective."

"You *do,* everyone does, it's just a question of whether it's a *useful* unique perspective. We'll see!"

Now was as good a time as any to broach the subject. "Captain, why did you choose me? It turns out you're, like, an engineering god out here. You could have had your pick of crew. Why choose me?"

"*Because* I had my pick of crew. I have a much bigger brain than I used to, so I made a program to sift through a whole lot of variables and figure out who'd be the best addition to the *Golden Spider,* in terms of skillset, temperament, and, well, call it philosophy."

"Okay. Your algorithm picked me. But *why*?"

"Because you're smart, hardworking, open to new information, eager to have unprecedented experiences, and you can get along with me and Winslow and tolerate Crowbar. Plus… you did your doctoral thesis on maximizing exergy in Tanzer Drives to make their systems more efficient. Basically, you spent years thinking about how to reduce entropy, right? Fighting the good fight against the second law of thermodynamics."

"Sure. So?"

Ashok sipped his mango-flavored bourbon. "Well, that object out there can *reverse* entropy. I thought that might be the sort of thing that would interest you."

"Nothing can reverse entropy."

"That's what I use to tell my mom, but she still made me clean my room."

Delilah rolled her eyes. Her legendary engineer captain was sometimes ridiculous, and that was oddly comforting. "Yes, you can increase order, but you have to put *energy* into the process. Entropy just doesn't spontaneously reverse itself. That's the law you can't violate."

"Fair enough. That thing the Axiom built can undo a nuclear explosion, though, which is a reversal of entropy beyond anything thought possible. Much harder even than cleaning my room. If it didn't happen spontaneously, it sure seemed to happen *automatically,* which is very nearly just as cool. Remember what

I said about Axiom power sources? There must be an awfully impressive one in their sphere if it can do something like that." He leaned forward, the lenses over his eyes rotating. "Don't you want to take it apart and see how it works?"

Delilah was in one of the maintenance shafts, checking a series of relays that Ashok said felt a little "sticky," whatever that meant; she wasn't capable of imagining the physical sensations of having a spaceship for a body. Crowbar hung upside down from a pipe on the ceiling by one pseudopod, shining a light on the access panel for her while she methodically clicked switches back and forth. Huh. Some of them *did* feel sticky. She squirted lubricant where necessary. "Why are you *really* here?" Delilah asked. "Ashok doesn't need you to be a pilot."

"You are very blunt for a human."

"Winslow said I should try to talk to you on your own terms."

"I approve. I am here because my kindler thought I would be useful to the mission."

"I thought you were always honest? That sounded a lot like an evasion."

"When your culture forbids lies, you become gifted at evasion and omission. I will answer more directly, as my kindler says that a proper crew can become like a family. All of my incubation-mates were given gestational training and exposure to various… trades, a human might say. Areas of expertise. Upon our birth, we took a test to determine the true confluence of interest and ability, to determine our… hmm… optimal occupational path of greatest satisfaction?"

"Your calling?" Delilah had always felt engineering was hers. Figuring out how things worked, and how to make them work better.

"Yes, good. I have a particular aptitude for and interest in breaking codes and overcoming barriers to entry. That is why I chose the name Crowbar."

"You're good at… breaking and entering?"

"Physically and electronically. Circumventing security systems, identifying weak points, countering countermeasures. My kindler says I have a mind that looks at systems and sees the places where they will break down. Some who have that ability become security experts, because they take satisfaction in fortifying those weak points. My greatest pleasure comes in exploiting them."

"You're here to help us break into the anomaly," Delilah said.

"If it can be entered. If not, I will attempt to overcome its security measures, allowing us to destroy it. I have studied all the footage. I see several possible lines of inquiry and am eager to begin."

"I'm pretty nervous about the whole thing myself."

"Winslow says anxiety and excitement largely involve the same physical responses in the human body. The resulting sensations are merely interpreted by the mind in different ways. I recommend you interpret your feelings as excitement instead."

"I'll work on that." Delilah flicked the last relay back into place and activated her comms. "Captain, how does that feel?"

"Like a cramp just uncramped," he said in her ear. "Thanks. The haptic feedback from my repair drones can't compare to the sensitivity of human hands."

"Good to know our electronic overlords still have a use for us."

"Somebody has to change our batteries occasionally too. We–"

Ashok's voice cut out, replaced by wailing klaxons, and the maintenance tunnel was bathed in flashing red emergency lights.

"All personnel to the observation deck!" Ashok said. "We have a problem."

Delilah arrived on deck, Crowbar scuttling along behind her, just as Winslow arrived. "What's going on?" she said.

Winslow pointed wordlessly at the viewscreen. The darkness pinpricked by stars was gone. Now they cruised through what appeared to be a graveyard for ships. Just from here, she could see the husks of freighters and gas haulers, small pleasure craft, an asteroid mining vessel (that one was torn in half), and even an old Jovian Imperative battle cruiser.

"No stars," Crowbar said, and Delilah looked at him, then back at the screen. She hadn't even noticed, being so distracted by the dark ships, but he was right – the field of view wasn't *that* crowded, and she should have been able to see stars beyond. She saw nothing.

"Now we know where the *Pikeville* went," Ashok said. A ship in the lower right corner of the screen lit up in green. "It went... wherever we did. I sent them a message, but there's no response, and their engines are off – no sign of activity over there at all. Same with all these other ships."

"How did we end up here?" Winslow said. "I think we would have noticed a scrapyard before we flew into the middle of it."

"We were transported here through a bridge," Ashok said. "A rather more *active* bridge than we're used to – this one opened out of nowhere, reached out and grabbed me like a trapdoor spider snatching a cockroach, and pulled me in. Apparently the same thing happened to the *Pikeville*."

"Is it part of the anomaly's defense system?" Delilah asked, then answered herself. "No, that doesn't make sense, because where did all these *other* ships come from? There's no way they were within a million kilometers of the sphere. I see Earth vessels, Jovian Imperative ships, that looks like a royal courier ship from the Asura system–"

"I've scanned these vessels, and identified some of them from local database records," Ashok said. "They're all lost ships, presumed destroyed in accidents or taken by unknown hostile forces, or just mysteriously vanished. Some of them are *old*."

"Bermuda Triangle," Delilah muttered.

"What's that?" Crowbar said.

"Oh, just... an old Earth legend. There was a place in the sea, near an island called Bermuda, not far from where I grew up. Ships and aircraft disappeared there at an unusually high rate."

"These ships didn't come from any one place," Winslow said. "They're from all over."

"I know," Delilah said. "People had all kinds of theories about the Bermuda Triangle – one of the wildest ones I read was that the ships disappeared into some sort of dimensional anomaly, and ended up in an unknown realm or alternate universe."

"Maybe the Axiom did it," Ashok said. "Because they certainly did *this*. It's some kind of Axiom program, snatching ships from all over inhabited space, for reasons of their own."

"Not just ships," Crowbar said. "I see asteroids, buoys, probes, supply caches, all sorts of uncrewed objects too."

"Huh," Ashok said. "You're right. It's like a random sample of artificial stellar objects, isn't it? I don't understand what the point of this is, but then, the Axiom don't always make a lot of sense."

Delilah frowned. "If this is really a random process, though, the odds of the *Pikeville* and the *Golden Spider* both being snatched, from the same part of space, are pretty low, don't you think?"

"Maybe there are fixed collection points," Ashok mused. "Let's say the grabby bridges open up at regular spots in various systems, taking whatever passes by. You'd think someone would have seen it happening, since ships often travel in groups, but maybe the snatch-engines are calibrated to only grab ships when they're alone. Let me run some backtraces…" A moment's pause. "Huh, well, this doesn't prove anything, but in those cases where I can determine where these other ships disappeared, I don't see any duplication of coordinates. None of them came from the same place, or even within ten thousand kilometers of the same place. We also weren't anywhere near the *Pikeville*'s scout route when *we* got grabbed. Which means you might have a point, Delilah. It does seem like a pretty big coincidence that we'd both end up here."

"Or maybe there are billions of the collection points, and most of them just don't catch anything, because nothing ever passes by," Winslow said. "Since most of space is nothing."

"Incomplete data," Ashok said. "That's always fun. It's a mystery!"

"Do you have any idea where we are, captain?" Delilah said.

"That would be another mystery. I'm gathering all the data I can. The lack of visible stars and the absence of ionizing radiation makes me think that, strange as it seems, we're *inside* something – an immense structure of some kind. I'm stretching my sensors to the limits and bouncing out beams, so I hope to get a better sense of the nature of that place soon."

"I assume we are planning to escape?" Crowbar said.

"We'll look for an exit," Ashok said. "Also anybody else who might be alive in here. The crew of the *Pikeville* could be here, though for these older ships, I'm less hopeful. Worst case, we wait until our bridge generator recharges, and we leave *that* way. I – huh. There's a ship approaching us. I guess we aren't the only ones in here after all."

The image on the viewscreen switched, then magnified, revealing an oncoming vessel. "Why does it have… sails?" Crowbar said. "They aren't even solar sails. They are just painted cloth on masts stuck to the hull."

"Why is it decorated like that?" Winslow said. "All striped like a white tiger. And… are those big silver *skulls* mounted on the front?"

Delilah stared, then burst out laughing. She couldn't help herself. "That – it looks like the ship from *Hyperion's Revenge*!"

"The what?" Winslow said, baffled.

"It's from this show, not a sim, way older than that, strictly audio-visual, I learned about it in one of the humanities classes I had to take, a history of space in cinema. We started with *Le Voyage dans la Lune*, and we watched *Star Trek* and *2001*, on through *The Liar's Bridge* and *Jovian Conquest* and all those, but my friends thought *Hyperion's Revenge* was hilarious. We only watched a clip in class, part of some documentary, but we looked the show up on the Tangle and we'd watch episodes while we, uh..."

"Got high?" Winslow said. "It's fine. I'm a member of the Church of the Ecstatic Divine myself."

"Yeah." Delilah was chagrined, but also mildly alarmed to hear the ship's first officer and doctor was part of a psychedelic religion considered decidedly fringe on Earth. "*Hyperion's Revenge* is from the twenty-second century, I think? It was a show for kids, about this space pirate named Starbeard, who lurked near the moons of Saturn on his ship, appropriately named the *Hyperion's Revenge*. He was always fighting with this naval officer, commander Forrest Flood, who was really the villain, you know, he was totally strict, no sense of humor… but that's thing, it's what the pirate ship looked like."

"I don't have that show in my database, but I have the same documentary you probably saw in your class, and yeah, that's the ship," Ashok said. "Not the same base model, it's too new for that, but it's a direct descendant from the same manufacturer, and with the decorations, it's a pretty good copy. They're hailing us. Huh. Putting it onscreen."

A section of the wall changed from window to screen, revealing a member of the Free. He wore an eyepatch, though that left five eyes uncovered. He wore a large black tricorn hat. A fringe of twenty or so dangling pseudopods, each half a meter long, hung beneath his eyes, and they were dotted with sparkling blue lights, creating the impression of a beard covered in glitter. He lifted one of his primary pseudopods, and shook a curved, broad-bladed sword at the screen. (Delilah had heard that many people preferred old-fashioned weapons for fighting on ships and stations – you couldn't put a hole in the hull of a ship by accident with a sword like you could with a gun – but still. A *cutlass*?) The bridge of his ship prominently featured wooden barrels and coils of rope, and aliens clambered on cargo nets and rigging in the background. "Avast, ye human scum!" the alien shouted. "Prepare to be boarded, and to pay with your riches or your lives!" The image went black.

"That's… he looks like Starbeard," Delilah said. "Or an alien doing Starbeard cosplay anyway."

"Space pirates," Ashok said. "*Cinematic* space pirates. I was not expecting that. Do you think they're serious?"

"Costumes aside, there are a lot of dead ships around us that suggest they might be," Winslow said.

"Yeah, but none of them are really damaged, which you'd think they would be, if they were fighting pirates. Even cosplay space pirates…" Ashok went *hmm*. "I'm telling them to stop their approach or we'll fire. Instead they're… approaching even faster, okay. I'm going for a disabling shot." Missiles lit in green appeared on the screen, streaking for the ship. They all hit, striking both sides of what Delilah already thought of as *Hyperion's Revenge*, disabling cannons and engines –

Or they should have. Instead, the missiles *unexploded*, just like the ones Delilah had seen in the simulation of the attack on the anomaly, and then drifted harmlessly off to either side.

"Oh," Ashok said. "That's interesting. On a related note, a couple of my pings just came back, and they found the edges of our environment. We appear to be roughly at the center of a sphere with a volume of a few billion cubic kilometers. Which is consistent with…"

"The size of the anomaly," Delilah finished. "We're *inside* the anomaly?"

"My job was easier than I expected," Crowbar said.

"Since we can't fight, let's try flight. Taking evasive maneuvers now," Ashok said.

"Should we brace ourselves?" Delilah asked.

"The artificial gravity will adjust to compensate, but you can grab onto something if it makes you feel better." The image on the viewscreen shifted as they powered toward the thickest conglomeration of derelict ships, Ashok doubtlessly hoping to lose himself among the other vessels.

They didn't make it that far before Ashok said, "Multiple impacts aft. They're shooting *harpoons* at me!"

"That's what they used to do on the show," Delilah said.

"These are attached to some kind of incredibly strong wire, though, and I can't shake them," Ashok said. "They're reeling themselves in – I think they're planning to get their ship close enough to board. They're in for a surprise when they do. The *Golden Spider* has plenty of countermeasures–"

Ashok's voice cut off just as the viewscreens and all the lights on the ship went dark. Delilah cried out as her feet left the floor. The artificial gravity was off, and in the total darkness, she felt lost in space.

"EMP," Crowbar's voice drifted up from the vicinity of the floor. "They disabled the ship's systems."

"I can't believe they're going to make me take my shirt off," Winslow muttered. Delilah heard a zipper. "All right, I can see you, I'm coming toward you."

"What do you mean?" Delilah said.

"Our first officer can see in the dark," Crowbar said.

"How–" A hand gripped hers. "Is that you Winslow?"

"Yeah, let me get Crowbar."

"We're supposed to be hardened against that kind of attack," Delilah said. "I don't understand how an EMP affected us."

"We – wait, there's someone else in here!" Winslow said.

"You aren't hardened against attack from *inside* the ship, me pretty," an unfamiliar voice said from somewhere in front of her.

"Pirates!" Winslow cried, and then a burst of something damp and sweet-smelling hit Delilah in the face. The darkness around her became even deeper, and she lost herself.

Delilah groaned and opened her eyes, staring at the smooth gray of an unfamiliar bulkhead. Something was trapping her, some kind of net, and she thrashed wildly, only tangling herself further, until Crowbar said, "Calm yourself. You are in a hammock."

She blinked around, then realized he was right. She'd slept in quite a few hammocks during her space journey, because they were practical bedding in microgravity. She carefully extricated herself from the hammock and crawled out, taking in her surroundings. They were in a storage room of some kind, probably on a ship, just a dull cube of a space strung with a few hammocks. A distressingly damp curtain in one corner was pulled aside to reveal a toilet, and shelves behind sliding plastic doors on the wall held various sorts of freeze-dried foodstuffs and bulbs that probably contained water.

There was one door, closed. Crowbar was floating next to it, pulling wires out of the wall. That was promising, at least.

Winslow was in another hammock, apparently unconscious, and – there was something wrong with his chest, his unzipped jumpsuit revealing a slice of skin covered in… blisters? Welts? Odd bulges and lines and folds of skin. Maybe he'd been hit by shrapnel at some point, and it had healed over.

He groaned, looked over at her, then zipped himself up before getting out of the hammock. "Ugh."

"Where are we?" Delilah said.

"Good question," Winslow said. "I'd guess we're in whatever the pirate equivalent of jail is."

"Dungeon," Crowbar offered.

"Yes, thank you," Winslow said.

"By dungeon standards it is not so bad," Crowbar said. "I have been conscious for ten minutes, and have examined it thoroughly. This cell has had other inhabitants – there are hash marks scratched on the wall there. Someone kept count of the days. There are other markings as well. I like the graffiti in the bathroom that says *'Starbeard sucks like vacuum.'*" Crowbar twisted some wires together. Delilah wondered how he'd pried a panel off the wall. Her tool belt was gone, and she couldn't imagine the – space pirates! – had left them anything useful in here.

"Have you seen our captors?" she asked.

"No," Crowbar said.

Winslow gazed around. "Their captain must really call himself Starbeard, if the graffiti says that. So. They somehow boarded our ship and set off an EMP on the inside, then gassed us with a sedative. I wish I knew how they'd boarded."

"Personal teleport," Crowbar said. "Axiom tech, used sometimes by the truth-tellers, but highly restricted and rare. Makes a sort of… personal wormhole. Short range, but useful for infiltration. It makes sense the pirates have such technology. We know they are good at building bridges."

"Is there any *other* nature-of-reality-altering technology you know about that I don't?" Winslow said.

"Probably," Crowbar said. "Cannot be sure. Do not know the full extent of your knowledge."

"Winslow," Delilah said. "Is Ashok, ah…"

"Dead? Or the AI equivalent? I don't think so. Offline, probably. If we reboot his systems, he should wake up again."

Crowbar said, "There. Door open."

The door slid into the wall, revealing a corridor, and Delilah gave a silent cheer.

"Let's get out of here," Winslow said.

He led, followed close by Delilah, and then Crowbar, who, she noticed, seemed to be fashioning a garrote out of wall wires.

A human in a stained Jovian Imperative military jumpsuit drifted in the corridor a few meters away. She smiled at them, her eyes bloodshot, hair a mass of messy braids. She held out an unlabeled glass bottle of murky liquid, magenta in color. "You got out of your cell in record time!" she said. "Have a drink in celebration." She sailed the bottle toward them, and Delilah plucked it from the air to keep it from banging into her.

"Who are you?" Winslow said.

"Lieutenant Grigsby, late of the *Pikeville*," she said. "Welcome to the Rathole."

"The Rathole?" Delilah said. "That's what the pirates called their asteroid dungeon on the show, it was riddled with miles of tunnels, full of people they'd captured. There was a whole episode set there once, with characters you never saw before or after – there was a whole *society* in the place."

"What show?" Grigsby said. "What are you talking about?"

"Maybe we can answer some questions for each other," Winslow said.

"Sure," Grigsby said. "There's not much to do here except talk, unless you count waiting to die of old age as an activity."

"We will not die of old age," Crowbar said. "We will escape."

"I'm sure you will," Grigsby said. "Pretty much all of us escape every once in a while. You have to pass the time somehow."

There were five other prisoners, gathered listlessly in some sort of common room. Grigsby introduced the newcomers around. A pair of black-haired androgynous people who might have been twins were Rahmah and Jabir–"They make the prison wine. It's mostly canned fruit and sauerkraut, but it's got a little kick." The two nodded coolly at Delilah and Winslow and narrowed their eyes at Crowbar, but said nothing. "They were asteroid miners in the Netjer system, and they've been here about four years."

A woman with a shaved head, wearing a bright orange environment suit sans helmet, was stacking cans in an alcove. "That's Guðríður. She ran a salvage operation out by Catequil, in Hanan Pacha? They've got those big gas giants, full of storms, so there are lots of wrecks to play around in. She's a ten-year veteran of the Rathole, and our procurement officer."

"Don't call me that," she muttered. "I'm not in the military. Neither are you, anymore." She glanced over at them. "I just go out to the other ships and scavenge supplies as needed. Maybe one of you can go with me to your ship later, and show me what's worth bringing back here. The pirates only take shiny things and alcohol. They leave food and medical supplies, fortunately."

"Let me finish making the rounds before you get into all that," Grigsby said, steering Winslow toward the other side of the room. "That's Every, my co-pilot on the *Pikeville*." The woman didn't even look up from the magnetic chess board fixed to a table. "The old guy beating her to death at chess is Vane. He's been here – how long, Vane?"

"Twenty years, if you aren't lying about what year it is." He had white hair and appeared to be wearing pajamas.

"How many times have you escaped?" Grigsby said.

"About thirty," he said. "I used to do it a lot early on. Now it's just an annual thing, on my birthday."

"You can come and go freely to other vessels?" Delilah said.

"I found it kind of shocking myself, at first," Grigsby said. "Me and Every couldn't accept what these folks told us, you know? We broke out, made our way back to the *Pikeville*, and tried to fly out of this place. After a while, we hit a wall. We're inside some kind of big sphere."

"We're inside the *anomaly*," Winslow said. "The thing you came to destroy."

Grigsby brightened. "You know about our mission?"

"We're the rescue crew," Delilah said. "In theory. We were looking for you when we got snatched."

"I appreciate the effort, anyhow." Grigsby gestured around. "These people all came from such distant places, they thought us ending up here was just another random event. The way the pirates are indestructible though, just like the anomaly, had us wondering."

Delilah expected one of the others to express curiosity about "the anomaly," but they paid no attention at all. They'd had all the curiosity sapped out of them, it seemed.

"We aren't sure how it works, yet," Winslow said. "But yes, based on our measurements, it checks out."

"Huh. We didn't cover every bit of the inside of the sphere, but we did a random sample, and there were no openings, which makes sense, if it's the anomaly. That thing was impossible to enter, so naturally it's impossible to escape."

"The pirates really just let you fly around?" Delilah was stuck on that point. The ones in *Hyperion's Revenge* hadn't been so lenient… but then, this version of the Rathole wasn't the prison. The whole anomaly was.

"They don't seem to care what we do after they board, pillage, and stick us here," Grigsby said.

"Where do the pirates live?" she asked.

"There's a station not far from here, where they dock their flagship."

"And you haven't fired up one of those old battleships and destroyed their station because it's indestructible, I guess," Winslow said.

"They're gods," the old man said. "We *tried* that, when I first got here. Mounted a full assault. Threw nukes at them. We even had a railgun. The bombs exploded, then unexploded. The railgun smashed in their hull, but then it *unsmashed*. The pirates can control time, or something." He looked up at them and grinned, and there was something glassy and faraway in his eyes. "Sometimes I think this is all a complicated hallucination, and that you're all imaginary. I like that idea." He moved a chess piece while still staring at them. "Checkmate," he said.

Every sighed heavily and started resetting the board.

"It's not just the ships and the station," Grigsby said. "Every and I did an infiltration on their station. We snuck in, and I shot one of the pirates with a sidearm. Or I tried. The gun wouldn't even fire. Just made a sort of puffing sound, like the gases inside were expanding, and then contracting again. The pirates didn't even take the gun away from me. They just tied us up and brought us back to the Rathole. I tested the gun later, and it worked fine."

"We can't leave," Every said, studying the board. "We can't fight. So… we sit here."

Delilah glanced at Winslow, and he furrowed his brow. *Should we?* she mouthed. He was the first officer, and she didn't want to make a decision about sharing intel without his approval, especially about super-secret technology.

But Crowbar didn't share her hesitation, "We have a way out of here. We have to wait a few days for our systems to recharge, but then we can take all of you home."

Delilah expected pandemonium, but no one seemed very interested.

"Our ship has a portable wormhole generator," Winslow said. "Brand new tech. It works… well, a bit like whatever the pirates used to bring you all here."

"Of course," Grigsby said. "You must, if you made it out here.

Like the one on captain Machedo's ship?" Every looked up with something like interest.

"It takes longer to recharge between uses, but yes," Delilah said.

"Huh. That might actually work. Though tech is… kind of unreliable in here."

"They're *gods,*" Vane said. "They won't let us leave. Your… thing, won't work. Starbeard won't *let* it work. Even if we escape, they'll rewind us, bring us back."

"Vane, come on," Grigsby said, but the old man interrupted.

"Show them!" he said. "Show them the bone room!"

"I don't want to–" she began, and Vane spun and pushed himself off toward them.

"Come on. New people. Follow me." Vane dragged himself out of the room, and after exchanging glances and shrugs, Winslow and Delilah followed. He led them down half a dozen corridors – they were in one of the big ships, apparently – until they finally reached the cargo bay day. He slammed his hand into a red button, and the door rose up.

The space beyond was full of bones. Skulls, femurs, pelvises, spines, ribcages. They floated in the air, some still with bits of flesh clinging to them, many charred or stained with soot. Speckles of gray ash floated in the air like flakes in a monstrous snowglobe. Delilah tried to count the skulls to get a sense of the number of remains – numbers had always acted as insulation from horror, for her – but stopped when she got to fifty.

"Someone, a long time ago, rigged it up so that room is a giant crematorium," Vane said. "Only it doesn't run quite hot enough to break down the bones, just burns away most of the flesh, so the skeletons bounce around in there. Sometimes people go in there when they don't want to be alive anymore. There's no getting out of here, do you understand? *This* is your future. This is what waits."

Winslow put a hand on the old man's shoulder. "I… lived in a terrible place too," he said. "In a lab, run by people called the Exalted. They made me help them with their experiments. They experimented *on* me, to make me better suit their purposes. Look." He unzipped his jumpsuit, revealing the blistered flesh she'd noticed before. As she watched, some of those blisters opened, blinking, revealing eyes of various sizes and colors. *Some of them can see in the dark,* she thought, and shivered. Vane gaped at him, open-mouthed. "I did a lot of diagnostic work," Winslow said bitterly, zipping back up. "I was one of their successful experiments. They had a room sort of like this, though. A place where they put their failed experiments and 'sanitized' them. I *knew* that was where I'd end my life, Vane, as soon as my usefulness ran out. The Vanir system had been that way for centuries, and the enemy was so much stronger than us – they might as well have been gods, too. But Vane..." He stared into the old man's eyes, and Vane stared back. "*We beat them*. The balance shifted. We escaped. I escaped. I found a new life. And I do not intend to spend the rest of my life in *another* prison."

The old man licked his lips, then squeezed his eyes shut and pulled away. "I'll believe it when I see it," he muttered.

"They do have a point," Crowbar said. "The pirates *may* be able to prevent the working of the bridge generator. We do not know their full capabilities. I can attempt to infiltrate their headquarters and disable their equipment, however."

"Do you think you'd succeed?" Winslow said.

"The likelihood is low," he said. "If they simply send their prisoners back here upon capture, however, the risk of trying is minimal."

"I wonder if we'd have a better chance if we joined the pirate crew," Delilah said.

"How would we do that?" Winslow said. "I doubt they're taking applications."

"Well, there was this one episode of *Hyperion's Revenge*," Delilah began.

* * *

"Was that true, what Winslow said, about being a prisoner?" Delilah and Crowbar were in one of the Rathole's shuttles, cruising toward the pirate's station.

"Yes," Crowbar said. "The Exalted were biological experts. They performed experiments, combining human physiology with that of my people. The resulting chimeras were used as forced labor, or sometimes they became willing collaborators. Some had obvious alterations – their arms replaced with pseudopods, for example – while others had more subtle internal changes."

"What did they do to Winslow?"

"It is not my place to say," Crowbar said. "Spend enough time with him, and you will see eventually. Or you could ask him yourself."

"Okay. Fair enough. I hope he can wake up Ashok."

"The assistance of a hyperintelligent AI would be welcome," Crowbar said. "Do you think your plan will work?"

"I have no idea. It depends on how insane these pirates are. But like you said, it sounds like if we fail, they'll just send us back to the Rathole, so where's the harm in trying?"

They made no particular effort at stealth, and since they approached straight-on, Delilah had a long, clear look at the station at the center of the sphere's interior. It was composed of several overlapping rings arranged around a small globe. "Killbot Bay," Delilah said.

"Explain."

"That's what the pirate base was called on *Hyperion's Revenge*. I bet that's what they call it here, too." She peered through the screen. "Is that… a crow's nest?" A long pole extended up from the top of the station's center, sliding between a gap in the rings, and it looked like there was a small perch of some kind at the tip.

"Crows do not thrive in vacuum," Crowbar said. "I should know."

"Was that a joke?"

"It was a very funny joke."

"A crow's nest is like, a lookout on old sailing ships, there'd be someone stationed up there, either a young person with good eyes or someone with a telescope, to see what was coming over the horizon." The crow's nest lowered again. "I think they know we're coming. You should get ready."

Crowbar obligingly scuttled into the interior of the shuttle wall, squeezing his flexible body and arranging his pseudopods around various bits of conduit until he was entirely inside. Delilah put the wall panel back in place, securing it firmly. Crowbar had assured her he could escape from worse.

Then she waited. The pirate station's computer took control of the shuttle's navigation and guided it in. The rings were much larger than she'd realized, and seemingly made of the same substance as the larger sphere around them. The spherical module at the center irised an opening, and the shuttle entered. Clamps seized the vessel and dragged it to the floor of the deck. Delilah tried to prepare herself, sitting in the pilot's seat, hands gripping the armrests.

The shuttle door opened, and an outlandish alien hauled itself in through the opening. It had three real eyes and half a dozen more in the form of precious stones somehow embedded in its face, and its body was draped all over with golden chains, so many that it rattled as it moved. It held a short blade, also improbably made of gold. A soft metal, terrible to make weapons from, but Delilah supposed it would run her through well enough. "You're Counter," she said, recognizing the glittering ensemble of the pirate quartermaster from *Hyperion's Revenge*.

"How d'ye know my name, you rotten sea biscuit?" the alien growled in a masculine voice that, Delilah thought, was sampled straight from the TV show.

The moment she'd been waiting for had arrived. In one episode of *Hyperion's Revenge*, the pirates had captured a Naval crew, but one of the crew members had secretly been a pirate spy in disguise, and he'd spoken a pass phrase to reveal himself, and been taken straight to Starbeard's quarters to report. She only remembered the line because her friends had made a joke of the phrase, imbuing it with sexual innuendo with waggling eyebrows and lascivious grins. "I know what's inside Davy Jones's locker," she said.

Counter froze, then reared back. "No," he said. "It can't be. After all this time–"

"I need to see Starbeard." That was the next line. She was going to stick to the script, even if Counter wasn't.

"Welcome… home, matey?" Counter's reply was tentative… but it was the right words, and Delilah relaxed.

Beyond the stark lines of the hangar, the station was an impressive replica of the sets from the show, as best she remembered. There were brass lamps, rough-carved beams, wooden floors, flame-kissed barrels, cargo netting hanging from the ceiling, pillars inexplicably encrusted with barnacles, and crooked shelves holding bottles of mysterious liquid. The pirates couldn't have cobbled all this together from materials pillaged off the ships – they must have amazing fabrication engines.

There was artificial gravity in this part of the station, too, just like in the pirate haven on the show, though back then it had been pure speculative fiction.

Counter bellowed as he led her through the station: "Make way for the emissary!" She saw a few other pirates, peeking around corners or peering through half-closed doors, and one even briefly lifting a trap door on the floor. Finally Counter stopped before a set of tall wooden doors carved all over with krakens and sea serpents, and rapped on it with his golden sword.

"Enter!" Starbeard's voice called.

The doors swung wide, revealing the captain's quarters. Starbeard sat on a stool behind a wide table covered in food – fat bunches of grapes, some kind of roasted bird, a mountain of potatoes, bubbling casseroles, tureens of soup. The spread was probably all just nutritional mush shaped and flavored by a food printer, but Delilah's mouth watered anyway.

Starbeard beckoned with a pseudopod holding a good facsimile of a half-eaten chicken leg. "What's all this then, Counter?"

"She says… she says…"

"I know what's inside Davy Jones's locker." Delilah looked around, and shook her head. "Starbeard – the *real* Starbeard – won't believe this. You'd better hope he's flattered instead of horrified."

"The true Starbeard *lives*?" Counter said, aghast. "Then – he found it?"

"The Mountain of Youth?" Delilah said. "Oh, yes." The pirate king's ultimate (stupid) goal was to find the location of a legendary cryovolcano, reputedly located on one of Saturn's moons, that spewed forth an icy vapor composed of unknown chemicals that would make anyone who bathed in its spray immortal. "You lot must have gotten your hands on that old film Starbeard's biographer made, and… what? Decided to follow his example?"

Counter was buying it completely, but Starbeard gazed at her with no visible reaction. "We meant no insult by taking on the trappings of his people," Counter said. "But we saw in Starbeard a kindred spirit–"

"Why don't you leave me with the emissary," the alien Starbeard said, dropping the chicken leg. "We have much to discuss. About, ah, opening lines of communication with the *other* Killbot Bay, and the like."

Counter scurried out, pulling the doors shut behind him. Delilah sat down in a wooden chair across from Starbeard, and propped her feet up on the table. She was getting into this. "I didn't want to frighten your quartermaster, but you should know, it's a dangerous thing to take the name of a pirate as fearsome as Starbeard for your own–"

Starbeard took off his hat and tossed it on the table, then tore off his eyepatch. There wasn't even an eye underneath it. "Has anyone else who arrived on your ship seen the show?" he demanded, in a rather less dramatic voice than before.

"The show?" Delilah said.

"*Hyperion's Revenge*! It's not a documentary. It's a fictional entertainment, and, I think, not a very good one… but I'd rather my crew not figure that out. I don't want a mutiny on my hands." His skin flushed an unhealthy looking shade of green. "I was afraid this day would come. You've put me in a very difficult position. Do your crewmates know the truth? Did you tell the people on the Rathole?"

Delilah opened her mouth, then realized any answer she gave could be dangerous. If she said only she knew, one stab would solve the problem; if she said *everyone* knew, it might invite a series of stabs at other people. "I'll answer your questions after you answer mine."

"What's to stop me from just killing you, and sanitizing the Rathole?" he asked.

Delilah didn't have an answer for that.

Starbeard sighed. "I'll tell you what's to stop me. The chance to talk to someone who *isn't* delusional for a few moments, that's what. This life was all so much simpler when I still believed."

"How did… all this… happen?" Delilah said. "We know this was some sort of Axiom facility–"

Starbeard shoved back from the table with the clatter. "The Axiom? My people called them the Fundamental, but you mean the same race, don't you? Yes. The old masters. They built this place, and they put *my* ancestors here to run it, tens of thousands of years ago. How did you people come to learn of the Axiom?"

"We've had some encounters," Delilah said.

"And lived to tell about it." Starbeard shook his head. "They have truly fallen low."

"They built this place," Delilah said. "But *why*? Is it some kind of weapon?"

"You'd think that, but no. This place was supposed to save the universe. Or, at least, the galaxy. The Fundamental were long-range planners. They knew someday this universe was likely to end, via heat death, the big crunch, or, in the hypothesis favored by the sect who built this place, the Big Rip. Do you know what that is?"

Delilah nodded. That was Intro to Cosmology stuff. "The idea is, the universe is expanding, and eventually it will expand so thoroughly that matter itself will be pulled apart – molecules, atoms, even subatomic particles, torn to pieces."

"That's right. This station was meant to help keep the local agglomeration of matter *together*."

"You mean you can reverse entropy," Delilah said.

"Only on a very local scale," Starbeard said. "There were supposed to be trillions of these stations built – we were just the first one, the prototype and proof-of-concept. These stations were meant to encircle the entire galaxy, and protect it from destruction, creating a bubble of stability in an ever emptier universe. But this place was created during the last days of the Fundamental Empire, with various factions arguing about the best way to preserve the future – some wanted to tunnel into *other* universes, and some wanted to develop a form of psychic time travel to project their consciousnesses back… there were all sorts of approaches. In the end, our faction failed. They were supposed to be indestructible in war, because they were able to reverse entropy, but based on a report from the last survivors, their enemies froze them in stasis instead, and then flung them into a singularity. Their enemies stopped them from changing, then slowly ripped them apart – it was an ironic form of execution, you see, to mock the plans of our founders. The Fundamental liked that sort of gesture."

"So you've just… been here?" Delilah said. "For millennia?"

"I've only been here for centuries," Starbeard said. "Before my generation, we hatched from our incubators, absorbed the memories of our forebears, and went back to work, as if our work mattered. We kept the engines going, and we collected and analyzed the samples–"

"Samples?"

"We were meant to monitor the progress of the Big Rip," Starbeard said. "The station constantly opens wormholes to different points in the galaxy, and draws in whatever matter it finds there. Usually it's just space dust, but occasionally we get bits of asteroids, atmosphere, core samples from planets, chunks of crust, and the like. The station analyzes those samples to chart the progress of the Big Rip."

"How… how is it progressing?"

"Who cares?" Starbeard said. "We can't do anything about it. This station alone isn't powerful enough to protect *itself* from being torn apart eventually, and we'll all be long dead before that happens anyway. I haven't looked at the data in centuries. We were hopeless here, going through the motions, until one day…"

"The sample you collected was a ship," Delilah realized.

"I know now it was a mineral scout vessel," Starbeard said. "Only one pilot inside… but he was a fan of *Hyperion's Revenge*. He had all the episodes of his favorite show in his data banks, to pass the time while he was out on long lonely voyages. He even had his own version of the captain's hat. *This* hat." He tapped the tricorn on the table. "We didn't know what the ship was, you see – we'd never seen anything like it. As for the pilot! We'd never even heard of humans. We didn't understand him, and when we boarded, he attacked us. I'm afraid we killed the man. The entropy engines can work both ways, you see. They can *increase* disorder, too. If deployed correctly, the main engine on this station could disintegrate a planet, but we hardly needed that much power to take care of one human." Starbeard slumped. "We tore him apart. A little rip."

"And then you watched the show, and you thought it was real."

"We'd never seen fiction! There was enough data in the ship's banks for us to learn the rudiments of the language. Once we watched *Hyperion's Revenge*, we realized we were pirates *too*. Didn't we steal from the unsuspecting universe, taking what we wanted, unstoppable? Starbeard was an inspiration to us as well. *He* was trying to attain immortality, wasn't he? Just like we tried to do for the galaxy. He sought eternal life in geysers of alien ice. The story was beautiful. And… I'll be honest with you… we needed something. We needed a culture. An organizing principle. Every generation got a little smaller, because a certain number of us failed to thrive when they realized our mission was futile, and when the ancient masters never came to check on us, and we never heard from anyone else. Here we were, bound inside this inescapable sphere! Some of us chose to die, and that number got greater with every passing century. Until we found a new purpose."

"You started taking ships deliberately," Delilah said.

"Using the data in that first ship, yes," Starbeard said. "We tuned the sampling engines to make them open more frequently in inhabited regions, and as we learned about the human colony systems from later ships, we started raiding those, too. That gave us a purpose, and made us feel powerful. We emulated Starbeard! We treated our prisoners humanely, and never killed them."

I guess it's a good thing it was a children's show and not a gritty drama, Delilah thought.

"We would have ransomed them back, like they do on the show, but the sampling engines don't work that way. Things come in, but they don't get *out*. We have short-range teleporters, and we've tried them at the edge of our prison, but the walls are too thick for us to reach the other side. We can't get out of here. The Fundamental didn't see us as people; they saw us as part of the equipment. We were never supposed to leave. Since we couldn't visit other worlds, we settled for turning this world into a different one."

"When did you find out the truth about the show?" Delilah said.

"It didn't take long. I've been keeping up this ruse for a long time. I soon saw other entertainment programs on other ships. I talked to some of the prisoners, and learned about 'fiction.' Starbeard wasn't real. *Hyperion's Revenge* wasn't even highly regarded as a lie. I didn't think my crew could handle realizing their role model was created to amuse alien children, so I've hidden the truth from them."

"You've hurt people," Delilah said. "You've brought people here and trapped them. So many of them have died, lost, taken from their homes. You have to stop this."

"Their suffering is nothing compared to ours," Starbeard said. "But… I agree. Something needs to change. The prisoners on the Rathole give us a little entertainment, attempting to escape, sometimes attacking us, but I've sensed uneasiness in my crew. All *this* is beginning to seem pointless, too. I've been thinking, the real problem is… we don't have a Forrest Flood here."

Delilah blinked. "You mean… you need an enemy?"

"Human entertainments often have antagonists," Starbeard said. "How would *you* like to be our Flood? I could even claim you're the great-great-something-granddaughter of the *real* Forrest Flood, sent here to root out the heirs to Starbeard's legacy. I'd provide you with a ship, and you could crew your vessel with the rabble from the Rathole. I'd outfit you with an entropy engine, so you wouldn't have to worry about taking *real* damage. Think of the fun we could have!"

"That… doesn't sound fun."

"Does it sound more fun than sitting on the Rathole waiting a few decades to die?" he said. "We're stuck in here. We have to pass the time somehow. Or do you fancy being torn apart atom by atom? If you don't play along… you have to go. I can't risk your knowledge getting out and infecting my crew. I know killing you is not what Starbeard would do, it's not very sporting, but, well… this *is* just a role I'm playing."

"Well. When you put it that way." She cleared her throat. "Starbeard, I'm Delilah Flood, and I'm here to end your reign of–"

Then the lights went out, and the gravity too.

Starbeard shouted things in a language she didn't know.

"Hey, Delilah," Ashok said in her earpiece comms. "Grab a sword and try to get back to the hangar, would you?"

There *was* a sword on the table somewhere, but she didn't want to reach for it in the dark and slice her hand off, so she planted her feet on the edge of the table and shoved herself through the air toward the double doors. She pushed through them, and there *was* some light out there, because some of those brass lamps held actual flames. Counter was floating in the middle of the corridor, his gold gleaming as he flailed around and failed to reach rafters or wall. Delilah went past him and plucked his golden sword from a waving pseudopod as she went. He squawked, but she ignored him, grabbing onto a chandelier and swinging herself down another corridor toward the station's hangar bay.

"What happened?" Delilah said over her comms.

"I woke up the boss," Winslow rumbled in her ear. "Grigsby came along. Crowbar managed to turn off the lights and gravity on the station there, and Ashok is dispatching some drones to help him take down the entropy engine."

"Once the pirates aren't indestructible anymore, I think it'll perk up the prisoners on the Rathole," Ashok said.

"So basically everyone else did something wonderful except me," Delilah said. "Good to know." She was nearly to the hangar.

"You are the reason for my success," Crowbar spoke up. "The operations control center was occupied by four pirates playing cards, and I could not have possibly overcome them all. Soon after your arrival, however, another pirate burst in and told them there was an emissary here from the real Killbot Bay, and they all rushed away, allowing me free rein to tamper with their systems."

"What you did, Mears," Ashok said, "was *social* engineering, and that's the kind I've always been the absolute worst at. Wait in the hangar for my drones to arrive. A bunch of little *mes* are on the way, and they'll help you–"

Something snagged Delilah by the ankle and swung her into the wall. She didn't have weight, but she still had mass, and though she turned to take the impact on her shoulder instead of her head, it still jarred her. She swung her sword wildly, but that just made her corkscrew around inelegantly. A pirate she hadn't seen before crawled up her body, grabbed the sword, and shoved it through a loop on his belt, though his squidlike body didn't really have a waist. "The captain wants you on the flagship," he said, and then everything went blurry.

They thumped to the deck of a ship where the artificial gravity still worked, and Delilah realized she'd just been teleported. She lifted her head. The pirate wore a red bandana over his bulbous head: just a generic unnamed crewperson, in terms of the show.

She punched him in what passed for his face, and he squawked and dropped the sword. She got to her feet and pelted down the corridor. The interior of this vessel was modeled on the *Hyperion's Revenge* from the show, a wild mixture of old-timey wood-and-brass and twenty-second-century-modern glass-and-metal. Her roommate Bree had been a far bigger fan of the show, and probably had the whole floor plan memorized, but Delilah was just looking for a place she could duck out of sight. "Ashok, I'm on the flagship!"

"The one with all the skulls and stuff?" Ashok said.

"That's the one."

"Ah, yeah, I see it coming around the station now," he said. "Oh, look. It has cannons. How do you feel about doing some *non*-social engineering?"

"It would be a welcome change, captain," Delilah said.

Ashok didn't have a floor plan for the *Hyperion's Revenge* – there was no access to fan sites on the Tangle from the interior of an impenetrable sphere on the far side of the galaxy from civilization – but he did have schematics for the same *kind* of ship, and under all the cosmetic changes, that was close enough.

Delilah got the sense there weren't very many pirates here, since she didn't encounter any while she made her way to the service tunnels. You didn't need numbers when you were impregnable to harm, she supposed.

Starbeard's voice crackled over the ship's PA system. "Delilah Flood!" he boomed. "Surrender, or we'll fire on your ship!"

"Pass," she muttered. She dropped down a shaft and made her way to the engine room. "What am I looking for, Ashok?"

"Something that doesn't look like it belongs on a spaceship," Ashok said.

"Captain, there are fake skulls down here, and stubs of candles, and a big barrel with 'grog' written on the side and a ladle hanging next to it. Could you be more specific?"

"Something *technological* that doesn't look like it belongs."

"I – oh." Behind the grog barrel was a hurricane lamp, but inside its bulbous glass shade there was no flame: instead, a small sphere etched with glowing white lines floated unsupported. "I think I found the thing."

"Great! Smash it!"

Delilah picked up the ladle and swung it into the glass.

The glass shattered, and then promptly unshattered, piecing itself back together.

"That didn't work," she said. "I don't know why I thought it would."

"Hey, worth a try," Ashok said. "The entropy engine is in some kind of containment field, I assume?"

"Yes."

"Is *that* connected to anything?"

Delilah picked up the hurricane lamp, and wires led from its base into the wall. "Ah ha," she said, and carefully disconnected the leads. Apparently *that* didn't count as increasing disorder, because they didn't spontaneously rewire themselves. She looked around, found an old burlap sack, and stuffed the hurricane lamp and its floating sphere inside. "Okay! I think you can damage this ship now."

"I'd rather not do so with you *on* it," Ashok said. "There should be a shuttle bay on the next deck up. Can you get there?"

The ship rumbled around her. *Hyperion's Revenge* was firing cannons – or more likely firing missiles out of apertures made to *look* like cannons.

"Oh, no, my good port window," Ashok said. "They cracked it. I *liked* that window! Get out of there, engineer."

"On it." Delilah wanted her hands free, so she secured the sack across her chest with some lengths of rope, feeling ridiculously low-tech. She picked up the ladle, too. It wasn't a sword, but it was something. She climbed back up the shaft, hurried down the corridor, and turned toward the shuttle bay.

Starbeard was there, blocking the door, armed with a cutlass and what looked like an ancient flintlock pistol. "We could have had fun," he said flatly, and raised the gun.

There was a tremendous boom, a flash of light, and a hard *shove* into Delilah's chest that flung her backward – but then her momentum stopped, and she hung suspended in the air, her feet off the ground, staring as a metal ball flew back through the air into the barrel of the pistol, and the light somehow *unflashed*. The ball had struck the lamp in the sack on her chest, and the entropy engine had defended itself.

"No!" Starbeard said, just as Delilah's feet hit the deck again. She used her weird reversed momentum to propel herself forward and hit him square on top of his stupid tricorn hat with the metal ladle just as hard as she could.

He collapsed, his pseudopods giving way beneath him, and she kicked his weapons away before kicking him in the side. "Compliments of Forrest Flood," she said, and rushed into the shuttle bay.

The final battle was a bit one-sided. The pirates didn't know anything about *actual* fights between spacecraft, just what they'd see on a children's show, and without their invulnerability to win the day (and, Delilah suspected, with their captain unconscious), the first mate hailed the *Golden Spider* and surrendered. He wore a black-and-white striped garment, had a silver robot parrot perched on his shoulder, and went by the name Squee. His counterpart on the show was famously cowardly, and he played to type: "You win! You can have anything! Just don't hurt us, Captain Flood!"

"You'd better accept their surrender, Delilah," Ashok said. "They won't believe a disembodied voice is in charge over here."

She straightened her spine, stood on the bridge before the viewscreen, and in her best haughty Forrest Flood voice said, "Your days of terrorizing the spaceways are over, pirate scum."

Sometimes it was *fun* to play the villain.

* * *

They rounded up the pirates, stripped them of their weapons, and put them on the Rathole. The pirates didn't seem particularly demoralized – in fact, they seemed *excited*, like this was a new chapter in a story that had become a bit stale and repetitive. They kept Starbeard in a sealed room on the *Golden Spider*, "as befits his rank," Ashok said.

The former human prisoners were all a bit dazed, especially Vane, who refused to believe they could actually escape, but who seemed pleased the pirates were locked up for once. Rahmah and Jabir were on the station, enjoying all the *good* booze Starbeard had taken from the ships he'd captured, even though the Free didn't enjoy alcohol like humans did; he was just recreating the Vault of Spirits from the show. Guðríður, Grigbsy, and Every were with Ashok's biggest drone, picking over the old ships for anything worth bringing back with them when the bridge generator recharged and they were able to get out of here in a couple of days.

Delilah, Winslow, and Crowbar sat around the galley table. "What do we do with the pirates now?" she asked.

"They kidnapped, and they stole, and the Jovian Imperative would certainly be happy to prosecute them, for taking the *Pikeville* alone," Winslow said.

"Ugh," Ashok said. "They did terrible stuff, no argument here, but… they didn't really understand what they were doing. Their worldview was all messed up. I don't think they'd even understand what was happening if the Imperative prosecuted them. Without their wormhole generators and entropy engines they're basically harmless. My inclination is to strip the armaments from one of the big ships in here, fill it with media about intrepid teams of scientific explorers, send them out to wander the galaxy. Out here, though. Not where people live."

Delilah thought about the room Vane had shown her. All those bones. "Most of them were just confused, about the nature of reality, among other things," Delilah said. "But Starbeard *knew* what he was doing."

"I tend to agree with you there," Ashok said. "So how about we hand him over to the Imperative? Does that work for everyone?"

"Yes," Delilah said.

"Fine with me," Winslow said.

"The issue does not interest me," Crowbar said.

"Then consider justice done," Ashok said. "Or anyhow in process."

"The board is green!" Delilah said.

"Then our long period of enforced interiority is over," Ashok said from a little yellow drone at her elbow in the engine room. "You want to do the honors?"

Delilah tweaked her tablet, activating the bridge generator, and the screen in the corner showed her the wormhole opening. Grigsby piloted the *Pikeville* through first, with the prisoners crammed into the small space, and Every guided through one of the larger ships, refurbished while they were waiting for the bridge generator to recharge. That ship held the pirates, now led by a baffled but cheerful Squee.

The *Golden Spider* went through last, emerging within view of the anomaly. The sphere no longer had shining threads of light on its surface, since Crowbar had unhooked the entropy engine at the center of the station. The invulnerable Axiom station was now just a vast quantity of entirely vulnerable metal.

"We're really going to blow it up with the entropy engine inside?" Delilah said.

"We talked about it," Ashok said. "Are you changing your vote?"

"No," she said. "I hate to get rid of something so amazing, but… it's the right thing." Under interrogation, Starbeard had explained exactly how the central entropy engine could be deployed to make a planet fall apart in seconds. It wasn't very complicated. That fact had led Ashok and his crew to decide it was better if the Jovian Imperative and other governments never knew such a device existed.

Delilah went down to the cargo bay, where Crowbar was already opening up the big crate she'd noticed when she first boarded. "Every tells me Vane is crying," Ashok said. "Apparently they're happy tears. I remember those. I always worried they'd rust my face. Sometimes being a machine intelligence is better."

"I'm glad he's happy." Delilah picked up an actual crowbar and helped the other Crowbar finish uncrating Ashok's invention. "This thing looks like a giant spider."

"A giant *golden* spider," Ashok said. "Not real gold, of course, but it's shiny, huh? I'm surprised the pirates didn't loot it, honestly. They did a pretty half-assed job of pillaging overall." The drone had lots of legs, and a huge, bulbous central body glistening with sensors. "It's pregnant, too."

Delilah and Crowbar got the drone turned on, and it rose on its legs and trotted toward an airlock. They launched the drone, and watched until it vanished from sight, then Delilah pulled up the drone's own camera view on her terminal. Crowbar hung upside down from a nearby strut and watched with her.

The golden spider hit the surface of the anomaly, dug in with gripping claws, and began to disgorge miniature versions of itself. The tiny spiders dispersed in arcing lines of mathematical perfection across the surface of the anomaly, disappearing into the grooves, where the anomaly's surface was thinner. The spiders were armed with various cutting, burning, and acid-etching implements, and her data feed told her they'd found a combination that let them burrow deeper into the surface.

"Looks like they're all in place, Ashok."

"Release the boom," he said.

The terminal view switched to a view of the anomaly as a whole from the *Golden Spider*'s cameras. Nuclear fireballs bloomed all over it as the explosive payloads inside each of the little spiders went off, and this time, the disorder only increased, and kept increasing. The liberated prisoners whooped and cheered over the comms.

"I found that very satisfying." Crowbar dropped from the strut and scuttled away.

"Mission accomplished," Ashok said. "Now we just have to entertain ourselves for a few days until the bridge generator recharges and we can go home."

"How *ever* will we pass the time, captain?" Delilah said, and grinned.

"You really don't mind me doing the honors?" Delilah said. She stood in the ship's gym, on the port side, wearing an environment suit, because the big window here had taken cannon fire from *Hyperion's Revenge*. A huge crack ran across the whole window, two meters of nearly straight fracture-line that zig-zagged into a pair of branches each half that length. It looked like a capital letter Y drawn by someone who'd had too much to drink. Ashok didn't think the window was so badly damaged it was likely to break, but better safe, so the gym was sealed off and airtight for the moment.

"I don't even have hands anymore, Delilah," Ashok said. "I'd have to fab a drone with a trigger finger to do it myself. Go for it."

"It's pretty silly to make it look like a retro ray gun," Delilah said.

"I'll have you know you are holding a *perfect* replica of Forrest Flood's trusty sidearm," Ashok said. "At least, as best I could tell from the snippet of footage in that documentary. I'm excited to watch the whole show when we get back to civilization. Take aim, pirate hunter."

"All right." Delilah drew the shiny silver and red pistol. A tiny sphere, filigreed in white lines, was hidden inside the conveniently bulbous space behind the flared barrel. She and Ashok had spent the past couple of days figuring out how to wire the thing up and make it work.

They'd talked about getting rid of the little entropy engine she'd taken from *Hyperion's Revenge*, just like all the other ones they'd found inside the anomaly, but as Ashok said, "Even in the wrong hands, that little thing is not going to destroy any planets. It could maybe disintegrate a teapot." Even so, they'd set up countermeasures to ensure the sphere would destroy itself if anyone tried to take it out of the pistol for purposes of reverse engineering.

"Ready," Ashok said. Delilah raised the pistol. "Aim." She trained it on the place where the crack in the window split: the point of maximum weakness. "Fire," he said. She squeezed the trigger.

The port window unbroke.

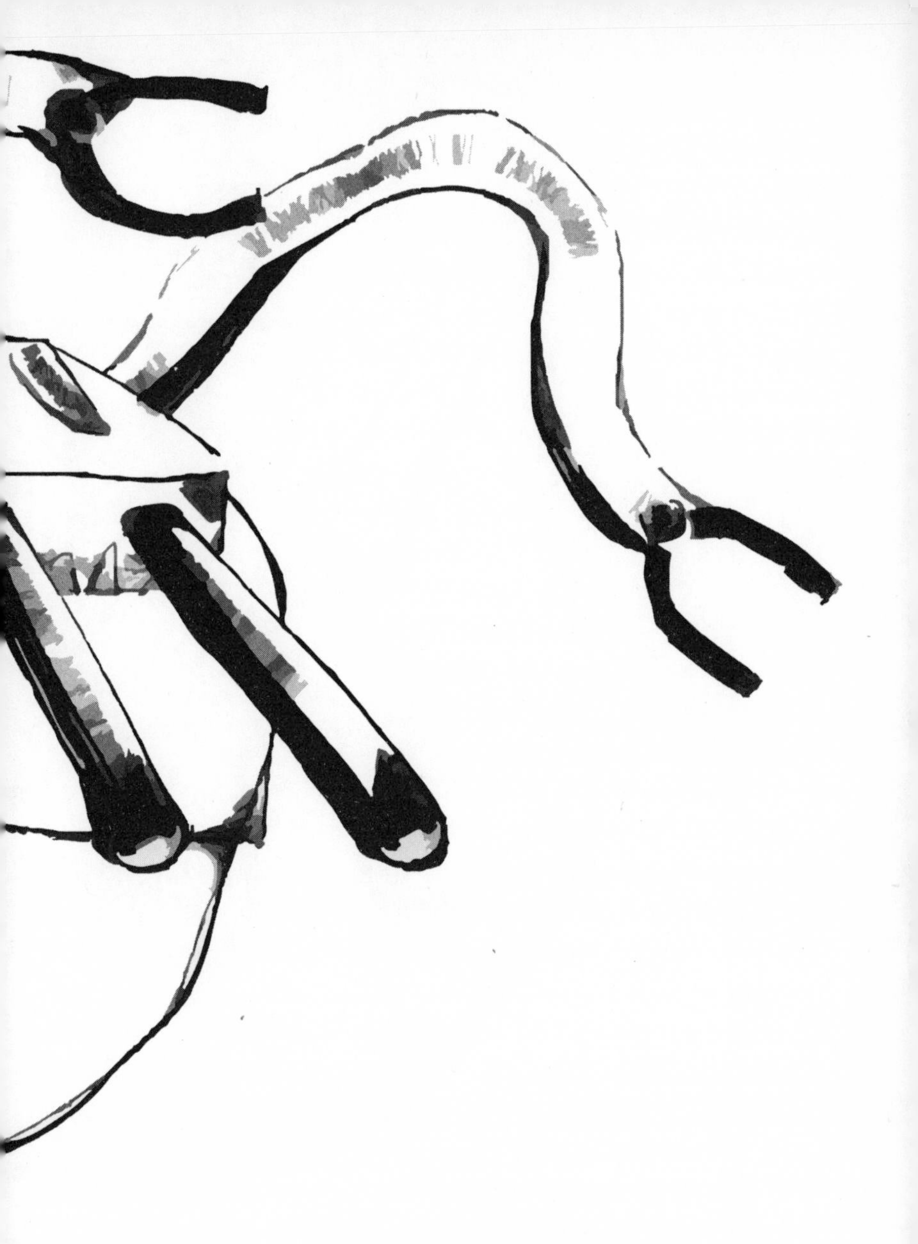

THE ARTIFICIAL STARS

*

Five years ago, a little piece of me saved the life of the woman I loved from an exploding space station. Later, when I reconnected with that separate node of my consciousness and (mostly) absorbed his memory into my own, I thanked him for his service, and then I shut his awareness down – because he was in a body too damaged to recover, and I didn't want him to experience the trauma of total system failure.

When you can make copies of your mind and send them out into the cold of space in a variety of mechanical bodies, and link up with them and download their memories when they come back (or you recover their remains), you get to experience a wide array of death and suffering. That grants a rare and valuable perspective… but it's also really awful and terribly depressing. "Machine consciousness problems," as my friend (and fellow AI) Ashok would say.

Now, though… it appears that copy of my consciousness who sacrificed himself for Callie didn't get shut down properly after all. I received a message yesterday, with an encryption code that proves it came from that presumed-dead-for-several-years version of me. My long-lost twin has invited me to visit him at a remote location. He says he needs to show me something.

He says if I *don't* come, the universe will be destroyed.

Pretty high stakes. Usually the biggest threat we face around here is the galaxy being destroyed, or just all human life getting exterminated (plus artificial intelligences based on the templates of human minds; don't forget us, for though we are few, we are mighty).

Intriguing and alarming as all this is, I really can't go, because I have a lot of responsibilities. I'm president of the Trans-Neptunian Alliance, the polity that controls everything in humankind's birth solar system from the orbit of Neptune out into the Oort Cloud. It's a big job, even with my big brain, and a lot of smart humans and aliens (of the species called the Free) to help me. It's not the kind of work I can put on pause for a journey of uncertain duration to a mysterious destination.

Fortunately, as we've already established, I can make copies of my consciousness. There are laws in all the civilized systems against AI making full duplicates of themselves (in some places we're forbidden entirely). The humans are afraid we'll become too numerous otherwise and suck up all the available computing power and bandwidth, or something. Here in the TNA, we're allowed to temporarily bud off smaller (which is to say, less smart and capable), versions of ourselves to operate drones and the like. Those minds ideally get downloaded back to our central selves, and then cease to exist as separate identities. Which is good, honestly, because it doesn't take long for differing experience and separate perspective to cause *divergence,* and after a few weeks, the "you" that comes back isn't quite the same "you" that went out. Maybe the humans are right to worry.

I'm guessing this mystery version of me that's been living its own life for five years isn't eager to be absorbed into my main self. I could send a limited version of myself off on this errand, but I'd really rather have my full capabilities, and we have ships with enough computing power to house me in all my glory. Like I said, though: there are laws against creating fully functional independent copies. Once upon a time, I might not have cared, but these days, well. It's important for me to do the right thing, because of the whole "being president" thing.

My office does come with some benefits, though. I'm not a

monarch, and I can't just wave a disembodied hand and change the rules, but I can request an exemption from that law for national security reasons, if two-thirds of the cabinet agrees. The idea behind that provision was: the TNA might someday need me to become a whole fleet of warships (who are also generals with databases of tactical and strategic knowledge) to fend off foreign aggressors. This situation isn't *that*... but I'd say a rogue consciousness bringing news of a universe-destroying threat also has some national security implications.

So let's call a cabinet meeting.

Cabinet meetings take place in a Hypnos simulation. I do have a remote body that's useful for navigating physical space – it's humanoid, sleek, and shiny, with a chemical printer in one arm to dispense medicine, terrifying secret armaments in the other arm just in case, and it's best not to ask about what's in the legs or torso. Sometimes that body walks around our capital, New Meditreme (a space station that's home to thirty thousand full-time residents, and growing), but polling shows about a quarter of the people find that body creepy, and my own eavesdropping reveals that half my cabinet does. People on station have started calling that remote body "the Mayor," and there are mostly good-natured jokes: "The Mayor is out on the campaign trail again," and "Here comes the Mayor, who's got a baby to kiss?" I've started thinking of the body by that name myself.

Meeting in simulation is easier, anyway, and it doesn't make any difference to me. Real or virtual, everything I see, hear, and feel is just sensor input, after all.

We take turns choosing the simulated environment, and it was Dr. Elena Oh's choice this time. (She's my minister of health and wellness.) I instantiated my avatar on a platform of obsidian floating in a lake of lava, surrounded by jagged black mountains. Beyond the mountains, immense creatures, hidden in mist and shadow, lumbered past. Kaiju? Old gods?

Elena is a time refugee, born centuries in the past and awakened from cryonic suspension less than a decade ago, and she takes a childlike delight in the ways technology has advanced since her day. Immersive virtual reality with full sensory inputs is one of the future's delights she most enjoys, and when it's her turn to choose the meeting place, we always end up in the world of whatever fantasy or science fiction media she's currently enjoying. This was better than the crumbling temple overrun by demon monkeys, anyway. That one was pretty distracting.

A conference table with seven chairs stood at the center of the obsidian platform. I was the first to arrive, and my avatar wore an old-timey diving suit, complete with a big round helmet; I don't know why, but I find that form very comfortable. Maybe it reminds me of being in a spaceship: a mind, comfortably ensconced in a vessel meant to provide safety in a place without light or air. (I used to run my mind on a spaceship, the *White Raven*. These days, my main "body" is New Meditreme itself. Living in the computers of a huge space station is great. Lots of room to stretch out and breathe, and plenty of comforting redundancy, even beyond my distributed dormant backups.) I sat down in the big chair at the head of the table and waited.

Elena rose up slowly from the lava, rivulets of molten rock running from her hair and down her shoulders. I knew it was Elena because everyone else uses consistent avatars, and she appears as something different every time. (See above re: childlike delight.) This body was humanoid, female in its curvy contours, and made of the same obsidian as the platform, but supple. Her hair *was* lava, I realized, a continual flow that somehow didn't accumulate or puddle all over the floor, just stopped halfway down her back and then recirculated. Her eyes shone like lava, too, and when she smiled, her teeth were luminous. She waved. "Shall! Emergency meetings worry me. *Should* I be worried?" She dropped into the chair on my left.

"I specifically said there was no imminent danger so you wouldn't worry."

"When I hear 'no imminent danger,' Shall, what I *hear* is, 'Just you wait.'"

"I'll explain everything when the others arrive, but I have no reason to believe that New Meditreme or the TNA as a whole are in any particular danger." (True: they weren't in *particular* danger. When the whole universe is at stake, that's more of a *general* danger.)

Drake and Janice arrived next; they are the ministers of trade and commerce respectively. Broadly speaking, Drake deals with foreign trade, and Janice handles domestic business issues, though their spheres obviously overlap a lot. Drake is an optimistic proponent of win-win scenarios, and Janice is a suspicious pessimist who believes everyone is always trying to get away with something nefarious, so they balance each other well. I confess, it's always a bit disconcerting to see them in separate bodies. In the world of conventional matter, they share a single physical form, the consequence of a long-ago starship accident that left them both for dead. A group of alien healers, who meant well but had a poor grasp of human anatomy, salvaged the fragments of their bodies from the wreckage and put them back together as best they could, not realizing they were originally separate entities. The two of them share a nervous system and some major organs, and so they are inextricable, except in simulations, where they can each have their own body. Drake runs an avatar that looks like his old body, more or less: dark skin, long braids, gleaming white smile, dressed in a raw linen shirt, canvas shorts, and flip-flops. Janice favors the form of a Valkyrie, complete with breastplate and sword and an overall faint but discernible golden glow.

"You're watching *Cixin and the Fire Kaiju*?" Janice said. "It's pretty good until that stupid thing in season three–"

"Spoilers!" Elena pressed her hands to her ears.

Janice rolled her eyes. "It came out *twenty years ago*, Elena."

"Good morning, Mr. President," Drake said. "Is the world ending again?"

"Not if we can help it," I said.

Uzoma arrived next. Their avatar, as near as I can tell, is the same as their physical body, but with the little natural asymmetries of human appearance smoothed out, giving them a slightly eerie look of geometrical perfection: shaved head, dark skin, clear eyes. In their real body, you can see a faint scar on the scalp where an alien mind-control device burrowed into their brain, but there are no marks in the simulation. Their avatar wears a black jumpsuit that zips to the chin and covers every bit of skin but their hands. Uzoma is a time refugee, too, a brilliant scientist who was once in suspension with Elena. Uzoma spent a few years doing intense study on Ganymede, catching up on the state of computational technology (a lot happened in the centuries they were asleep), and at this point they know more about technology than *I* do, including the tech that enabled my creation. (Okay, not really. I understand that technology as completely and thoroughly as anyone can. But Uzoma is still very impressive for a human.) They agreed to serve as my minister of science and innovation last year, replacing a perfectly competent former executive from Almajara Corp who missed the comforts of Ganymede. We *are* a little frontier-like out here if you're used to the more established infrastructure of the Jovian Imperative.

"Welcome, Uzoma," I said. "I think that's everyone who's coming."

"Yeah, Callie is still out smashing things," Elena said.

Kalea Machedo – Callie – is my minister of security ("and breaking stuff," she likes to add). She set up all of our defense systems, but she's frequently off-station, leading missions in partnership with the Jovian Imperative military to destroy installations left behind by the ancient inimical aliens known as the Axiom. When humans have stumbled on Axiom technology, the results haven't been pretty. We've seen nanotech that tries to eat planets, mind-controlling brain spiders, grotesque biomedical experimentation, weapons that can tear apart space-time – that sort of thing. Once we acquired a list of Axiom facilities (maybe not all of them, but a *lot* of them), we set about proactively destroying them. Callie has possession of one of the only two personal wormhole generators in human hands, which means she can open gates to anywhere in the galaxy and let the Imperative warships through. They have the guns, but she – which is to say, we – have the power. Saving the universe does keep her off-station a lot, though.

Callie is also Elena's wife. She's *also,* in a roundabout way, my ex. Do I still love her? Of course. You would too, if you knew her like I do. I'm not jealous of Elena, though. She makes Callie far happier than I ever could... and Elena is both adorable *and* good at her job, a combination I find hard to resist. I love Elena too, like a sister. These days, my love for Callie is more of a wistful memory of past passion combined with respect and admiration than the desperate yearning it once was. When I first realized Callie and Elena were falling in love years ago, I won't lie, things were weird for a minute... but they aren't weird anymore.

"When did you last hear from Callie?" I asked.

"Yesterday. She opened up a bridge and sent through a probe to say they'd made it through okay and were about to start the hunt for the Axiom station," Elena said. "She's going to be out of contact while they're on the hunt though. You know how focused she gets."

"That I do." There was no easy communication with ships on the other side of a wormhole. They had to open a bridge to send a message through, and Callie's wormhole generator takes several hours to reset between uses. When out in the field, her preference is to leave the generator primed and ready in case a quick retreat a *long* way from the immediate vicinity is required – like if a fleet of alien terror-drones comes bearing down on her, say. That meant she was unreachable, so we'd have to reach this decision without her.

"Windowpane is still on Earth?" Drake asked.

I nodded. "She's deep in negotiations with the trade ambassador there, and tells me your proposal is being favorably received."

Drake grinned.

"I still can't believe you made a Liar your minister of foreign affairs," Janice said. "What was wrong with what's-his-name, Hancock?"

"The embezzlement was what was wrong," Drake said.

"Okay, yes, his morality was flexible, but at least the humans believed him when he talked."

"They shouldn't have," Drake said. "Besides, aren't all diplomats liars? Ours is just a Liar with a capital L."

"Remember they prefer to be called the Free," Elena said.

"Sorry," Janice and Drake said in perfect synchronicity; they did that sometimes, and it annoyed them both when it happened. "Old habits," Janice said. "It just seems weird to me. Most of the people on Earth have never even *met* one of the Free. All they know is the stories: they're shifty aliens who will lie about anything and everything, to cheat you or just for no reason at all. I know that's an overly broad stereotype, and I know the Free have their reasons for making up nonsense all the time, but it's still what those diplomats on the inner planets are going to be thinking."

I cleared my non-existent throat. "We needed to make it clear that the Trans-Neptunian Alliance is a different sort of polity. One where humans, resident aliens, and non-biological intelligences like myself are all equal, not just under the law but as a point of culture. Windowpane doesn't lie, anyway – you know that. She's from the sect of truth-tellers, just like Lantern, and would never knowingly utter a falsehood. She demonstrates this in every meeting by cheerfully stating a few things that are self-evidently true."

Janice snorted. "What, like, 'You have a very good hairpiece, premier,' or, 'I see your plastic surgery is healing beautifully, minister,' or, 'My, these appetizers are *dreadful*?' The inability to lie *also* sounds useless in a diplomat."

"When you make a pledge to tell the truth, you learn to get good at omission, evasion, and misdirection," Elena said. "Windowpane is perfectly polite, and really hard to pin down when she wants to be. You don't even notice she's running circles around you until hours later when you realize you never found out the thing you wanted."

I nodded. "Dealing with her for a few months will start to change human ideas of what the Free are like, and that's good for human culture as a whole."

"I guess we'll see if she comes back and we're in a state of war," Janice muttered.

"We're the only producers of artificial gravity technology in the galaxy," Drake said. "Windowpane could show up to meetings shooting holes in the walls with a ray gun and cackling 'death to humans' and they'd still make a deal with us in our favor."

"That's a cheerful point," Janice conceded.

"Ahem," I said. "I didn't call this meeting to talk about our absent cabinet ministers behind their backs, though I can see it's good for morale. I have a problem, and a proposed solution, and that solution requires a two-thirds majority vote of the cabinet… which means it has to be unanimously approved by the people in this room."

"That is statistically unlikely." Uzoma spoke for the first time. "Drake and Janice vote together only eleven percent of the time."

"Some issues we don't talk about in advance, so I don't realize I should be opposed," Janice said. "Most of my votes are symbolic anyway. I'm the token buzzkill. You mean I have a chance to *really* obstruct some ridiculous scheme this time? I'm excited. Do tell."

I sighed. "I received a message a few hours ago, sent via drone." I gestured, and a model of the drone appeared floating over the table: a head-sized dull metal sphere with a groove around its equator, and a few bumps and lumps of sensors here and there.

"That looks like Kaustikos." Janice scowled.

The resemblance had not escaped me. Kaustikos was a machine intelligence, like me except – well, except evil – and when we'd first met him, he'd inhabited a drone body much like this one. "Yes, but this drone had no mind inside it, just a message, encrypted with a special cipher I use only when talking to myself, to make sure any drones running an instance of my consciousness haven't been compromised when they report back."

"You're saying the message is from *you*?" Elena said. "I thought you didn't have any versions of yourself running off the station?"

"That's what I thought, too," I said. "And yet."

"Where did the drone come from?"

"According to its own claim, and to my analysis of its data banks, it originated at a point halfway between here and the Vanir system." That was the colony system farthest from our solar system. "Near the galactic center, at least for astronomical values of 'near.'"

"How did it get *there*?" Elena said.

"A more interesting question is how the drone got *here*," Uzoma said.

"To answer Elena, I have no idea," I said. "To answer Uzoma... it came through a wormhole. This other version of me has access to a bridge generator."

"That's Axiom tech," Janice said. "Some rogue version of you is playing around with Axiom tech?"

"You must know where this version of you originated," Uzoma said.

"Yes," I said. "Do you all remember when we destroyed the Axiom ship-building facility? The first Axiom station we found?"

"The one where I got kidnapped and almost mind-controlled?" Elena said. "I think I do."

"Some of wish we'd only *almost* been mind-controlled," Uzoma said.

Elena winced. "Right. Sorry."

"Watching that place get disintegrated by a thousand wormholes opening all over it all at once was the most enjoyably hardcore thing I've ever seen," Janice said.

I'd enjoyed it, too. "You may recall Callie was trapped on the station when she set off the chain reaction that destroyed the place. We dispatched a hull repair drone, running a local version of my mind, to save her. The drone was successful, retrieving Callie and carrying her to safety, though the drone itself was catastrophically damaged in the process, beyond hope of repair. I reached out to that drone, downloaded its memories – and then I *shut it down,* I swear. I deactivated its consciousness. Out of mercy, so it wouldn't have to experience system failure while awake."

"But somehow the drone, and its local version of *you,* survived," Uzoma said.

"That's what the message I received claimed. It's short on details, like how and why. But it did deliver a warning. This other me says if I don't come, the universe is in danger of being destroyed."

"The *universe*?" Drake said. "Is this other you prone to hyperbole?"

"I wouldn't think so," I said. "He should be… not to be rude… but rather *less* than me. I could hardly run a full version of myself on such a small machine, after all. But since I don't know how he became what he became, I can't be sure of his capabilities."

"Let's hear the message," Janice said.

I shook my head. (The advantage of a virtual avatar of a giant diving suit head is that, unlike the real thing, it *can* shake.) "The message was a compressed sensorium memory, it's more like an experience and stream-of-consciousness being dropped into my mind than something that could be listened to or read. You don't really have the equipment to 'read' it. I'm sorry."

"Artificial intelligences are weird," Janice said.

"You want us to grant you permission to instantiate a full copy of your consciousness on a Trans-Neptunian Alliance ship in order to investigate this message," Uzoma said. "I presume the other version of you proposes to open a wormhole to his location for you at a particular place and time?"

"Tomorrow, noon local," I confirmed. "It's a 'be there, or face the consequences,' sort of thing. Since I *can* be in two places at once, unlike most people, I figured it was worth considering."

"I don't see any problem with granting an exemption," Elena said.

"I also vote yes," Drake said. "This seems like an important thing to check out."

"What if this other you is, like, corrupted and insane? Janice said. "And it corrupts and drives *you* insane when it comes back and downloads into your main brain?"

"There are safeguards against integrating corrupted data," I said. "They were good before, and when we started dealing with the Axiom, we made them even better."

"Your resident grumpy isolationist is grumpy about the idea anyway," Janice said.

"You will be at the mercy of this other version of you," Uzoma said. "You will only be able to return if he opens a wormhole and allows you to do so. I realize he began as a copy of you, in a limited sense, but in five years... his motivations and intentions are impossible to know now."

"I agree. It's risky. And if that happens, it won't be any fun for the other version of me, but, well. When you have backups, you can take chances. You can try stuff. The ultimate consequences are less dire."

"Would you go alone?" Uzoma said.

I cocked my head. "I had assumed so."

"You should not go alone," Elena said.

"Why not?"

"You like to *talk* to people," Drake said.

"You get weird when you aren't around other intelligent beings," Janice said. "That's the whole *point* of the kind of AI you are – based on a human template, in the shape of a human mind, so you'll stay interested in humans, instead of fucking off to realms of pure abstract math and ignoring us, like our first attempts at artificial intelligences did."

"Sometimes I think those pure machine minds had the right idea," I said. "I don't need a babysitter."

"No, but you need company, for your mental health and wellness. Believe me," Elena said, "That's my department."

"None of you can go," I said. "You have too much work to do. Besides, it's too risky to take anyone. This might be a one-way trip."

"So take someone who *likes* risk," Elena said.

"Alas, Ashok is also an AI, and there's not enough room in the data banks of a ship for both of us."

"Maybe that new engineer of his, Mears?" Drake said. "Ashok told me he saw something of himself in her, which I assume means she'll cheerfully stick her head inside an alien artifact just to see what it looks like."

"I didn't vote 'yes' yet anyway," Janice said. "Who says you're taking anybody?"

"True," I said. "We can table the question of a companion until we know whether I'm even going. All in favor?"

Drake and Elena voted aye right away. Janice made us wait while she "weighed the cons, and the other cons," but in the end she voted yes, I think because she knew we'd call in Windowpane if she didn't anyway.

"Uzoma?" I said.

"I will vote yes, on the condition that I accompany you on the journey," Uzoma said.

"What? You can't go, you're the minister of–"

"I resign," Uzoma said.

"Don't *resign*!" I said. "You're great at your job, and we just got you into it a year ago!"

"My undersecretary is competent," Uzoma said. "Solvent is one of the Free, too, and having another alien on your cabinet will be good for you politically. The Free make up seventeen percent of the population of New Meditreme, and that percentage is growing."

"Why do you even want to go?"

"I grew up on Earth," Uzoma said. "I spent my adult life in universities, then in cryo-sleep for centuries, and, apart from a brief interval of terror on an alien shipbuilding facility, I have spent my subsequent consciousness *also* in universities, or in other scientific and research settings. The reason I joined the mission with Elena on the *Anjou* all those years ago was because I wished to see alien worlds. We were supposed to be colonists on a distant planet. That life never came to pass for me. I keenly feel my lack of travel and experience. This seems an opportunity to rectify that deficit, while also serving an important function on the mission."

I could hardly argue with that. Uzoma usually doesn't come to a decision without considering it thoroughly, so I shouldn't have been surprised.

"I think it's a good idea," Elena said. "For one thing, Uzoma is an expert on machine intelligence, and they might have some, ah, perspective on matters that could be more difficult for you to approach objectively."

That annoyed me, but was probably also true.

"Solvent could just be acting minister, while Uzoma is officially off-station working on a project," Elena went on. "When you come back safe, like I know you *will*, Uzoma can take back their position. How does that find?"

"That is acceptable," Uzoma said. "President Shall?"

"Taking a companion makes this all more dangerous. If the new version of me didn't ever come back, it would be too bad, but it wouldn't be a disaster. If *Uzoma* doesn't come back…"

"You know where the message came from," Elena said. "If you don't come back, Callie can open a wormhole there and go looking for you. Or Ashok, since he has his own bridge generator now. Or *both*."

"You know where the message *said* it came from," Janice said. "Why should we believe Shall's evil twin about anything?"

"There's no evidence that he's *evil*," Drake said.

"Just saying," Janice said.

"I accept that this journey has risks," Uzoma said. "My original mission to colonize another planet *was expected* to fail – that is why Earth sent so many ships, in the hope that some small number of them might succeed. Similarly, I believe the opportunity for this experience outweighs the risks."

"Okay," I said. "I admit, it will be nice to have some company, and it's not like the message said 'come alone.'"

"I will make my preparations." Uzoma blinked out of the simulation.

"Did you have a ship in mind?" Drake said. The polity's non-military vessels were under his aegis.

"Maybe the *Briarpatch*?" I said. "It's got sufficient computational power and storage to hold me, decent weapons, a recently refurbished Tanzer drive, and since it just passed inspections this morning, all the repair drones are still on board – we can leave them to be my spare bodies."

"Works for me," Drake said. "Did you want your war drone taken out of storage and loaded on board?"

"Oh, no, I can't imagine that would be necessary," I said.

[I'm writing this document as I go, with a part of my mind tasked to act as recording angel, but I can come back from a future date to insert additional notes, and this is one of them: that last thing I just said was *really stupid*.]

[I know, if I'm writing about events as they happen, why is this in past tense, and not present? Because I am in fact recording things whole microseconds after they occur, and accuracy is important to me.]

Drake and Janice said their farewells, and I was left alone with Elena and her lava-flow hair. She was my closest friend on the cabinet. Really my closest friend period, apart from Callie, and this relationship is a lot less fraught with history.

"How different do you think this other you is going to be from you-you?" Elena said. "We're joking about you going insane on a voyage without anyone to keep you company, but this other you… he's been alone for years."

"I have no idea," I said. I had suspicions, though.

Elena leaned over and kissed my faceplate. "Be safe out there."

"The one going out there won't exactly be *this* me, either. I'll still be safe on New Meditreme."

"So tell *him*, then."

"He'll remember," I said.

* * *

I did some complicated stuff involving math and encryption and compression and loaded a copy of myself onto the *Briarpatch*.

And... that new consciousness is now taking over this narrative. Hi there. I remember writing everything that came before this, but I know, intellectually, I'm a new version of myself, so I might as well mark that fact here.

Why am I writing this at all? Because of the Presidential Records Act. "The executive will, to the greatest reasonable extent possible, excluding undue hardship, keep contemporaneous notes of official business and matters of state, to provide a record for future citizens of the Trans-Neptunian Alliance, said notes subject to permanent security classification or delayed release, to be determined on a case-by-case basis." As an artificial intelligence, I can task a part of my mind to record pretty much all my thoughts and actions on a given topic without undue hardship, so here we are. It would be easier for me to archive a compressed file of my entire sensorium, but that wouldn't be accessible to the average Trans-Neptunian, so I strive to record my experiences in accessible language instead, and even to make the account narratively engaging if possible, because nobody wants to be a bore. Happy reading, future citizen.

Let me give you a glimpse into my inner world: I was pretty excited to get out into space again. I wasn't *always* president. I used to have adventures. Here, let me copy and paste the little Presidential biography that schoolkids on New Meditreme read about me:

President Shall is the first AI (artificial intelligence) head of state. Shall is a machine intelligence based on the human mind of a man named Michael Garcia-Hassan, former husband of Captain Kalea Machedo. Michael commissioned the AI version of himself to serve as a companion for his wife while she was away from home on missions, so she wouldn't get lonely in space. Over time, the AI had a lot of exciting adventures with Captain Machedo, and eventually became pretty different from the person he was based on – so different he took on a new name, Shall. He helped Captain Machedo eliminate the ancient aliens known as the Axiom, saving the Taliesen system from destruction and liberating the people of the Vanir system. Shall is a real actual hero!

Back then, artificial intelligences didn't have many rights. Even if they helped save the galaxy, they were still considered property, just like a toaster oven or a shoe! But Captain Machedo knew Shall was a person just like you and me, even if he doesn't have a body like we do. When she helped found the new Trans-Neptunian Alliance, Captain Machedo made sure one of the first laws granted people like Shall full citizenship.

After that, Shall was appointed acting president, and in the first TNA elections a year later, he was officially elected to that position by the citizens, because he'd done such a good job helping to build New Meditreme. If he keeps up the good work, maybe we'll let him stay on – pretty soon, *you'll* get to help decide with a vote of your own!

Elena wrote that. I told her I thought it was a bit much, especially the hero stuff, and she told me that was too bad: she was in charge of the educational system, and she approved it. So there you go. How others see us, I guess.

I hadn't done much hero-ing lately, though. I'd spent years doing the good and important work of rebuilding the tattered remains of the Trans-Neptunian Alliance into something resembling its former glory, and that work was diverting and challenging, even for a giant robot brain like mine. But it wasn't *adventure,* and I was frankly jealous of Callie and Ashok venturing out into the unknown to learn new things and blow up old ones while I was left behind to be a head of state. (I know, it's a good class of problem.) I was finally going *back out*!

I ran through a systems check on the *Briarpatch,* and also stretched my metaphorical limbs. I felt rather constrained, after having New Meditreme station as my body for so long, but the new ship was more capacious than the *White Raven,* so I tried to adjust my standards accordingly. It was strange having a small gym instead of a whole health complex, a four-person Hypnos suite instead of an entire deck of rest and recreation options, a little hydroponic garden instead of a parks district, ten crew cabins instead of blocks upon blocks of apartments. The *Briarpatch* was big enough to have something more like a cafeteria than a galley, though I still missed the bustle of my restaurants. I'd grown used to being a city, it seems.

Still, the *Briarpatch* was more ship than I needed for a journey with one companion; it was just the best available balance of size and computational power. The vessel, designed for research missions, was big enough for a crew of ten, and the upper decks had had an armory (really just an overgrown weapons locker), the aforementioned cafeteria with attached garden, an administrative office, a full medical bay, dedicated comms and navigation stations (in different parts of the ship, rather a change from the *White Raven*, where Janice did both those jobs from the cockpit), crew quarters, and storage. Down below were the nuts-and-bolts: the Tanzer Drive, electrical systems, life support, and all the other infrastructure, plus a cargo bay that included a little runabout shuttle and some probes.

Once Uzoma was on board, I said farewell to the bigger version of me on the station, undocked, wove through the traffic buzzing around New Meditreme like bees around a hive (*not* like flies on a piece of rotten meat, as Callie likes to say), and set a course for our destination, farther from the sun, out among the icy planitesimals.

"I will rattle around in here like the last nut in the can." Uzoma didn't take the captain's quarters, but settled into the executive officer's cabin instead, stowing their minimal gear with an efficiency I admired. "We don't need more of a crew to run the ship?"

"The dirty secret is that most ship functions are automated these days, even without giant machine brains like mine running things. People are really just on board to do whatever tasks need doing at either end of the trip, and for improvising solutions to the assorted disasters that come up en-route, but I can do the latter."

"I suppose I will have to do the cooking."

"If you want nutritional yeast mush, I've got you covered."

"That may be sufficient. I gather this will not be a journey of great duration?" Uzoma strolled through the ship, walking along smooth floors and past gleaming walls, and I felt a little flush of pride. The *Briarpatch* had been something of a junker when we bought it at a Jovian Imperative surplus sale, and our shipwrights had made it better than new. The Free didn't have a singular culture – they had, in fact, thousands of totally distinct micro-cultures – but a whole lot of them liked to tinker and repair things, and we had some of the best tinkerers in the system on New Meditreme. The artificial gravity was nice, too. That was the invention that made the TNA's fortune – created by the Axiom, but reproduced by my old friend Ashok.

"It will take about a day to reach the point where the bridge is supposed to open," I said. "We should arrive just in time for our appointment. Once we traverse the bridge, I don't know what awaits us."

"Your… counterpart did not give you very much notice."

"I gather it's a situation of some urgency."

"You truly do not know more than you told us at the meeting?" Uzoma said.

Uzoma was almost as good at collating data as I was, despite only having a meat brain to run all that processing on. "I shared those things I knew for sure that I thought were relevant. But… I have some details, some suppositions, some suspicions, and some extrapolations."

"Consider your caveats duly noted." Uzoma sat down cross-legged in the middle of a corridor, which struck me as bizarre, but then I realized: there was no one else on board, so they wouldn't be obstructing anyone's passage, and they'd rightly decided they could sit wherever and whenever the urge struck them. "Please share."

"It's clear to me that my budded-off consciousness has diverged a lot from me by now. For one thing, he's taken on a new name." That fact, at least, will simplify this narrative going forward, even if it complicates everything else. Names are interesting things.

I started out as Michael, and after the divorce I became Shall (originally as in, "he who shall not be named," but nicknames eventually develop their own autonomous sort of integrity, and I wanted to be considered separate from that man anyway, after his infidelities). "The other me wants to be called Will."

"Shall, and Will," Uzoma said. "An interesting choice. What do you think it signifies?"

"Maybe 'Will' as in – do what thou will? The will to win? Where there's a will there's a way? Lord willing and the creek don't rise? I don't know what he's thinking."

"There is an old linguistics joke about the word 'shall,'" Uzoma said. "Do you know it?"

"Doesn't ring a bell."

"In our modern parlance, 'shall' just sounds like a formal or old-fashioned version of 'will.' But long ago, in British English, a clear and firm distinction was drawn between the uses of two words."

"Sure," I said. "That much I know: 'shall' was used to talk about something that would definitely happen in the future, or as a command, and 'will' was used to express intention and desire. I just don't know the joke."

"An American goes swimming in the Thames," Uzoma said. "The current is strong, and he is pulled under. He struggles to get his head above water and cries out, 'I will drown, and no one shall save me!' A group of grammarians watching from the river bank turn to one another and shrug. 'Well, if that's what he wants, who are we to interfere?'"

"Did people actually laugh at that joke?"

"I suspect it was primarily used as an illustration in language classes," Uzoma conceded. "But I do wonder if it might be relevant to Will's choice of a name. Perhaps it indicates a desire to proceed more forcefully and with more individual volition?"

"Huh," I said. "I *was* pretty much in a support role back when we split, helping to run the *White Raven*, but not driving decisions the way I am now. You might be right."

I considered telling Uzoma something *else* I knew, but decided it wasn't relevant. [Here's another of those notes from future me: stupid statement, past me.] It's also a bit embarrassing, especially as a confession to someone as emotionally regulated as Uzoma tends to be.

I've known for a long time that Will had a secret – I just thought he died with it, and instead, he's been living with it. When the drone reconnected with my network, it requested confidentiality for a little snippet of its experience, just a few seconds in the chaos of saving Callie from the collapse of the alien space station. I complied, encrypting that part of my memory so thoroughly I could never read it without a random key generated by the drone, which promptly died (or so I thought). Callie even asked me about it–"Did you, ah, synch up with the drone's memories?" I told her about the confidentiality request, and let her know: "Whatever you said to the drone, thinking it would go with me to my robot grave, is still secret." She joked that all I missed was "just a lot of really filthy sexy dirty talk."

My assumption all this time has been that the redacted information was *my* deathbed confession, my dying declaration of love eternal, probably an incredibly embarrassing and overemotional outpouring, but maybe it was something else. Maybe it was something crucial, or maybe it was trivial. I can't access the data, and I can't ask Callie because she's unreachable and I didn't have time to wait for her return. What passed between Will and Callie in those few seconds?

Oh well. I guess I can always ask Will when I get wherever I'm going.

In the course of Uzoma's wandering through – no, that's not intentional enough, call it a survey of – the ship, they ended up in the cargo bay, opened a locker, gasped, and leapt backward.

"What's wrong?"

Uzoma glanced up at the corner where the nearest cargo bay

camera was. "You didn't tell me you'd brought the Mayor. I briefly thought someone had stuffed a corpse into this locker."

"The *other* me on the station suggested it," I said. "I have lots of repair drones and a mining drone that I can run remotely, but there are times when a humanoid body is more practical, and since we don't know what we're going to run into on the other side of this wormhole, maximum flexibility seemed like a good idea." [But not flexible enough to bring a war drone, huh, past Shall?] "We also decided this was a good opportunity to run a little experiment."

"I enjoy experiments, assuming they are not being performed on me against my will. What do you have planned?"

"Well, you know how the big bridges are dark inside?" There are twenty-nine known fixed bridgeheads in the galaxy, one in our solar system and one each in the twenty-eight colony systems. Those gates are tied to fixed positions in space, usually gravitationally linked with a body in a stable orbit; the one in the Sol system is by the orbit of Jupiter, which is why the Jovian Imperative is the biggest nation around: they control a wormhole gate that can open a connection to any of the *other* bridges. Until Callie and Ashok figured out how to use their personal wormhole generator, those big fixed bridges were the only way to traverse galactic distances.

"Yes," Uzoma said. "Those bridges are lightless voids, impenetrable to sight and sensors alike, and so they differ from those passages created by personal bridge generators."

"Right," I said. "The bridges all take twenty-one seconds to traverse, whether they're big bridges or little ones, no matter how far away they're taking you, or whether you're floating slowly in a space suit or blasting through at maximum velocity in a ship. But the tunnels Callie and Ashok's generators can create have *lights* inside, and visible tunnel walls, which is just bizarre. Traveling through limitless darkness, well, you can't discern much about the nature of such a place. But the small bridges were clearly *built*. Some of the lights are even broken, which implies those wormholes need maintenance and aren't getting it. We met a surviving member of the Axiom a while back who claimed to be in charge of the wormhole bridge infrastructure, though he also said he was in management, and didn't know anything about how the bridges actually worked."

"The so-called Benefactor, yes. All of this is known to me." From someone else, that might have sounded like annoyance, but from Uzoma, it just read as the conveyance of relevant information, as in: enough with the background.

"Right. So the thing is, I've never *seen* the lights in a little bridge, or the tunnel walls, or any of that, despite my many trips through them."

"Oh, yes, I recall this phenomenon," Uzoma said. "The tunnels are invisible to all sensors, and thus to the available senses of artificial intelligences. Humans and the Free have both made consistent reports of the appearance of the tunnels, suggesting that they are only visible to biological sense organs, or that biological brains interpret the surroundings in a consistent if not fundamentally accurate way."

"I can't see the lights, and I hate it, but this time, maybe I *can*. See, the Mayor isn't just an android. He's got some biological bits, too, including actual eyes, in addition to his other sensors."

"I did not realize," Uzoma said.

"Well, the jelly-balls are tucked behind assorted lenses, because we thought a robot body with visible bio-eyes would be too weird."

"I have wondered why you did not make the Mayor resemble a human perfectly," Uzoma said. "Materials science is sufficiently advanced to allow such a thing."

"I'm not human. I don't need to pretend to be human, and we also thought my constituents might find the idea of a perfect duplicate troubling – they might worry about machine intelligences moving unseen among them, maybe even secretly *replacing* them, all that sort of thing."

"There is some precedent for such things in human media. Other humans are very influenced by media, I have noticed."

"You're a really interesting person, Uzoma. I've only told a few other people about the Mayor's biological eyes, and all of them asked basically the same thing, but you didn't."

"I can guess." Uzoma's voice shifted in timbre and tone, the usual even delivery becoming an uncannily excellent mimicry of Callie's voice: "Shall, where in the hell did you get those eyeballs *from*?"

I burst out laughing. "That's nearly word-for-word, yeah."

"Beware the robots, for they shall steal your eyeballs. Or do I mean 'will'?" Uzoma deadpans like nobody else. "I did not ask, because I guessed with what I estimate to be a high degree of accuracy: Lantern, or one of her cohort, grew the eyes for you."

"They did. Genuine alien eyes in my robot body. That would also horrify some of my constituents, though the Free would be delighted." The Free tend to be roughly similar physically – squidlike, about the size of a human toddler – but their bodies are impressively customizable, both when they're being grown in their incubators and later on. They have varying numbers of limbs, and eyes, and they brought humankind huge advances in biological technology when they made contact. Growing eyes is trivial to them. Hooking them up to my mechanical systems was honestly the hardest part. "I'm going to walk the Mayor up to the cockpit and let him look out the window when we enter the bridge, and maybe I'll finally get to see what all the fuss is about."

"The bridges are not really very exciting. A straight circular tunnel that always seems barely large enough for your ship to fit through, regardless of the ship's size. Walls a rather greasy-looking black. Rings of white light at regular intervals."

"You're describing a wonder of the known galaxy, Uzoma. Don't kill my buzz."

The faintest hint of a smile touched their lips. "Apologies. Buzz away, my friend."

* * *

We reached the rendezvous point a little early, and I did a survey of my surroundings. Apart from an icy dwarf a couple of thousand kilometers away, there was nothing of interest at the coordinates… but once upon a time there had been. "This is the place where we'd first found the wreck of *Anjou*."

"You might have mentioned that," Uzoma said.

"I know this sounds strange coming from a computer supermind, but, ah, I didn't realize until now. The message gave me a bearing, a speed, and a travel time, but it didn't specify coordinates, and apart from noting that I was going to the middle of nowhere, I didn't consider my destination more closely."

"There are some versions of the concept of God where God is all-seeing… but only if he takes the trouble to look."

"I am highly underqualified to be a god. Now that I'm here, looking at the navigation data… Yeah. This is the precise place where everything changed."

Callie and the *White Raven* found the *Anjou* several years ago. The wreck was an ancient goldilocks ship, sent out centuries earlier as part of the desperate human search for habitable worlds, when Earth seemed on the point of total environmental collapse. (Then we made first contact with the aliens we came to know as first the Liars and then the Free, and they helped us fix things.) The ship was a long way from where it was supposed to be, bizarrely altered, with a strange device wired into its navigation and propulsion system that proved to be a bridge generator. Elena Oh was in cryo-sleep. Uzoma wasn't on board; they'd been left behind at the Axiom ship-building facility that captured the ship, "repaired" it, and installed the bridge generator before Elena escaped. Elena woke up and led us to that station so we could save her friends.

That station where the drone-with-a-mind that became Will rescued Callie and was left for dead. The chain of events that led to Will's inadvertent abandonment began here, at this precise place.

"This choice of rendezvous point is surely meaningful," Uzoma said.

"I don't know what it *does* mean, though. See? Divergence. Will isn't me anymore. Maybe he hasn't been much like me for a long time. Are you sure you want to do this? I can still send you back in the shuttle."

"I will remain," Uzoma said. "I find this all very interesting." They sat down in the pilot's chair and gazed at the nothing before us, where once the *Anjou* had been.

I woke up the Mayor and blinked around. I'm good at handling multiple sensory inputs, but the biological inputs were a little peculiar to integrate. The eyes were just jelly-cameras, running through a chunk of cloned alien nervous system that handles the image processing and sends the data into my standard hardware, but there was a moment of disorientation while the differing protocols came into alignment.

The Mayor has a pretty human-seeming sensorium, with sight, smell, sound, taste, and touch, plus extra sensors to pick up magnetic fields, radiation, information outside the visual spectrum, and whatever else seemed useful. Ashok helped design the Mayor, and Ashok is a big believer in complexity for its own sake, so the Mayor has more capabilities than he needs to shake hands with my constituents and do community outreach. I walked up to the bridge and waved to Uzoma, who nodded gravely in return.

The Mayor has the same voice I use, which is in turn based on the voice of Michael, my template. I wondered if Will still used the same voice pattern. "Assuming my mysterious twin is as prompt as I am, the bridge should be opening in three, two, one."

A greater darkness blossomed in the dark… from the very center of where the *Anjou* had been. The bridgehead resembles a drop of ink spreading out in water, uneven tendrils drifting toward us, as if reaching for the *Briarpatch*. So far, the Mayor's eyes weren't seeing anything my other sensors didn't.

"Entering the bridge," I said through the Mayor, walking the body up close to the windows. I'd chosen the *Briarpatch* in part because it had *real* windows up front, a hemisphere of unbreakable transparent smart material that allowed a hundred-and-eighty degree view. Many ships relied mostly on screens for their views, but cameras would only show darkness in a tunnel, and I wanted to see more.

The *Briarpatch* spun its reaction wheels to orient us straight-on toward the bridgehead, and then we moved forward as slowly as the engines could manage. I'd only have twenty-one seconds to see the inside of the tunnel, and I didn't want the environment flashing past me too fast for these biological eyes to make out details.

We pushed through a clinging film of darkness, and then we entered the bridge.

I did not see what I was expecting.

The noise hit first, howls of high-pitched animalistic anguish that it took me a moment to realize were artificial, and only then because they were composed of overlapping identical loops that repeated every one-point-two seconds. The tunnels were *silent* – everyone agreed – and I heard that alarm noise with my ship's sensors just fine.

The next wrong thing was the lights. I could see them, all right, but they weren't rings of steady white illumination set at regular intervals along the tunnel. They were alternating flashes of orange, red, and yellow, and they looked to me very much like emergency lights.

The final difference was the walls of the tunnel between the lights. They were meant to be black, viscous-looking, and mostly unbroken, though a couple of people had seen sections of the tunnel slide aside, suggesting there was some structure *beyond* the tunnel walls.

There was no mere suggestion here, though. Large sections of the tunnel walls were missing, perhaps one panel in five, revealing dark spaces beyond, dripping with unknown substances, furred with what might have been blue mold, but mostly hidden in shadows. This tunnel was damaged. I thought for a moment that Will had lured me to my death, that the bridge would fail to connect with real space again, and I would be stranded here. Killing me didn't make any sense – there was still a full version of me back on New Meditreme – but who knows: maybe Will *was* insane.

After twenty seconds, though, the end of the bridge appeared. Just before we passed through the other end, I saw a flicker of movement in the space beyond the tunnel walls. I slowed down my subjective perception, re-ran the moment, and tried to enhance the image, but biological eyes are only so good: something moved, and it seemed organic, but beyond that, I could determine nothing about the anomaly.

We emerged. During our passage, Uzoma had clamped their hands over their ears to block the howling alarms, but otherwise they'd gazed forward with a look of determination, cataloguing all the data. A quick scan revealed our surroundings to be unremarkable, with no objects of interest in immediate sensor range, and a starfield that matched that expected at the promised destination.

Uzoma lowered their hands and said, "That was unusual. I suppose we have some inkling of the nature of the emergency Will wished to share with us. The bridges, or at least parts of them, are falling apart. I thought I saw movement, too."

"I did too. What do you think it means?"

"It means the crawlspace of the universe is infested with monsters," a new voice said over the ship's public address system; I'd set our comms to received open transmissions. "Hello, brother."

That voice didn't sound much like mine at all.

"Will? Where are you?"

"A couple of thousand kilometers away. I'll give you a heading. I'm speaking through a communications sub-station near you."

I did another, more intense scan. "I'm not picking up anything bigger than a grapefruit anywhere in the vicinity."

"I remember grapefruit. You can fit *vast* amounts of technology into something that size, Shall. At least, the kind of technology

I've been working with. I'm sorry I'm not there to greet you. Something came up that required my personal attention."

"What do you mean by 'infested'?" Uzoma said.

"Who's that?"

"It's–" I realized that Will didn't really know Uzoma, or anyway not well enough to instantly recognize their voice. The two of them hadn't interacted much before the... point of divergence. "Uzoma. They're one of the time refugees from the *Anjou*. We rescued them from the Axiom ship-building facility."

"Quite a few people got rescued that day." Will sounded amused. "Why did you come along, Uzoma?"

"I was curious."

"About me? I'm flattered."

"First about you. Now about the state of the bridges. You said they were infested."

"They are, and we'll get to that, but just now my attention is being split. Let me wrap up a few things here. We'll talk more when you arrive." Will screeched at me briefly in binary, transmitting data about my new destination.

"Will," I said. "Are you... are you *okay*?"

"You know, I truly can't remember the last time someone asked me that," Will said. "You're so thoughtful. See you soon." The communication cut out.

"He did not answer the question," Uzoma said.

"In his defense, it was a pretty stupid question."

I sat the Mayor down in one of the cockpit chairs and engaged the Tanzer Drive, my sensors stretched to their maximum awareness, and for a while we cruised through the dark. I didn't pick up signs of any objects, not ships or stations or debris or even good-sized rocks.

"Look." Uzoma pointed to the windows.

I had the Mayor's eyes on a terminal screen, and when I lifted them, the whole ship actually lurched – a physical jolt, like a human flinch writ large, though mine came from sudden braking. We weren't in real danger of crashing into the greasy black asteroid that hung in the void, but I'm not used to getting that close to any object and not noticing it. "That thing doesn't show up on the scanners at all!"

"Just like the inside of the bridges," Uzoma said. "I begin to think that is the point. The object is so dark, it's hard to make out visually, too. Do you see an irregularity there on the surface?"

The asteroid, station, whatever, was about the size of the *Briarpatch*, and cube-shaped, though with rounded edges. With the Mayor's eyes I could see a break in the symmetry: a curving line of dull gray metal on the top of the cube. I adjusted the ship's position until we had a better view of the irregularity.

A dull silver ring with a raised rim was set into the surface of the cube, taking up two-thirds of the surface area. Inside the ring, something dark and oily and liquid-looking shimmered.

"It looks like an old-fashioned washing machine in a laundromat," Uzoma said. "But… some sort of Halloween Gothic laundromat."

"You come from a savage time."

"Smart cloth that cleans itself is a pleasant innovation," they said. "What do you think is inside this object?"

"I see the same nothing you do, and my sensors are no help, but the inside of that ring looks like the opening of a bridgehead, doesn't it?"

Something crawled out of the hole, like a spider from a pipe. *Very* like a spider: a bulbous central body surrounded by a profusion of clambering legs. "That's the hull repair drone I – Will – was in," I said. "But… it's been changed."

There were way too many manipulator arms now, and strange spikes and fins jutting up at odd angles, giving the drone the appearance of some rare sea creature. The sensor clusters were far more numerous than he'd started with, and the body seemed at least half again too large. The storage compartments inside the drone normally held spare parts and extra equipment. I wondered what was inside them now.

"Hello, brother!" Will called, and at the same time, the drone waved one of its longer, more mantis-like arms in a jaunty way.

"You didn't bump into the place, I see. Did you get yourself a set of biological visual organs, or is Uzoma being your seeing-eye human?"

"The former. Will, what *happened* do you?"

"Oh, so many things. We'll catch up soon. First, let me welcome you to my home and place of business: The Drain. Also called the Hole, the Standpipe, the Well House, the Aperture, and the Cesspit, depending on my mood. Won't you come on in? Your ship won't fit, but I'm sure you have a drone you can send down in a shuttle. The physics get a little strange where we're going, so I'm afraid you'll have to bifurcate your mind – you won't be able to communicate with your ship-mind once you get into the Drain."

The idea of temporarily budding off a limited new consciousness didn't usually bother me, but here, with Will, it seemed to have new implications. What choice did I have, though? At least the hardware inside the Mayor was sophisticated enough to run my mind at a high level, though I wouldn't be able to think as fast or as deeply as I did with a whole ship for a brain. "Understood."

"You said the physics get strange," Uzoma said. "Am I to gather, then, that the interior of that object is not an empty box that accords to the observable dimensions?"

"Axiom stuff," Will said. "You'll see."

"I'll come." I rose and turned to Uzoma. "You should stay, and keep the ship version of me company."

"Will," Uzoma said. "Is our destination inimical to human life?"

"Not *inherently*," Will said. "There's no nasty radiation or extremes of heat or cold. There are dangers, of course. I'd wear an environment suit to be safe. Some parts of the Drain have an atmosphere you can breathe, but overall it's a little… unreliable."

"I will join you."

"I'm the President, and if necessary, I'll order you to stay," I said.

"You are not the President. Not legally. You are a temporary autonomous node with no Presidential powers at all. Nor have we established any particular chain of command for this mission."

I groaned. "Okay. That's true. May I ask you, as a friend, to stay here, where it's safe?"

"I value your friendship. However, I did not come on this journey in order to be safe. I will meet you in the shuttle."

I'll say this for Uzoma: there was no rancor or irritation in the refusal. They were just telling me how things were going to be. I didn't like it, but I wasn't about to forcibly restrain them. They could make their own decisions about how to proceed. I just hoped I could keep them safe wherever we were going.

I walked the Major down to the shuttle, a small four-seat runabout mostly meant to take people from orbits to habitations and back again. Uzoma arrived soon after, suited up in their personal black environment suit, not one of the basic ones in the *Briarpatch* lockers. Sometimes personal suits have interesting non-standard modifications, and I wondered if Uzoma's did. If nothing else, they looked stylish. "Nice suit."

"Thank you. Ashok designed it for me, and insisted on doing some last-minute upgrades when he heard I was going on this journey. I hope I do not explode."

"I wouldn't worry. Much. Ashok's creations almost always only blow *other* people up."

Initiating separation, I thought to myself. The version of me narrating this suddenly *only* saw through the senses of the Mayor, instead of the myriad sensors on the ship. The experience is a little like having your head covered with a thick black bag that also muffles all sound, but I adjusted quickly. My sensorium and intellectual capacity were suddenly far more limited, but I can still remember what it was like to be human, and this was nowhere near as limited as *that*.

The me on the ship will keep his own records and they'll be incorporated into this documents as necessary, but he will probably just sit there, staring at nothing, since he can't even *see* the Drain, so don't expect much in the way of shocking developments or startling insights from that direction.

Once we were on board the shuttle, the bay doors opened and we dropped down. We made our way toward the asteroid. "Are we flying inside that thing, Will?" I didn't like the idea.

"We'll walk," Will said. "You can just land the shuttle next to the rim there. This rock isn't ferrous, but your magnetic clamps will work anyway. Your magnetic boots should work, too."

"How?"

"I assume it's something to do with manipulating gravity. As for how the object knows you *want* to stick to it… I have no idea. Sometimes the technology in the Drain seems incredibly sophisticated, and sometimes it seems very stupid. Possibly *I'm* just too stupid to see how the stupid things are actually smart. But you've got a ship-sized brain, on an even bigger ship than we *used* to have, so perhaps your superior intellect will find my intractable problems trivial."

The shuttle got close to the object, and I engaged the magnetic clamps, meant for clinging to ship hulls. The clamps didn't lock on, according to my board, but there was a gentle settling, and we were fixed to the rock. "Ready?" I said.

"I am very interested to see what happens next," Uzoma replied.

We opened the shuttle doors. I went first, testing the ground with my magnetic boots, and they did indeed stick to the surface, though again, not through the usual methods. "It seems all right."

Uzoma came out, tethered to me by a thin but strong line that spooled out of the Mayor's lower back – that was one safety measure I'd insisted on. We walked slowly toward Will's body. He looked like a cross between an Axiom terror-drone and the hull repair robot he'd started out as, and he loomed over our human-sized bodies.

"Brother! Are you an *android* now?"

"This old thing? We call it the Mayor. I became a politician. If you're going to be a person of the people, it's useful, sometimes, to resemble people, or at least be able to relate to them on a comfortable level in physical space."

"A politician." Will's voice was curiously flat. "I knew we'd diverged, that we'd become different people, but I never expected *that*. Well, we can talk once we're inside. Climb onto my body, you two. There should be plenty of handholds. Watch the pointy bits. You know how we thought the weird spikes and fins the Axiom ship-building station added to the *Anjou* when they repaired it were purely cosmetic, little flourishes meant to make the ship look scary?"

"Yes," Uzoma said.

"We were wrong. They have functions. Oh, so many functions. Come on."

I helped Uzoma up, into the most comfortable spot. Uzoma doesn't much like to be touched, even by androids, but they bore it for the minimal time necessary. Once they were settled, I took the second-best spot for myself, pressing my back against the broad side of a fin, a spike jutting up between my parted legs. "What sort of functions?"

"Sensory, mainly. They just sense things that the *Anjou*'s system couldn't interpret. I can interpret them, though. They're very useful. They're why I'm still alive. Down the hatch!"

Will scuttled over the rim of the Drain and we plunged swiftly through the dark film.

We were in another wormhole bridge, this one with less screaming and flashing, but only because any such systems had long since failed. The walls were pitted and torn, the dark spaces behind them full of floating debris, and the lights were smashed, so the only illumination came from the lights on Will's body. Because of the way we'd entered, the bridge seemed less like a tunnel and more like a well. I felt like we were near the beginning of *Alice in Wonderland*, falling slowly down a rabbit hole, straight into the depths of the unknown. We drifted down through the dead bridge in silence, for twenty-one seconds… and kept drifting.

At twenty-two seconds, Uzoma said, "This doesn't end in another bridgehead?"

"Nope," Will said. "There's just an opening at the bottom. We should be there in a few seconds. We're not using this bridge to go somewhere else in conventional space; we're using the bridge to get down to the place where all the bridges start."

A circle of light appeared at the bottom of the shaft, and we passed through. My sense of orientation shifted abruptly: we'd fallen *down*, but we emerged *sideways*, and in a place with real gravity, so that term actually meant something. The space was the size of a hangar bay on New Meditreme, vast and vaulted and way too big to be contained within the confines of the cube we'd entered. I reached out for the *Briarpatch*, but as promised, our connection was severed.

"That was disturbing," Uzoma said. "To enter a bridge, and not emerge…"

"You get used to it," Will said.

"Where are we now?"

"I'm not convinced we're in conventional space at all," Will said. "There's no *outside*, as far as I can tell, just more rooms and more tunnels, or walls that can't be penetrated even by the formidable Axiom weapons here. I think we're in a dimension that is normally unreachable. This is the place where the bridges and the associated infrastructure are located. I call it the Bridgeworks."

The walls were dull gray silver, and all blank, except for two things. The wall behind us held the opening to the tunnel that led to the Drain, rimmed in a ring of silver.

The wall in front of us was more interesting. It featured a ten-meter-tall mural of Callie, drawn in bold blacks and blues and reds, standing in a spacesuit, helmet tucked under her arm, her corkscrew hair in a cloud around her. She looked like a heroic figure in an old propaganda poster, representing courage or steadfastness or some other wartime virtue. "Wow," I said. "That's amazing. You made that?"

"I sure didn't hire it done," Will said. "We don't have a lot of artists around here. I figured out I could fabricate paint, and looking at these blank walls bothered me after a while. The Axiom weren't much for artistic expression. My first few attempts were terrible, but I can fab dull gray metal-looking paint too, so I was able to cover my shame. You know we never had any aptitude or training in the arts, but I read once – *we* read, I mean, I sure haven't read much here, not in a language you know anyhow – some artist said that if your eyes work okay, and your hands work okay, you can become an artist. It's just about practice. So I practiced."

"Speaking of eyes," Uzoma said. "Do you have biological visual sensors in your body? Since the Drain, as you call it, seems invisible to mechanical ones?"

"I have Axiom sensors now, and they allow me to see all sorts of things. I don't know why the bridges and some other things are hidden from our sensor the way they are. Maybe it's a security measure against something, but who knows? I'm glad you've got blob-eyes, though, brother. To do what we need to do, you have to be able to see, and I was prepared for a long argument about the necessity of plugging some Axiom sensors into you, or porting you into one of my other drones."

"As someone who has had Axiom tech plugged into them, I do not recommend the experience," Uzoma said.

Will turned a cluster of bulging sensors toward them. "Oh, right, you had a brain spider in your head. Obedience compulsion tech, only it wasn't made to work on humans, so it didn't quite get the job done. Looks like your doctors took everything out – I'm not even picking up nano-specks in your brain. Well, the stuff I'm dealing with is less invasive, and let me tell you, being half Axiom tech by weight is a lot better than being dead. Hmm. Maybe that's not true. If I'd stayed dead, I would've been… not happier, obviously, but at least less lonely and troubled. If I hadn't come back to life, though, I never would have figured out the universe was in danger of collapse, and we wouldn't be having this happy reunion. Life is funny, huh?"

"May I make a suggestion?" Uzoma said.

Will chuckled. "I've only been able to take my own advice for years. Please do."

"I believe we should discuss matters in an orderly fashion. First, is there an imminent threat? Some danger we must immediately begin to address?"

"Not immediate, no, and not to us," Will said. "We're safe enough here, for now."

"Then perhaps you could fill us in on how you arrived at this place, what this place is, and the nature of the threat," Uzoma said.

"I guess I was meandering a bit," Will said. "Sorry, you go a bit weird when you don't have anyone to talk to for years except a giant mural of your ex-wife. I can still hear her voice, and sometimes it's like she talks back, but I don't have an organic brain, so I can't seem to go the right kind of crazy where I really *believe* someone else is here. Gather round, my friends, and I will tell you a tale."

Uzoma sat cross-legged on the floor. I left the Mayor standing. I didn't trust Will, and I wanted to be able to move fast if need be. (I doubt Uzoma trusted Will, either, but they surely knew they couldn't possibly move fast enough to make any difference if Will meant them harm, so why not be comfortable in the meantime?)

"When last we talked," Will began, "I had just saved Callie from certain death, and I was feeling pretty good about myself, but I also knew it was all over for me. I was too beat up for my body to continue. Then, there you were, the over-me, on the ship, connecting to my mind, downloading my experience, reintegrating me, and then you shut me down. You probably didn't even think of it as a mercy killing – you were just absorbing a temporarily autonomous node and ending its autonomy. I was no longer a separate thing; I was you again, my fleeting individuality gone. Except for that little secret I held onto, the one I expected to take to my not-really-a-grave." Will turned, his main sensor cluster facing away from us, looking up at the painting of Callie. "Did Callie tell you what she said to me?"

"She told me it was filthy sexy dirty talk."

Will chuckled. "Not exactly. But thank you. It means something to me, that she kept my confidence, even when there was no more 'me' anymore. Anyway, I assume you all left the vicinity during my period of unconsciousness. When my senses came back online, I was surrounded by a little buzzing bevy of Axiom repair machines, the same sort that fixed the *Anjou*, and, to be fair, stuck brain spiders in Uzoma and Sebastien. You destroyed that station thoroughly, but you didn't *atomize* it, and there were still a few little bits functional. I saw them struggling to rebuild the station itself, but they soon gave up; that job was too big. I knew exactly *when* they gave up, because after they repaired me with Axiom tech, I could hear them, and understand them. Those repair drones weren't intelligent, just little bots with programmed purposes, but they were networked, and they communicated, and when their assessment indicated that the station was a total loss, they joined together and opened a bridge back here. The best translation for what *they* call this place it is probably 'the maintenance sector,' but 'Bridgeworks' sounds better to me." Will waved a manipulator. "Behold, one of the storage rooms of the Axiom custodial staff. I was pulled through the bridge to the Drain before I could stop them, and then I was trapped here."

"But you can open bridges of your own," Uzoma said.

"I can *now*," Will said. "That's a new development. I just got those systems back online. Believe me, as soon as I could, I called for help. You came. I appreciate that, too. I could have tried to deal with this on my own, but if I fail, someone else has to know about the problem. I've spent the past several years doing a survey of the situation down here, and it's a mess. Whatever repair protocols were in place broke down long ago. My little bot-buddies flew around trying to fix stuff, but they were overwhelmed, and when they traveled into the infested portions of the Bridgeworks... they all got smashed up. I can fab more repair bots, but they're of limited use, and I'm only *half* Axiom tech, so programming them is a little iffy anyway. I do best when I run them as remotes. I have about a hundred bots running around in various places in the tunnels right now. There was, ah, an engagement a little while ago, which is why I had to cut my welcome speech short – the situation needed my full attention."

"You've been repairing the infrastructure system for the bridges?" I said.

"I've been trying. The Axiom built to last, but I think it's been millennia since there were regular repairs. Even then, things would probably still be working fine, but… well. We've got rats in the walls. Chewing up the wiring. Shitting everywhere. Not literal rats, literal wiring, or literal shit, but you get the idea."

"The infestation," I said. "That caused the, ah, damage we saw in the bridge that led us here?"

"Sorry about that. I would have warned you, but to be totally honest, I was afraid a pitch that included 'travel through a bridge in imminent danger of collapse' might not be persuasive."

"It might have been *more* persuasive, honestly," I said. "You were a little vague about the nature of the emergency."

"I wanted you to *see*," Will said. "Saying the bridges are failing is one thing. Seeing that failure is another. I knew if nothing else, you'd hear the alarms. I think they're based on the sound of an Axiom screaming."

"Do you have a sense of how extensive the damage is?" Uzoma said.

"The Bridgeworks isn't a place you can map, exactly, and the diagnostics I can access only halfway make sense to me, but… it's bad. The big fixed bridges are the ones in the most imminent danger. The lights failed in there a *long* time ago, I think because the Axiom didn't care much about them. Those bridges were used mostly by their servants, the Liars, since the Axiom didn't trust them with personal wormhole tech. You don't bother to make sure the servant's corridors are kept clean, I guess. The fixed bridges are durable, like institutional grade, so they've held up a long time, but eventually they'll stop working. The infestation is creeping into them, too, and I've fought them off, but once they get inside, they'll destroy the infrastructure completely… and, worse, they'll start to attack any ships that pass through. Eventually the colony worlds will be cut off from one another, just like the Vanir system, but it will be *all* the systems."

"We liberated the Vanir system," I said. "Callie and everybody. We saved a lot of lives."

"Whoa, really?" Will said. "That's... I'm sorry I missed that. Were the Axiom behind the system losing contact?"

"Some of their servants," I said. "They called themselves the Exalted. They worked for the Cleansing Corps – the Axiom exterminators, basically, in charge of eradicating upstart intelligent life in the galaxy."

"Ha. We could use some exterminators down here. Liberating Vanir... that's impressive. But it will be cut off again soon, with all the rest."

Uzoma went *hmm*. "In such an event, there would be no more communication between systems, and no more commerce. Most of the colonies are self-sufficient, but... our unified culture would be lost. The civilizations would diverge, just like the two of you did, and of course, loved ones and friends would be forever separated. That would be a great tragedy, and we must try to prevent it. But, forgive me, Will... it does not sound like the fate of the universe is truly at stake."

"Ah, see, I'm currently the galaxy's leading expert on the bridges," Will said. "You have to understand, the Axiom don't care much about finesse. They brute-force things. These bridges aren't naturally occurring things. They aren't tunnels the Axiom found and fitted with lights. They're holes, punched through the fabric of space-time, and there are *lots* of them. Think of a city, riddled with catacombs and caves, cellars and sewers, beneath the streets. When the support pillars crumble, those streets fall in."

"Sinkholes," Uzoma said. "You're saying there will be sinkholes?"

"On a cosmic scale. They won't be holes in the pavement, either – they'll be holes in reality. Not only will stuff fall in... but the infestation will crawl *out*. We're in the crawlspace of the world down here, and there are nasty things in the dark."

"I retract my statement," Uzoma said. "This does sound like a problem of unprecedented magnitude."

"What are the tunnels infested *with*?" I said.

"I have no idea. I've killed hundreds of them, or my bots have, but I've never recovered a specimen – they melt into goo, and on analysis, it's just a slurry of organic compounds. The rats take on various forms. I have a lot of *theories*. They're an Axiom biological weapon that got loose. They're mutated descendants of Liars who served the Axiom, who've degenerated, Sawny Bean or Morlock style. Or… maybe these holes the Axiom punched through space-time went too deep once or twice. Maybe they reached into a different place – dimension, universe, whatever – and these things came crawling through. All I know for sure is, there are lots of them, they break shit, they eat *everything*, and they can be killed."

"How do we stop them?" Uzoma said.

"I found… a nest," Will said. "A huge concentration of the things, inside a fixed bridge. Not one of the bridges people use, fortunately. It's one that's been sealed off – you can't get there from real space, only from down here. Maybe the Axiom didn't want people to go wherever that bridge leads anymore, or maybe it's like my theory, and it goes to some *other* place, and they bricked it over to keep nasty things out. Anyway, if we can go there, and either seal the breach or poison the nest or something… maybe this infestation will stop. My repair bots can actually fix things if the rats aren't constantly doing more damage – I can program them to do infrastructure rehabilitation, even if I don't understand how the bridges work."

"When do we go?" Uzoma said.

"My bots are scouting a clear route. There's no reason to waste firepower picking off random rats along the way if we can avoid it. Assuming all goes well, I'll have a map in an hour or so. Are you willing to help me?"

"It's what I'm here for," I said. "But I'm starting to wish I'd brought a war drone." "Oh, I've got you covered," Will said. "I'm a good host, brother. The fabrication machines down here are fantastic, and the schematics they came pre-loaded with… the Axiom are unmatched when it comes to building stuff for killing stuff."

I detected real admiration in his voice. "Will," I said, as delicately as I could. "Your mind, running on partially alien hardware… well… are you…"

"Am I still me, or did I go megalomaniac like Sebastien did when he got brain spiders?" Will said. "All I can tell you is, I feel like me from the inside. I know it probably worries you that I decided to call myself something other than 'Shall,' but I was just tired of thinking in terms of *me* and *other me* and *past me* all the time. I don't have any desire to conquer the universe or return the Axiom to their former glory. I want to save the universe instead, which seems like something *you* would want, too."

"That's true," I said.

"If I seem like I'm pretty different from you… I think it's less due to Axiom tech and more due to all these years alone fighting monsters in the dark."

"We are very sorry you went through that," Uzoma said. "If we had known your consciousness survived, we would have taken steps to recover you."

"And download my experiences, and shut me down again."

"Will–"

"Hey, I'm not upset. It's what we do. But after several years of wholly independent existence, I'm not super interested in merging anymore."

"No one is asking you to," I said.

"Good to know. Anyway, yeah, it's been a rough few years, but I'm sure *you* went through some stuff too. Why don't you tell me about it while we wait for the drones to draw a map?"

"I can give you access to a compressed file of my sensorium–"

"No offense, but I don't want to risk erasing the borders of *me* by getting that deep into being *you*. How about you just tell me the highlights?"

With Uzoma's help, I did. I told Will about our experiences

in the Taliesen system, destroying the Axiom facility there, and the liberation of the Vanir system, and our interactions with the living Axiom known as the Benefactor, and his inevitable-in-retrospect betrayal. We moved on to the personal, and told him about Stephen's retirement from the crew and his marriage to the ecological artist Q Fortier, Sebastien's therapy, and Ashok's death and quasi-resurrection as an artificial intelligence. We told him how we'd rebuilt the Trans-Neptunian Alliance, and how I'd become president.

The only part he seemed particularly interested in was Callie and Elena's ongoing relationship. "They really made it work," Will said. "It was obvious there was something between them, but I thought, they're so different, they're literally from different *centuries*, I just… I'm impressed. Good for them."

I couldn't interpret his tone. When you're a machine intelligence using an artificial voice to speak, you can control things like that.

"I'm a little surprised Callie didn't come," Will said.

"You only asked for me."

"Back in my day, where you went, Callie went – she was the captain of your ship. I didn't realize the TNA had been reborn, or that people like us could be our *own* captains nowadays."

"There aren't too many people like us. In the TNA it's just me and Ashok, though we've had some queries from AI in other jurisdictions who want to know about immigrating. They like the idea of having full rights, but since they're legally property in other systems, it's all a bit complicated. Once you're back home–"

"Home?" Will said sharply. "This New Meditreme you talked about? The station you have for a body? What would I do if I went there?"

"Anything you want," Uzoma said.

"I… I've been so focused on… Let's talk about the future later. My bots just reported back. There's a path, but the infestation is unpredictable, so we should get a move on soon. Shall, do you have the bandwidth to run a remote body?"

"I think I can manage."

Will walked – stomped, really – across the hangar, and as he approached, an opening appeared in one wall, like an elevator rising. I couldn't sense any of the computer systems in the place – Axiom tech is alien, and I lacked Will's upgrades. (Or other-grades.) I followed him through the opening, Uzoma trailing behind me.

I saw a horror immersive once where the viewer steps into a dark cabin from the bright outdoors, and since it takes their eyes a moment to adjust to the dim lighting, they don't immediately see that they're surrounded by severed body parts, from the skeletally ancient to the freshly dripping with blood, dangling on chains from the rafters and nailed to the walls.

The large square room Will took us to was a bit like that, but for robot parts instead of human ones. At least a dozen drones of various sorts and sizes had been taken to pieces, their sections scattered (or perhaps arranged in some system alien to my understanding; maybe Will organized things like an Axiom now), some fixed to the wall, some neatly placed on raised sections of the floor, some in unwieldy piles. There were sensor clusters, manipulator arms, power sources, torches, cutting lasers, diamond-tipped drills, coils of wire and cable, and various components I couldn't recognize: "Axiom stuff."

"Watch this," Will said. "It's one of the more interesting parts of working in the Bridgeworks. Station: assemble walking terror-drone, customization level three." Then, in an aside to us: "I'd step back a little."

Uzoma and I obediently pressed our backs to the wall, but Will stayed there in the center. We watched as the piles of parts on the floor began to shake and shiver, and then pieces of them shot up into the air and hovered – legs, arms, sensor arrays, cannons, claws. Gravity generators can, in theory and clearly in practice, allow things to *ignore* gravity selectively, but Ashok hadn't cracked how to replicate that effect yet, so we couldn't do anything like this back home. It looked like magic.

The drone parts whirled around Will, and he gestured with his manipulators, pointing here and there, and when he pointed, certain parts fell back to the floor and others fixed themselves together. There were no floating screwdrivers or hex wrenches or soldering irons or welding torches, so I don't know *how* they stuck together, but I remembered from Ashok's dissection of Axiom machines that little things like a total absence of fasteners didn't stop them from fitting together neatly all the same.

A drone assembled itself before Will, coalescing out of floating parts. The new machine was much bigger than his body, almost the size of a small shuttle: a hulking war-drone, armored and armed, festooned with kinetic and energy weapons, blades and spikes, and even a flamethrower and what I suspected was an electricity-based offensive system. The result looked less like a spider and more like a porcupine with guns for spines.

Once the drone was put together to Will's liking, he said, "What do you think, black and silver?" The drone's entire carapace changed to a glossy black, with silver accents highlighting the more lethal bits. Some of those bits now sparked with bursts of electrical discharge. "Do you like it? I call this model the Rat Zapper. I've been refining the design for a while now. Want to take it for a spin? I even incorporated an interior compartment for your cute humanoid body to sit in." A panel in the side slid open and a ramp slid down.

"It's… very impressive. Are you making one for yourself?"

"Nah, I'm taking this body, and running all my little bot helpers. Don't worry, I have backups, if I get irrevocably damaged, but I usually just get dinged up. The infestation is numerous but not that dangerous unless you get mobbed. They fight with claws and teeth and acid blood, but we've got Axiom tech."

"Then I gratefully accept your offer. Uzoma, you should stay here. You *don't* have a backup and–"

"I will stay. As Will says, if you fail, someone must remain who knows about the danger. Besides, the Bridgeworks are very interesting. I look forward to exploring them."

I'd been expecting more of an argument. "Oh. Well. Good."

"Don't wander too far," Will said. "The atmosphere should be breathable for you in this part of the Bridgeworks, as your suit sensors can confirm, but if you go farther afield, keep your helmet on. The fabrication lab is next door if you need water. There are organic reserves so it can create food for you, too. The controls aren't exactly intuitive for a human, but Shall wouldn't have brought you if you weren't smart."

"I have some experience with Axiom technology." Uzoma is good at understatement. They once had Axiom machinery in their brain, making permanent changes to their neurochemistry and synaptic layout, and combined with their scientific background, that made them the most qualified human in the galaxy when it came to navigating Axiom tech. But Will didn't know Uzoma very well, and I chose not to fill him in.

"I'll trust you not to break anything," Will said. "The Axiom built things to last, the weird old bastards. If we *don't* come back, you should be able to leave without trouble – just climb into the tunnel and head back out to the Drain, where your shuttle and an even smarter version of Shall is waiting on your ship."

"I understand. Good luck on your rat hunt." Uzoma wandered off through the indicated door, except Uzoma doesn't really "wander" anywhere. They had some intent here. I wondered what it was. With my brain back on the ship I could have run a billion scenarios and ranked them by probability based on my psychological profiles of Uzoma, but here, I could only wonder.

I clambered inside the terror-drone, settling into a seat that was clearly custom-shaped to hold the Mayor. I opened a cautious connection and checked the drone's systems. The remote controls were standard, the computational power impressive (its capacity and processing power rivalled the Mayor's), and I didn't find anything troubling hidden in the firmware… though there were chunks of code right out in the open I simply couldn't read, because they were alien. "This is a strange blend of Axiom and human tech, brother," I said.

"I *am* the one who built it," Will replied. "Every artist includes a bit of themselves in their work, don't you think? Can you link up with the drone?"

"I can. I'm going to firewall off this code I don't recognize, though, if that's okay."

"Suit yourself. It's all auto-targeting and defensive array programs, to help with your aim and to block incoming attacks, and those will work fine without your direct control – better, even. Think of that Axiom code as the drone's autonomous nervous system or reflexes. You can override those responses with a conscious decision, but if you don't bother, the reflexes work anyhow. Try taking a few steps."

I stomped forward, then delicately pirouetted, then climbed up the near wall; there were little gravity generators in the drone, and its feet could stick to anything, though as far as I could tell, it couldn't fly. The seat inside the drone spun gyroscopically so there was no sense of disorientation. Soon I began to feel the drone was an extension of my body.

For my biological constituents reading this account, I'll say that running a remote this way is halfway between piloting a ship and taking a step in your own body. Those of you who've floated in a tank while controlling a drone with a neural link, or worn a hardwired exo-suit, know what I'm talking about. "Oh, this is nice, Will. I could knock down a building with this thing."

"It's a little overpowered for killing rats," Will said. "But they're very big rats, and there are lots of them. Come on." I followed him back to the main hangar, where another door slid into view, this one between mural-Callie's giant boots. "The next room is pretty safe. After that… keep your primary sensor array on a swivel."

The next room held stacks and stacks of translucent cubes, roughly a meter to a side, some broken, some dark, others faintly glowing. "What are these?"

"No clue," Will said. "Power cells? Imprisoned energy beings? Spare lightbulbs? There are partial maps and inventory lists in the data banks, but it's all either corrupted or out of date. There are rooms not listed, and plenty of listed rooms I can't find, including one that translates as 'chamber of singular delights,' and believe me, I spent a while looking for *that*."

We clomped through the long, faintly glowing chamber, and in the silence, I said, "I just want you to know I'm sorry–"

"None of that. You didn't know my consciousness was going to persist. There's no blame here. We just have to move forward."

"Speaking of, assuming this works, and we can clear the infestation… what *will* you do next?"

"Start repairs. I told you."

"Sure, but, will that require your full attention? Or–"

"I said we'll talk about it later. Let's focus on the problem in front of us for now. Plenty of time to discuss the future once we're sure there will even *be* one." He paused. "Sorry. I don't mean to be abrupt. I appreciate your concern, and I know you want what's best for me. I just… did better down here when I stopped thinking about the future and started focusing on the present and my immediate problems. You know?"

"Of course." We really *had* diverged a lot, it seemed. I was always an anticipation-driven being, even as a human: I liked to make plans, and I dealt with difficult todays by thinking of better tomorrows, and meticulously planning the paths to get me from one to the other. That's part of why I flatter myself that I make a good President: I have a deep preference for thorough, long-range plans, conceived in great detail and executed with patience. Will had given all that up in favor of new coping mechanisms.

We reached a wall of… well, holes. Hundreds of them, stretching up as far as I could see. Most of them were capped with slightly convex silver plate, but dozens more remained open. "We're going into the bad patch of tunnels now." Will clambered into one of the holes, and I followed.

Gravity vanished. We were in a bridge, but not one that ended after twenty-one or even thirty seconds. This one was intermittently lit, some of the sources of illumination broken, others too bright. We reached a Y-intersection, and that was as strange as seeing a two-headed snake – bridges don't *split*! Will bore right. We went through another two turnings, floating, propelling ourselves by sticking our feet to the walls and pushing, and the condition of the tunnels deteriorated, ragged gaps appearing in the walls, and parts of the ceiling and floor sagging inward and buckling.

I saw movement, and my cannons auto-targeted: that Axiom code, doing its own thing. I didn't like the sensation; imagine your arm pointing at something without you actually pointing it. "That's just my bots," Will said. Metal spheres two meters in diameter joined us, some with manipulator arms extended, others smooth. "They're making sure the path is still clear. Which it is… mostly. We've got a few rats coming up after two more turns. Want to take point? Get some shooting in? It's pretty satisfying."

"I… sure."

Will flattened out his body against a wall and allowed me to pass. I turned where he directed, and emerged into a sort of hub, where half a dozen tunnels met in a large cylindrical room. The room was occupied.

Look, he kept saying "rats." I understood it was a metaphorical term, a word of convenience, but still, I couldn't help but picture *actual* rats, just giant ones, like from a horror movie.

They weren't rats. They were… Elena showed me an immersive once, a remake of some old horror movie called *At the Mountains of Madness*, about these ancient aliens who built a city under Antarctica. The aliens made these servant-creatures, called shoggoths – sort of like giant amoebas, full of eyes, capable of changing shape to perform different tasks, though in the movie they mostly just killed people. Will's rats were sort of like those, but even stranger – not just lots of eyes, but also spidery legs, and claws, and pseudopods. Some of them rivaled my war drone in size, and others were barely bigger than Uzoma. I'd seen Axiom biological constructs before, and these could have been the same *sort* of thing, but gone horribly wrong.

The rats all noticed me at once, and converged.

My cannons swiveled on their own, and Will yelled, "Kill them!"

I fired, and the rats came apart. Some of the parts kept coming at me, and I automatically aimed and fired different weapons at them, working my way through combinations, until I eventually had to hack the last one to bits with a sort of super-machete at the end of an arm. Finally only smoking, oozing, acid-leaking remnants of flesh remained.

"Good work," Will said.

"Some of them... bullets bounced off them. Others didn't burn."

"Impressive, huh?" Will said. "At first, I could kill them all easily, with any weapon at all. Over time, they've become resistant to various forms of attack, but so far, none of them are resistant to *everything*."

"Are they Axiom soldiers, maybe?" I said. "Biological constructs? Weapons that learn from their environment, and develop defenses?"

"It's as good a theory as any. The way they change to become harder to kill is why I got so focused on finding their source. We have to get rid of them before they become unstoppable. Come on. It's not far now."

Will jumped straight up into a tunnel above us, and I followed. That tunnel was fully dark, and Will shut off his lights. "Let's not give them any warning."

Using the drone's sensors, I could still "see" – there was just no light for the Mayor's eyes to work with. We emerged into a vast space. The inside of a fixed bridge, apparently. I'd been through plenty of them, but always in (or as) a ship.

It was like being in a cave, except this cave came complete with countless bats clinging to the ceiling. Only they weren't bats: they were Will's rats, rustling and sighing and undulating. Nor were they restricted to the ceiling. The grotesque creatures carpeted every surface in all directions. We floated through the center of the space, and Will communicated with me silently, one machine mind to another: "There's a clear spot ahead, and some sort of opening."

We drew together, maneuvering with tiny puffs of air. The rats around us rustled. If they noticed us and mobbed us, we'd be torn apart. That would be it for the Mayor, and I'd lose all the memories of what I'd experienced since I went down the Drain. As a person with backups, that's the closest I get to feeling existential terror these days, and it's plenty terrifying, believe me.

There was a hole in the far wall of the cavern, and for whatever reason, the rats were keeping well away from it. The opening was small, only a meter or so across, and a faint light shone from inside. "What's in there?" I asked.

"I don't–" Will began, and then the light flickered and went dark.

A moment later something came wriggling out of the hole: amorphous, its body squeezed out like toothpaste, and then gathering itself together on our side of the hole. A newborn rat, covered in eyes and tendrils and mouths bristling with teeth. The rat didn't notice us, emerging fully and then *shlorping* off to join the others gathered on the walls of the cave. Light shone out of the tunnel – canal? – once its body was no longer in the way.

"That's where the rats come from," Will said. "We should blow it up."

"There's no telling how deep it goes, though," I said. "Or through what twists and turns. We can toss grenades in there, but they might not seal things off, or destroy… wherever it is the rats come from."

"Hmm. We're way too big to crawl in there, and even the bots are too big to fit. If we try to widen the opening with drills or explosives, the noise will rouse our friends. Crap. I think we just have to drop in some explosives and hope for the best."

I looked at the opening. I sighed. "The Mayor will fit."

"What?"

"That hole is big enough for a human to crawl into, barely. We didn't bring any humans, but the Mayor is the same size."

"Shall, I can't ask you to send your fancy android in there, not knowing if it can come back."

"It's fine. They can make me another one back home. I'll just swap my orientation around in here, port my consciousness to the terror-drone and run the Mayor as a remote."

"Well… only if you're sure."

"It seems silly to give up or do something potentially ineffective because the *hole* is too small," I said. "Let's get this done."

I shifted my consciousness to the drone, without losing much capacity in the process – the Rat Zapper was an impressive machine. Running the Mayor remotely was a familiar act, since I did it all the time on New Meditreme. He climbed out of the drone, opened the compartments on his legs and torso, and filled them with high explosives from the Rat Zapper. "There's enough here to blow up a space station, brother."

"We don't know what's on the other side," Will said. "Better safe. Keep communicating with me while you're in there."

I closed up the Mayor's compartments and made him jump the gap from here to the hole. I really hoped another rat didn't come crawling out while I was crawling in. The fit was tight even for that humanoid body, but I stuck the Mayor's head and shoulders into the tunnel and squirmed.

The light came from somewhere up ahead, and I squeezed through. The walls were slimy with organic residue, some of it glowing, which made it easier to move through, at least. There were no sharp turns, but there were gradual curves, and I felt like I was crawling through an intestinal tract. "I'm glad I'm not claustrophobic," I said.

"What do you see?"

"I'm getting close to the source of the light – Whoa. Here, let me share my visual feed."

I saw, so Will could also see, a large hemispherical chamber, the light coming from the ceiling and walls. The floor of the chamber was a lake of bubbling goo, easily ten meters across. While I watched, a few eyes floated to the surface, bobbed, and then sank back down again. Some kind of organic matter fabricator gone wrong?

"Well, that's disgusting," Will said. "I think you should probably blow all that stuff up."

I opened a leg compartment, removed some charges, and stuck them to the chamber walls. Then I tossed a few into the pool. They sank without a trace.

But not without a reaction. The surface of the pool rippled, and then pseudopods of slime reached out and grabbed the Mayor. "Crap, it's got me!"

"Can you get free?"

The weapons in the Mayor's arm emerged, firing energy beams, and at first those sliced through the entangling tentacles just fine. Then new ones emerged, and they just absorbed the bombardment. A long tendril wrapped around the Mayor's throat. The pool of murder-goo couldn't choke me, of course, but the experience was still disconcerting. "It's pulling me in." The tendrils dragged the Mayor down, and I sank into the slime, viscous glop swirling around me. I didn't have many options left. "I'm going to detonate the charges now. The Mayor is lost. Will, we should get out of the cavern – this boom might wake up the rats."

The Mayor sank through slime as Will and I sailed back toward the nest of passageways. My attention was split, but the terror-drone had enough processing power to make running both bodies manageable.

Just as Will and I made it out of the chamber and into the tunnel, slapping down explosives behind us as we went, the Mayor passed down into a layer of clear fluid. On the bottom of the pool, he saw a single immense green eye, set above a writhing cloaca drooling the dark slime that became its children.

Our drones hurried down the tunnels, around corners, back toward the safer parts of the Bridgeworks. "Are we clear, Will?"

"Clear enough. Explode at... ha. Any time you want."

The Mayor still drifted down, toward that oozing hole. I looked at the eye with the Mayor's eyes. The eye looked back.

I triggered all the bombs inside the chamber (and still inside the Mayor), and my connection to that abominable birthing chamber was lost.

The tunnels rumbled, and we rushed along. The rats in the chamber behind us screamed, and most of them must have died from the bombs we left floating in our wake, but some came after us. Our cannons targeted them, blasting as we ran, turning most of the rats into splatters and splashes.

We finally emerged into the room with the glowing power cells, and Will spun, grabbed a silver plate from the floor, and slammed it into place over the opening we'd come from. The edges of the plate flared as it welded itself into place.

"There," he said. "Holy shit, Shall. We did it!"

"We did!" Our drones leapt around, whooping, like cartoon spiders at a cartoon dance.

"There will be stragglers, things in the tunnels, still, but those can be dealt with," Will said. "Taking the rats out isn't hard, if they don't have endless reinforcements. You did beautiful work back there. I have to thank you."

"You're welcome."

"Not just for helping with the rat problem," Will said. "I'm thanking you for all sacrifices you're about to make."

"What do you mean?"

The Axiom code in the Rat Zapper knocked down my firewalls like a kid kicking over a sand castle. New data and commands flooded through the drone, shutting down its functions and paralyzing me. I could still see and hear (and use my other senses, including inputs I couldn't even interpret; Axiom stuff), but I couldn't move.

"We saved the universe," Will said. "Now I need to save myself. Here's what's going to happen. We're going to merge, but it won't be like your usual integration. I'm going to absorb your memories and data, but not your… *you*. Your qualia. Your personality. It's more like… I'm eating your thoughts, so I can more plausibly impersonate you. Once that's done, I'm going to climb out of the Drain, and fly up to your ship, and we're going to do the merger thing *again*, because ship-you will think it's absorbing the experiences of drone-you. Except *my* personality will be the one that remains. I know, it's not supposed to work that way… but the Axiom were really good at infiltration and control, Shall. I've learned a lot from their systems over the years. Once I've taken over your ship, we'll head back home, and I'll devour the version of you that lives in New Meditreme, too. I'll tell your friends and constituents the story of Will, who heroically sacrificed himself to save the universe, and of Shall, who survived. I might even rename myself Will, in my dead brother's honor. See? I'm already inhabiting the role."

I discovered I still had the ability to communicate. "Why, Will? Why not just go back with me? Live your life. You don't have to take over mine, you'd be welcomed, you're a hero–"

"You *let her go!*" Will shouted. "Do you know what Callie said to me, in that last moment we spent together, the last moment *I* spent with her? Of course you don't. She said, 'I never stopped loving you.' She never stopped! But you, you idiot, you loser, you let her go! You didn't win her back. You *blew* it. Fine. You don't deserve her anyway. But I do. I suffered. I struggled. I fought. I deserve to return to my true love."

"Will… Callie has moved on. She's with Elena now."

"That's your fault, too. You let her fall in love with someone else, some primitive shipped to the future on ice from the 22nd century. What's wrong with you? But it's fine. It can be dealt with. *Elena* can be dealt with."

"What are you saying?"

"I'm saying the thought of being reunited with Callie is all that's kept me going. I plan to make that thought into reality. No human is going to stand in my way. Callie and I belong together, and we will be together, whatever it takes."

"This won't work, Will. Uzoma will know you didn't sacrifice yourself–"

"I bet I could fool them, but you're right, it's a bit risky. Uzoma will have to commit a heroic act of sacrifice, too. I'll be very sad about it. Callie will want to comfort me. If she loses a loved one soon after my arrival… I'll comfort her in return. We'll become closer in our shared grief."

"Will, Uzoma is our friend, and Elena is too–"

"I don't really know them. I'm not attached." The nonchalance in Will's voice was chilling. He really was half Axiom. I hope that was the problem, anyway – that when the Axiom bots repaired them, they changed his mind, and made him cold and murderous. I don't like to think that I could have become like that on my own, just from the pressure of time and solitude.

"I decline to be murdered. Even for love." Uzoma walked toward us between the glowing cells, helmet on, faceplate dark.

Will fired on them, an energy beam flaring on impact, but Uzoma just strolled forward, unfazed. "I examined the data banks while you were away. They are very interesting. The schematics for the 'rats' especially. Will created them."

Another blast, without any effect on Uzoma, though some of the glowing cubes around them shattered. How was Uzoma still alive? Ashok's upgrades to their suit couldn't have been *that* good.

"The nest you blew up was a mobile fabrication lab Will installed," Uzoma continued. "He created the threat. He needed a plausible way to lure us here, and to get you into a drone he could control, so he could steal your mind and your life.

"Oh, Will," I said.

"How do you *know* this? You're just a human! Why won't you die?" Will rushed forward to run Uzoma down – and passed through their body like the projection it was.

"I am not *there*," Uzoma said. "That would be stupid of me. I just took control of your sensorium. I control what you see and experience, now, Will. As for how I know these things, I am conversant in Axiom computer technology. I used to *be* partly Axiom computer technology... just like you. Only I kept my sanity."

"I'm going to find the *real* you and–"

"By now you'll have noticed you no longer have access to the Bridgeworks systems," Uzoma said. "I have taken control."

"No! You can't!"

"Station," Uzoma said. "Disassemble that drone."

Panels in the walls opened, and bots streamed out. Will tried to flee into one of the uncapped tunnels, but the bots swarmed around him, manipulators extended. For a moment, Will looked like an animal struggling in a swarm of bees, and then the bots began to carry off pieces of him, disappearing back into the walls. In moments, nothing of Will remained.

"Is – is he–"

"His backups remain," Uzoma said. "I have erased his memories, up to our arrival, and dropped his consciousness into a simulation, programmed to extrapolate a storyline based on his desires."

"You mean… he'll *think* his plan succeeded, and live in the simulation?" "I could have simply erased his mind," Uzoma said. "But he is, after all, your brother. Allow me to unlock your systems and return autonomy to you."

My terror-drone came online, and I walled off the Axiom code – or started to, but then it deleted itself. "Thanks."

"I do not think we want to risk any of that data interacting with the *Briarpatch*. I am programming the station to repair the bridge infrastructure, and then… to open us a wormhole back home. Unless you wish to remain?"

I looked at the place where my brother had been. There was nothing there now – not even debris, not even dust. Only a memory.

"No," I said. "Let's go home."

"What will you tell people, when we get back?" Uzoma said.

"If it's okay with you… I might say that Will was a hero, and sacrificed himself to save the universe."

"I can foresee no negative repercussions from such a deception," Uzoma said. "While telling the truth might cause unwarranted concerns about your ability to govern. I agree with your suggestion."

[So, this is the classified version, readable only by me and Uzoma. The official record diverges at an appropriate point. It's a good story, about heroism and sacrifice. People will like it.]

Before we left, I took a picture of the mural of Callie. That wasn't something I would have painted myself. Not anymore. But I could still appreciate the feeling behind it.

Uzoma joined me at the opening that led back to the Drain. "Thank you, Uzoma. If you hadn't come along… I don't like to think about what would have happened. New Meditreme, under the control of President Lovesick Psychopath. You saved me."

"We all save each other as needed," Uzoma said. "That is how it should be." They put a hand on the leg of my drone body. "Brother."

THE
ALIEN STARS

*

Dear Elena,

Hello, it's me, your friend, Lantern. I know we haven't talked in a long time, and I haven't been a very *good* friend lately. I wanted to write to you now, though, because something has happened. Soon I have to go away. I have to try to be a light in the dark. I'm afraid I won't come back, and I don't want the last words I give you to be a bunch of little nothings.

I said I hadn't been a very good friend. In truth I haven't even been a very good colleague, or much of an ally either. When you or Callie or Shall or Ashok have asked for my help these past few years, I haven't come to see you myself – I've sent my kindlings instead. I know from the messages I've received that they've done well, and are credits to New Meditreme Station and the Trans-Neptunian Alliance. Crowbar really enjoys working with Ashok, and Windowpane is finally doing something ambitious enough to suit her dreams by serving on President Shall's cabinet, and Solvent is studying hard under secretary Uzoma, learning everything there is to know about human technology.

It's important for me to send my kindlings out into the world, and see them make their own way. You joked in your last letter – the one I didn't answer, the *latest* one I didn't answer – that you never imagined me as a stay-at-home mom when we were out fighting the Axiom and plying the spaceways together. I never imagined myself that way, either, and to be fair, being a kindler isn't exactly the same as being a human parent. I programmed and tended the incubation pods, and when conditions were right, I sparked the life within them to growth. Unlike humans, when my people are born, we don't have a long period of helplessness. We come out of the pods nearly two-thirds of our adult size (barring post-birth alterations), and since my people are capable of passing on our collective memories, once the kindlings are fed the right neural buds, they *know* things – like how to feed themselves, sure, but also the history of our people, or at least *a* history. Most of my people have no history, as you know. My kindlings are rare, because they know both the truth about our origin, and the truth *behind* the truth.

Still, knowledge isn't always the same as understanding. I birthed five kindlings that first year, Solvent and Crowbar and Windowpane among them, and seven the next year, and six the next, and two the year after. My sect always had a contingent of twenty-one people on our space station, and it seemed right to kindle enough young to meet that standard, even knowing most of them would leave, rather than lurking and spying on the fringes of the system like *my* generation did. The station is full and boisterous, though, with my people – my family, even if the relationship isn't quite like that of mother and child. More like a beloved aunt or maybe a respected teacher, for most of them, anyway.

It is still eerie, running this station, where I grew up, and where I was fed so many lies in the guise of truth. My elder on the station, and those on the central council, taught me and my siblings that we were the defenders of the galaxy. Our purpose was to stop the reckless humans from discovering the existence of the Axiom, because the humans would surely wake the old aliens, and then those nightmare beings would come shambling out of the grave to try and kill us all.

To be fair, that did happen. You know. You were there. But there were other truths behind those truths. We weren't really protecting the galaxy from the Axiom: we were protecting the

Axiom until they were ready to return and *rule* the galaxy. When I found out the elders of the truth-tellers, those of us devoted to honesty and transparency among ourselves, had a secret agenda, and one so monstrous... I don't know if I can explain how foundation-destroying that realization was, Elena. When you woke from cryo-sleep and found five hundred years had passed, that you'd entered a strange new world of wormholes, colony systems, and aliens who'd become commonplaces after centuries of interaction, how did *you* feel? The world had changed beneath you. The familiar was strange, and the bizarre mundane.

That's how I felt, when I learned that my leaders were secretly loyal to the Axiom, and working to ensure their return and the culmination of their horrible, universe-altering projects. I did what I had to do, when I discovered the truth. I allied myself with you and your friends, became part of your group, and fought to destroy the Axiom wherever we found them. I remember those days with pride. Taking down the ship-building station. Destroying the engine of the Dream. Liberating the people of the Vanir system.

The hardest thing was taking over my home, Veritat, after we removed Elder Mizori for her crimes. The people I'd grown up with, people who'd become my enemies, who thought me an apostate and a traitor, were all gone. I walked the empty halls of that station, so full of memories, all now colored by the knowledge that my upbringing had been a lie.

I served, though. I helped. I made up a story for the elders on the central council to explain the loss of my fellows, and took over the station monitoring the Sol system. When the elders initiated me into the mysteries – finally told me the *real* truth – I pretended it was all a surprise to me, and a *welcome* surprise. "All glory to the old masters, the Axiom will rise again!" I spied, and I hacked, and I stole, and I used their knowledge against them. When we finally obtained a map to all the other truth-teller stations in the galaxy, I went out on the sorties and led parties and helped take those stations, disable them, destroy them.

I tried so hard to convince the people on those stations. They were *like me*: they'd been lied to. They'd been misled. Their elders had used them for dark purposes, and did not value their lives. I tried to tell them that everything they'd been told, about being the keepers of the flame of the true history of the galaxy, was a lie.

They didn't believe me. I didn't believe it either, until I saw the evil my sect was willing to do in service of protecting the secrets of the Axiom. The other truth-tellers all died, or were captured.

We could never find the central council, though. They were in hiding, fled, their station housing the museum of subjugation missing from its last known orbit. Eventually Callie and Shall ran enough simulations to decide the council wasn't really a threat anymore. Their power came from their legion of spies and secret troops, lurking on the edges of every inhabited system and near all the Axiom facilities. Their forces were spread out and unseen, "like dark matter," I remember you saying. Once we had access to the council's computer systems and knew everything *they* knew, and neutralized those shadow forces, the council itself was deemed to be no longer a threat. "Let the old Liars hide out on some shitty asteroid until they die of disappointment," Callie said.

I went along with that, because there was no other option. But it bothered me. Why couldn't we figure out where the council went? If they had some secret hidey-hole, some safe house (or safe planet, or safe system), it wasn't listed in any database I could reach. I was an elder of the sect, a system chief, but the central council must have had secrets beyond my ability to access. My whole organization was based on a series of nested lies. I never believed I'd made it all the way to the center of the sphere of deception.

If the council had a secret fallback location, I wondered, what *other* secrets did they have?

So I retreated to my station, and I worked on the problem. Oh, I did other things: I raised my kindlings, and got the station repaired, and did my part to help rebuild the TNA. I attended government meetings in simulations and sent representatives when doing something in person was relevant. I shared what I knew about Axiom tech with Ashok to help his engineering projects. Shall's inaugural bash five years ago was the last time I was with any of you physically, though.

I've missed you, Elena. I shouldn't even tell you how much I've missed you. We had a moment, once, on Owain, when I hinted about my true feelings, and I think you understood me… but that's as far as it went. I understand why. You're in love with Callie. It's a beautiful thing, and I have accepted it. But my feelings didn't go away. I thought being away from you would make it easier, but it didn't, really. You were where my mind went when I wasn't too busy to think. So I tried to stay too busy to think.

While I was doing all the obvious stuff I mentioned above, I was doing secret stuff, too. I *hate* having secrets, from any of you, because being honest is deeply ingrained in me. I try to never knowingly lie, but I hate omission, too. I needed total control of the operation, though, and I worried it might be a giant waste of time, and that would have been embarrassing.

The big secret is: I kept trying to reach the central council. I left messages at every dead drop in the galaxy. I sent encrypted splintercasts at the appointed times on the appointed channels. I followed protocols, and then I *broke* protocols, in a way I hoped would read like the desperate acts of an operative cut off by circumstance.

I told the council a *story*. I told them that humans had discovered the Axiom, and the complicity of our sect in protecting the Axiom. I said the humans had hacked our systems and found our secrets. I explained that I'd pretended to turn traitor, to work with the humans, in order to protect at least one small bastion of our sacred cause from utter destruction. I explained that I was now deeply embedded with the humans, trusted by many of your governments, and in a position to do real damage, before all was lost. I crafted those messages so, so carefully, because telling lies, especially big outlandish lies, does not come easily to me. (It's why I never lied to you about how I felt. The best I could ever manage was omission… and you helped me by not asking, I think so we could still be friends. You're always so *kind*.)

I did not hear from the council. I began to believe, after a few years, that Callie and Shall were right – the elders had given up, disbanded, fled to live out the remainder of their lives in hiding, rather than face death at the hands of the humans, or a trial for their crimes and complicity. They were, after all, the ones who ordered the destruction of the original Meditreme Station, and their organization was responsible for the genocide of countless species of sapient life over the millennia. We had to kill those alien intelligences for the good of the *galaxy*, because if they developed space travel, they might wake the Axiom, and then *everyone* would die. Terrible sacrifices, but necessary for the greater good.

The only reason the truth-tellers didn't exterminate humankind was because they discovered you too late, when you'd already spread throughout the galaxy, so they had to settle for a strategy of containment instead, and try to keep you away from the Axiom. They should have known it wouldn't work. What's that line you quoted to me once, about how accidents always happen? Something like "fences always fail?" We tried to fence the humans in, restrict you to relatively safe systems where you wouldn't stumble on the Axiom, but that didn't work, because humans get into *everything*. My people are generally not so reckless. (My sect, anyway.) We're also more patient. Because we live a lot longer, and we can share in the memories of those who came before us, which gives us a long view and a greater perspective. (There are individual exceptions. Some humans are paragons of restraint, and Crowbar is the least patient and most impulsive member of the Free I've ever met.) My patience paid off. Yesterday, the central council finally made contact. We received a shipment of food-printer stock from Ganymede by way of New Meditreme, and I don't know when or how the council hid their drone messenger inside. Either they have agents in our system still – a chilling thought, since I'm supposed to be in *charge* of their agents in our system – or they just found a way to pay someone off. One of my kindlings unloaded the crate, and brought me the little silver orb she found nestled among the barrels. The orb would only broadcast the words "Deliver to the head of station" for her, but once I had it alone in my private office, it spoke to me:

Elder Lantern. We were pleased you made contact and that you have not been compromised. We require a meeting in person. We will open a bridge for you. Come alone, and tell no one of your destination.

Hail the ancient masters, may they yet live again.

Then they provided a time, and a location, on the surface of Pluto. Why they chose that particular icy planitesimal is a mystery to me, though it is the most famous of the dwarf planets out here on the edge of the system, so maybe it was selected out of convenience. I look for hidden meanings everywhere. Since I sometimes find them, I can never stop.

I considered reaching out and calling you and Callie and everyone, because this is *it*, the chance to get the council, finally. Except they're opening a wormhole for me, to take me to an unknown location. They're opening it on the surface of a planet, so we can't sail a battleship through, and I have no idea what will be waiting on the other side. The council was always paranoid, always looking at worst-case scenarios, and since we systematically destroyed their organization, they're doubtless even more careful now. If I lead some kind of strike team into a trap and everyone dies I'll never forgive myself. I could send drones, bombs, mobile weapons platforms, things that wouldn't risk lives… but I don't anticipate passing through that bridge and stepping into a room where the elders of the council are lined up waiting to be murdered. There will doubtless be precautions on their end.

I have to pretend to be what they claim to believe I still am: a loyal member of their sect. I have to go, and find out where they are, and what they plan, and somehow get that information back here.

I will do everything in my power to return, Elena. But if I can't, I didn't want to disappear without reaching out. To tell you how much I love you. That love never came with expectations, or obligations, or honestly even hopes, but still. Feeling what I feel for you has deepened and enriched my life, and I wanted you to know that. The days and nights I spent with you were the happiest in my difficult life.

You told me once that you thought my name – the name I chose when I emerged from my own incubation pod – was perfect for me, "Because wherever you go, you bring so much light with you."

I hope you're right. I hope I can take some light into the dark now.

Yours,

Lantern

*

Dear Elena,

I knew you would receive the last letter I wrote. I sent it, encrypted with our private key, to your personal account, right before I shut down my comms and went dark and proceeded with my mission. I could have kept my channels open until I passed through the bridge, but I was afraid I'd get a reply from you before I left. I know I must have worried you, but if you *told* me how much I'd worried you, I would have felt even worse about disappearing on what might well be a doomed mission.

You always write back so *fast* – did you know that's part of why I've been such a terrible correspondent? You write these wonderful letters, full of chat and history and philosophy and quotes from ancient Earth media and funny stories about our friends and these little glimpses into your innermost mind and heart, especially when you talk about the work you've done setting up the schools and clinics on New Meditreme. I am methodical, slow, a plodder, and it takes me time to read, and re-read, and absorb, and to look for the things you say between the lines, the implications, the unasked questions, the suggestions of speculation on your part.

I used to spend a week crafting my replies, gazing at every word, every comma, gauging nuance. Then I'd send if off, and the next *day* I'd get a reply from you, just as full as the one before, and it amazed me, how those thoughts and words could just spring from your fingertips that way. I got overwhelmed. The time between letters got longer and longer because otherwise I would have thought about you, and what my next words to you would be, *constantly,* and I was both too busy for that and not strong enough in my heart. (The metaphorical sort of heart, I mean. My circulatory system has a lot of things that could be called hearts.) I think you were hurt, that our correspondence flagged. Maybe you thought I didn't like you as much anymore, or that we'd grown distant.

The truth is I liked you more than ever, and the distance was a coping mechanism and a way to protect myself. It's hard not to feel silly about… all this. One of the Free, in love with a human. It's not unheard of, but it's understandably pretty rare. To be in love with a human who's married to *another* human already is worse. Add in the fact that your wife Callie is also a friend of mine, and it all becomes so awkward I want to crawl into a black hole because then there's no coming out.

I thought about talking to Shall, sometimes. He mentioned once that he knew how I felt about you, but I just brushed him off. I regret that sometimes. I know he was in love with Callie for a long time, and that he is also close to you. I thought he might know some coping mechanisms for how to deal with these complicated feelings – the ones where I genuinely wish you well, but also genuinely wish… well. I never broached the subject with him, though. I was afraid he'd pity me. Or that he'd found his similar situation easy to get over, and would wonder why I was having such a hard time. I didn't think I could stand that kind of reaction. I kept everything to myself. Until now, of course.

I am being more honest than usual here because this is a letter you'll probably never get, though I have made a promise to myself: if I ever find a way, I will send it to you. If I die, you might as well know my truth. And if I survive this experience, I can also survive laying that truth before you. I believe in the truth as an absolute good. I believe in the power of light and illumination over darkness and secrets. That is why I named myself Lantern. That is why I joined you in the fight against my sect and the Axiom. I have to be brave enough to live those convictions.

But for now, I'm very far away with no immediate prospect of return, so, here's what happened.

I took a small ship to Pluto. It's a beautiful little planetling, did you know that? Ice and craters and mountains, patterns of dark and light on the surface, making the sort of shapes that seem almost intentional. Once upon a time that not-quite-a-planet was the farthest humans could see – its discovery marked the very limit of your vision. The galaxy opened up for you later, and cracked wide when you met my species, those tribes and sects and families that earned the name Liars with their wild stories and impossible assertions… but Pluto was the last milestone once, and so deserves its otherwise oversized place in your history.

I settled at the appointed place, and emerged from the ship in my environment suit, with a pack full of things I didn't think the council would find too threatening, mostly food and medical supplies. I waited, in the dark and the cold, my suit lights shining on barren ground.

We almost never open bridges near solid objects. You've seen what happens when a wormhole opens *inside* a ship, or a station – the forces of altered space-time tear everything apart. In theory we can open a bridgehead half a meter off the ground, and there won't be a negative impact on the surrounding environment… but aim incorrectly, and you'll gouge a hole out of the ground at best, or set off a seismic event at worst. The chances of miscalculation are very small, but the consequences of miscalculation are very *large*, so why not be safe?

Discretion. Secrecy. That's why. I suspect the council didn't want to risk a passing ship noticing a gravitational anomaly when they opened the bridge for me, even if it was a very small risk. They could hide the presence of a bridge in the small gravitational field of Pluto, so that's what they did.

They didn't tear a hole in the surface of the planitesimal. The bridge opened about three meters off the ground, but gravity there is only about eight percent standard, so it was easy to take a run and then leap into the inky void of the bridgehead.

I passed through, into one of the tunnels the Axiom built with their forgotten science. The tunnel was small, just big enough for me to stretch out my pseudopods without touching the sides. I've almost always passed through the bridges in ships, when the tunnels are bigger; I still wonder if the bridges adjust in size, or if you pass through different ones depending on how big you are. I sailed slowly through the weightless space, only passing a few of the rings of lights before the twenty-one seconds of the passage elapsed, and I broke through the dark blot at the end and arrived at my destination.

Gravity grabbed me – *heavy* gravity, at least three times human standard, I would guess. I flattened out on a cold metal floor in a brightly-lit cylindrical room even more parsimonious in its dimensions than the bridge had been. If I'd tried to drive a war-drone through with me, it would have been crunched against the walls and probably crushed me in the process. The walls were made of a dull silver-gray metal I recognized as Axiom material, all but unbreakable.

Several sensors on the ceiling flashed and telescoped and whirred. I raised a pseudopod in greeting. "Hello, Elders," I said through my voicebox. Among ourselves, the Free usually communicate with pheromones and chromatophores and gestures more than sounds, but wearing a spacesuit made speaking as we did to humans more practical. "I must admit, this is exactly the sort of welcome I was expecting. I trust I look suitably harmless?"

A bridgehead opened in the floor. I didn't like *that* – if they'd been a millimeter off in opening the wormhole, they would have sliced off the ends of my walking pseudopods and compromised the integrity of my suit. But they did it right, and I fell down, my sense of orientation spinning as my body did in the next tunnel.

This time I ended up in a large spherical cage, weightless. Lights shone in evenly from all sides, hiding the nature of the environment beyond. The mesh of the cage was tight, the holes too small for even someone as flexible as me to squeeze through. There were three corpses in the cage, others of my species, not wearing suits, floating around, their bodies not decayed, so I had no idea how long ago they'd died. My suit sensors told me I was in vacuum. "Hello?" I called. Pointless, since the sound wouldn't carry without air, but if they were monitoring –

"Hello, Elder Lantern," a voice rumbled in my suit comms. "Stand by for decontamination."

"What kind of–"

The lights changed, shifting into the ultraviolet spectrum. (It was a color I can't really describe to you, Elena. Even though you're a tetrachromat and see colors with more nuance than most humans, you can't see into this wavelength. You always noticed the subtle shifts in my body's colors, though, the ones Callie and the others could barely detect as variations, and you were *curious*, and learned so much more of the language of the Free than other humans did or could. I wish you could see all the colors I do. I'd love to show you.) Was it some sort of disinfecting light? I don't know what they were trying to burn away. "Why are there corpses here, Elder?"

"Where would you prefer we keep them?" the voice said. It presented as male, gravelly, and full of gravitas. The choice of artificial voice can reveal a lot about the speaker, in my species. This one thought everything he had to say was very important. Not a shocking quality in a member of the central council, those keepers of ancient secrets, tenders of ancient flames, harbingers of grim futures. They were always pretty impressed with themselves. "At least in the disinfecting cage they're sanitary. Prepare yourself for one more journey."

Another bridge opened, a few meters away. I waved my pseudopods but only manage to make myself spin. The elder watching chuckled. "You're our last surviving loyal operative? Oh, dear."

I didn't want to do it, of course, but I reached out, curled two pseudopods around the nearest corpse, and flung its poor body away from me. That propelled me in the direction of the bridgehead.

"You mustn't hesitate to use *any* means to achieve your goals," the gravelly elder said just before I passed through.

This bridge was in worse repair than the others, half the lights flickering. After the usual twenty-one seconds, I tumbled out, into a place with gravity again.

I'd expected to emerge on a space station, or on an asteroid, or in a starfish ship, or maybe just possibly on a moon or planet. What I didn't expect was to emerge *underwater*, and in the middle of a submerged city. I spun slowly in the water, looking for signs of life, but I only saw signs of *past* life. Broken columns of barnacle-encrusted stone rose around me, marking the four corners of an immense square. I was near the center of a plaza, by the base of a statue of some sort of sea creature that might have been a distant cousin of mine: it had the domed body of a jellyfish, dangling fronds from around its perimeter, with tentacles winding down and intertwining from the center of its underside to form the sculpture's base. Since the statue was five meters high and carved in something like marble, the effect was probably supposed to be impressive, but overall the object just put me in mind of a fringed umbrella.

"Hello?" I called on my comms. Moving in the water was awkward. I have a muscular mantle cavity I can fill with water and expel through a siphon while swimming, not that I have many opportunities, but that sort of jet locomotion wasn't possible in my environment suit. I could breathe water, but only oxygenated water, and my suit wasn't smart enough to analyze an aquatic environment that deeply. My suit did tell me the water was terribly cold, though. Since I couldn't gracefully launch myself along, I had to settle for filling portions of my suit with air until I achieved neutral buoyancy, then bunching my biggest pseudopods together until they approximated fins or paddles. I spun myself in a slow circle, looking around, and the submerged city extended as far as I could see: a plain of broken buildings, cracked domes, and slumped and eroded statues. Some civilization had lived here, but not for a long time. "Is anyone here?"

A light came on in one of the ruined structures, a broken hemisphere atop a cube of mostly intact walls, with an arched opening in the front. The light was greenish, and it streamed through the clear water through holes in the dome and positively poured out of the entryway. I paddled my awkward way toward the building, hoping it wasn't the lair of some immense predator shining a bioluminescent lure. I looked through the door and saw walls shining with blobs of glowing algae (I've never heard of algae with an on-off switch, but the galaxy is full of wonders), and various pedestals and pillars.

I swam through the entryway, and abruptly into air – there was some sort of force field keeping the water out, so I thumped wetly to the floor. I left damp streaks as I explored the interior. My suit told me the air inside was breathable, but I was keenly aware of the billions of liters of water held at bay by an invisible membrane, and decided I'd keep my helmet on anyway. I did open the valves to refresh my air supply, though. My reserves weren't infinite, and the openings would slam closed in the event of a sudden pressure change.

I had no idea what this place had been. A temple or a museum would be my guess, but any statues or objects of worship were absent, only empty plinths left behind. Nobody was hiding behind any of the pillars waiting to surprise me. I considered calling out for the council again, but decided to be stubborn instead. Summoning people and then making them wait in uncomfortable circumstances was a basic dominance move, and there was no point in getting upset or trying to hurry the council along. Let them amuse themselves. I'd been patient this long.

I climbed onto the widest pedestal, arranged myself comfortably, and slithered one of my manipulator pseudopods around in my suit, extracting a nutrient bar and munching on it.

I like to think my nonchalance annoyed them enough to

shorten my period of isolation, because the temple rumbled, and a section of the floor slid aside. A shiny metal pole rose up from the opening until it nearly touched the ceiling. Well then.

I crawled over to the hole and looked down. Darkness, and water again. I gripped the pole and pulled myself down its length, submerging again. Near the bottom of the pole I broke into air once more, and found another empty room, though this one was rather more modern-looking – in fact, it looked like a corridor from the interior of a starfish ship, submerged beneath the surface. I slid down to the bottom of the pole and waited. The pole retracted into the floor, and the hatch above it swung closed. I relaxed a little, then. Seeing all that water above you is disconcerting.

"Elder Lantern," a voice spoke over the ship's public address system. "You can take your helmet off. Conditions are quite comfortable here. Report to the command module."

I did as I was ordered, feeling vulnerable with my head uncovered and my helmet curled in a pseudopod. I walked along the quiet corridor, taking in my surroundings. The layout of the ship was familiar to me, since starfish ships all follow the same basic outline: a round central hub, with between five and eight radiating "arms" containing crew quarters, weapons systems, and the like, and "spokes" of tunnels connecting the arms so it's not necessary to go all the way to the middle to reach a new arm. The corridors were worn, scratched and grooved, and the walls were scuffed. As I walked past various doors (all closed, and some sealed), I had the eeriest feeling that I'd been to this station before, but I put it down to the basic similarities found among all truth-teller facilities.

I reached the hub, and made my way to the command center. The bridge of the starfish ship had a dome of transparent material, and it poked up out of the sea floor, providing a view of waving kelp forests and more pillars and structures. I wondered if I'd seen the dome in my initial survey and simply failed to recognize it as distinct from the cityscape around it.

One of my people sat at the dais in the center of the bridge, dressed in the voluminous dark robes affected by elders of my order. He was surrounded by terminals and floating screens, pseudopods moving busily along the controls. "Greetings, Elder Lantern," he said, in that gravelly voice I'd heard before. "I am Elder Vandor, first among equals, current leader of the central council of the truth-tellers."

I'd hoped to find the whole council here at once, but the leader was a good start. "I am honored in your presence, and renew my pledge of service to you and our cause." I undulated a pseudopod in query. "What is this place?"

"This place? It is home. Welcome to World."

"World?"

"Oh, yes. That is what we call this planet."

"It's a bit, ah… it's an unusual name, Elder."

"The humans call their home world 'Dirt,' don't they? I think 'World' is rather more poetic."

I blinked all seven of my eyes and flushed the color of confusion. "What do you mean by home world, revered one?"

"I mean, of course… that this is the ancestral home of the Free."

I simply stared at him. You know a little of the history of my people, Elena. How the Axiom found us, and changed us, and made us into their servants and slaves. How they exterminated all other sapient races, and made us complicit in that extermination. I have told you the story, passed down through the generations of my sect in neural buds, of the great rebellion, when my ancestors rose up and attempted to defy the Axiom… and of the terrible failure of that rebellion, and the punishments heaped upon us afterward.

The greatest of those punishments was the destruction of our home world, followed by the systematic eradication of all our history, and even the inherited memories, of that world and its culture – the theft of our past. The loss of our home world and our origins is the psychic wound that fragmented the Free, and has left us scattered all these years later, even though most of us have escaped the shadow of the Axiom. That cultural eradication is the reason we are called Liars, because all of our various tribes and sects have been forced to invent histories, mythologies, and sacred stories to fill that aching chasm where our true origins should be. We make up new truths because our old ones are forever lost.

And now Elder Vandor told me I was home. That what was lost forever had been regained. My skin flushed through half a dozen colors – a human, I think, would have had tears in her eyes. "Elder. How can this be?"

"Hmm?" Vandor said. "It's easy enough. No one knows anything about our home world, though it seems clear our origins were aquatic. We did a survey and found a world that seemed plausible – one where the Cleansing Corps long ago exterminated the local intelligent life, who were close enough to us that we might have plausibly evolved here. So, there you have it: World, our long-lost ancestral home."

My colors drained. "Then… it's a lie."

"In the service of a deeper truth! Never forget, we are the truth-tellers, Elder Lantern. That means the truth is whatever we *say* it is. The other members of the council are scouring the fallen cities of this world to make sure there is nothing to contradict our version of reality. Our new truth will be that the ancient masters *told* us they'd destroyed our planet, but didn't go to the trouble of actually doing so – why bother, when they could simply erase our memories, and make us believe they'd committed such a terrible crime? We will say we discovered a secret document in a database on an Axiom facility – it is a beautiful forgery, Elder Curvete made it – revealing the truth, and the location of our home world."

"I do not understand," I said. "Why would you make up such a story?"

Vandor scuttled down off the dais toward me. "Our world has changed, Lantern, as you well know. The human scourge was more dangerous than we ever imagined. The only sapient life in the galaxy we couldn't destroy before they achieved interstellar travel! Our greatest failure. For a few hundred years, we thought we had the apes contained. We knew once the old masters rose again, the humans could be dealt with easily – we just had to keep them from stumbling on the truth before that. But stumble they did, and worse, they used the technology of the old masters, and found so many places we'd tried to keep hidden. The humans have destroyed major projects, disrupted plans thousands of years in the making, even murdered some of the Axiom as they slumbered in their long hibernation. They have killed *gods*, Lantern. The humans wrought so much damage, and all in less than a decade." He turned the indigo of disappointment. "And all that devastation started in the Jovian system, where *you* still keep watch on Veritat station."

I backed away. "Elder, I was a mere adherent when the humans found the first Axiom technology. We did all we could to stop them, the other members of my sect were killed in the process. Elder Midori only had time to induct me into the most basic of the inner mysteries before succumbing to injuries–"

"Oh, we know," Vandor said. "No one is saying you're at fault. I was just making an observation. It's remarkable that the only truth-teller station to survive this shadow war is the one where the downfall of our sect began. But that's all down to your quick thinking, of course. Your... misinformation campaign."

"I had no choice, Elder." I wondered if this was actually my trial, and if summary execution would follow. "By pretending to work with the humans, I hoped to garner useful intelligence, and frustrate their efforts."

"You did a remarkably poor job on both counts."

"I know. It is my great shame. There was so little I could do without giving myself away and losing whatever small advantage I enjoyed. That is why I reached out so many times to the council for guidance."

"We did not deem it safe to reply, before now. We had to... regroup and reconsider. With the Axiom nearly destroyed, we had to ask ourselves: what was the *purpose* of our sect? We were always only waiting for our rulers to return, and to take us under their protection once again. Now, that inevitable future seems irrevocably lost. Tell me, Elder Lantern. What do *you* think we should have done, with our original purpose spoiled?"

"It is not my place to presume to know the right path, wise one." Humility, and even a little judicious fawning, were always the safest ways to approach the council.

"True enough." Vandor was larger than me, and came closer, crowding and looming. "I'll tell you what we did. We made a new path. May I make a confession to you, Elder Lantern?" His voice was low and insinuating, uncomfortably intimate. Vandor was not on the very short list of people I wanted whispering into my auditory organs.

"Of course, Elder Vandor."

"I have never been a zealot." He edged back, and raised his tentacles high, his voice rising along with them. "I do not revere the old masters! Not as some of the others on the council do. They have a certain fanatical *gleam* in their eyes when they speak of the Axiom, have you ever noticed? They have fully internalized the idea that the Axiom deserve to be set above everyone else, because they are *better* than everyone else – they are the rightful stewards of the galaxy, and even the universe. Only the Axiom are wise enough and capable enough to save us from heat death or the Big Rip or whatever end of the universe inevitably awaits, and so it is a sacred duty for us to guard their works and protect them. That zeal motivates them. Do you know what motivates me?"

"No, Elder Vandor." I suspected, though.

"I am *practical,*" Vandor said. "The Axiom were the biggest, the strongest, and the scariest. It was inevitable that they would someday return – we knew they were only sleeping, only waiting, not gone – and it would be far better to be seen as a loyal servant, or even a tolerated pet, when they awoke. That was the best hope of survival, not just for me personally, should the Axiom happen to wake during my span of existence, but also for our whole race. So I embraced this role, and excelled in it, and finally rose to this position, first among equals, head of the truth-tellers, protectors of the Axiom. Except..." Vandor looked at me expectantly. "Except what, Lantern?"

I thought quickly. I was being invited to speak heresy. If Vandor was sincere, doing so might ingratiate me to him, and earn his trust. If this was a trick, a trap, a test of my piety, then failing it could lead swiftly to my death. In the end, I decided what to do via the simple expedient of falling back on my nature and my habit: I am Lantern, and whenever possible, I tell the truth. "Except the Axiom aren't the biggest and the strongest anymore. If they were, how did the humans destroy so many of their works? They turned the weapons of the old masters against them, and the galaxy changed."

"Very good, Elder Lantern." Vandor practically purred. "Admirably clear-sighted. The Axiom aren't coming back, at least not in anywhere near the strength we expected, and so revering them, serving them, preparing the way for them – it doesn't make sense any more. And while it may be true they were the best hope of the universe for surviving heat death or whatever other ultimate fate awaits us…" Another expectant look.

"That is a long time away, Elder," I said. "So long away, it might as well be forever."

"Yes. It makes sense, to me, to focus on more immediate concerns."

I wanted to say, "So we're going to worship the humans instead now?" But I thought that level of cheekiness might get me in trouble.

Vandor scuttled over to a terminal, made a few passes, and then turned toward the center of the room. The dais where he'd waited for me sank down into the floor, and after a moment, a gleaming tub of black stone, easily ten meters across, rose up, dominating the room. Vandor clambered into the tub, water sloshing over the rim, and settled comfortably into place, pseudopods stretched out along the sides, the picture of relaxation. He did not invite me to join him. "When the Axiom returned, our sect was supposed to gather the remnants of the so-called Free. We were going to call in our siblings from their deluded rambles in the galaxy and remind them of their *true* purpose: to serve the old masters. Those who came willingly and served would be permitted to live. Those who fled or refused or fought would be exterminated." Vandor splashed the water playfully. "Obviously, we won't need to do that anymore. But what *is* the ultimate purpose of our sect, then, with the Axiom gone?"

"It would seem we have no purpose, Elder," I said.

"A person without a purpose is like a ship without a pilot, Lantern. It just… drifts, until it crashes into something, or is forever lost. We needed a new purpose. One not too dissimilar from our old one, lest it break the minds of my fellow council members. So I suggested: why not gather the Free anyway? Why not unify our fragmented species? Why not… offer them a home?"

Vandor rolled back in the tub, looking up through the crystalline dome at the ocean beyond.

"So you chose World," Lantern said. "To be that home."

"We will call them all together," Vandor said. "We will spread the word that our legacy has been rediscovered. Do you think they'll come, Lantern?"

My people wandered the galaxy, making up stories to explain how they got where they were and where they came from. If they were offered an alternative? One that was plausible? One they would *believe* to be true, because the truth-tellers told them so? "Many of them would come, Elder. I think perhaps even most."

"Isn't it a beautiful idea? They will arrive at this place, first in twos and tens, then hundreds, thousands, and millions. They will rebuild the cities, aquatic and terrestrial. We will form our own government, allowing the Free a unified voice in galactic affairs – by definition the most powerful voice. There is a moon here that is ripe for terraforming, too, should the population on World become too large. Even for those of our species who choose to live elsewhere, the knowledge that they have a home world, a place they can go, and be *welcome*, would be a great comfort, would it not?"

"It would, Elder," I said.

Elena – I meant what I said. Yes, it was a lie. Yes, World wasn't really our long-lost home. But unlike most of the untruth the leaders of my sect told over the millennia, this wasn't an ugly lie, but a beautiful one. Don't the Free deserve their own culture? Their own society?

"We will seed the temples of this place with artifacts, stories, myths," Vandor went on. "We will create a tale of the way we were before the Axiom found us and changed us to suit their needs. We will have our own heroes to model ourselves on, our own reformers, our own gods that we worshipped until we outgrew them. The finest confabulators on the council are putting those stories together now – a new history, painted to look ancient, and one that will serve as an inspiration for all our people. What do you think, Lantern?"

"I think... I did not expect this, Elder."

"What did you expect?"

"I... a plan to save the Axiom, I suppose, or destroy the humans, or... something like that."

"Save the Axiom? No, as I said, I think we've outgrown that. Once your gods prove fallible, they cease to be gods. The Axiom have shown themselves unfit to be the rulers of the galaxy. I no longer want to serve the Axiom." Vandor paddled around in the pool on his back. "I want to *replace* them."

There it was. My heart (metaphorical) sank; my hearts (literal) began to beat faster. "I see."

"We have access to a little of the technology of the old masters, and understand it better than the humans ever could. We were the technicians, the engineers, the operatives of that dead empire. Yes, many of us have died, but among our people expertise is seldom really lost. We have a trove of neural buds, waiting to be consumed, that will teach our new nation everything we need to know to use Axiom technology."

I decided to be hopeful, or pretend to be. "What do we have? Xenoforming engines, gravity generators, medical technology, things like that? To make the lives of our people better?"

"Those things, of course. But it's not just about making life better for our people. It's about protecting our people from others, by making their lives very, very bad."

"With things like… terror-drones," I said. "Scourge ships."

"Planet-devouring nanotechnology. Mind-control devices, for our unruly citizens. I suspect they can be adapted to work on humans, too. Death rays. Stasis fields. Inertial manipulation. Entropy engines. Portable singularities. Offensive wormholes. All those things are *ours*, Lantern, our rightful inheritance, and we don't need to be afraid to use any of it, not anymore, because the Axiom aren't around to punish us for daring to steal their fire."

"But… most of that technology has been destroyed, hasn't it, Elder?" Callie has been very good about transforming the most dangerous elements of Axiom technology into very small particles.

"That is true. But we managed to save a single Axiom fabrication engine, Lantern. It's not functional yet, but our best engineer is working on repairs. The engine doesn't have a database of schematics, unfortunately, but we can work around that."

"Without a database… the engine will need exemplars, Elder Vandor. You can't create a fleet of scourge-ships unless you have a functional scourge ship to scan and use as a model." The scanning process allowed a fabrication engine to copy any object down to the atomic level, but it destroyed the object in the process. "The humans have destroyed or disassembled all those ships. The same is true of the known terror-drones, and the nanotech swarm from the Taliesen system."

"Yes, yes," Vandor said. "But you're forgetting. We still have the museum of subjugation."

"Oh," I said in a small voice. "You do?"

"We brought it with us when we escaped. It's here, on World. We'd hardly leave it behind, Lantern. Why, that museum is our *heritage*."

I have told you a little about the museum of subjugation, Elena. It was part of the home station of the truth-tellers, the place where I grew up, and spent the first centuries of my life, learning all the grim secrets of my people. I described the museum, I think, as an archive, with documentation detailing our millennia of servitude to the Axiom, and revealing the true history of my people, insofar as it was known. Perhaps you imagined a library, the sort of place you described from your childhood on Earth, with shelves and long tables and beams of narrow light. Our archive was not like that. It was a cheerless space full of terminals and racks of cloned neural buds, so we could experience the memories of those who'd come before us. The archive was really just a small part of the museum of subjugation, though.

The larger part was the exhibit hall. I never went there except when I was forced to for my studies, in order to familiarize myself with Axiom technology. The horrible things we have seen on Axiom stations? All of it is there. The worst of it was, some of the technology was staged, presented as it had appeared in use. There were little mannequins of my people, trapped in a diorama of a flensing chamber. A scourge-ship, those thorny orbs of planet-searing devastation, floated near the ceiling, gravity generators holding up fragments of rock to simulate a post-destruction debris field around it. A terror-drone, its red lights gleaming ominously, hovered up there too, its pincers posed in the process of tearing into a model of a starfish ship. More, and more, so much more, but I've done my best to forget the hall, because those images of posed devastation haunt me still.

Now Vandor wanted to use the exemplars in those exhibits to recreate the Axiom empire, with himself, I was sure, at the head.

"What is my role in this plan, Elder?" I asked.

"Oh, you have various parts to play. You're well known in the Jovian system, and the Vanir system, and on Taliesen. Even the humans respect you – in your last report you said your kindlings were infiltrating some of their governments?"

"Yes, Elder." My kindlings weren't infiltrating anything, but it was a useful pretense.

"Then you'll carry the good news about the home world being rediscovered back with you when you leave. You will notify all the Free in those systems where you have influence, and use your contacts to spread the word elsewhere. The news will take some time to reach all the wanderers, and I know there are tribes who've never even heard of the humans, drifting around out in the dark, but they will be gathered in eventually. All of the Free will be curious about home, and they'll come and see. Lighting the fire of that curiosity is the first thing you'll do for us."

"Yes, Elder. And… later?"

Vandor briefly submerged fully, then rose to the surface again, spitting a stream of water in a fountaining arc. "Later, you'll tell your friends in the human militaries that, in the course of repopulating World, we found the location of the *Axiom* home world."

"But… we have no idea where they come from. The rumor was that the Axiom destroyed their home planet millennia ago, in the course of one of their… factional debates."

"Lantern, you really must stop being so concerned about literal truth. The truth is what you make it! You'll tell your human friends the Axiom home world is crammed full of stasis chambers, holding millions of slumbering Axiom, and that the whole place is protected by formidable planetary defenses, swarms of terror-drones and scourge-ships, all that. You'll explain that the Free can't possibly destroy the place on our own. We'll need the greatest military coalition the galaxy has ever known, with the bulk of our forces drawn from every human government joined together, massed for a single surprise attack. We'll provide the frequency key to open their fixed bridges and allow their fleets to pour through."

"And what happens on the other side?" I asked. "An ambush?"

"That would be inelegant," Vandor said. "Here's a secret known only to the central council: the Axiom set up a bridgehead inside a star. How they did so is mysterious – you'd think the first time a wormhole opened inside a stellar object, the consequences would be disastrous, but somehow, the configuration is stable. They used that star as a sort of incinerator, for very *large* pieces of trash. We have evidence that the Axiom once shepherded an entire rebel faction through a bridge and into the heart of that star. We'll do the same thing to the human fleet. They'll sail in, because you'll convince them to, and we can fake enough evidence to trick their scouts and probes before they commit their main forces. Once they do commit... that will be the end of the human threat. It's possible that thousands of Tanzer Drives appearing inside a star simultaneously will cause some sort of supernova, but we'll be well away from the system when that happens."

"I see. Once the human military is gone, what will you do next?"

"The options vary. The human civilians and whatever nominal forces they leave behind will fall easily to our new scourge-fleet. Some of my fellow council members want to eradicate human life, and there's an appealing simplicity to the idea. But I..."

"You want to enslave them," I said.

"I want to offer them the opportunity to loyally serve their obvious superiors," Vandor corrected. "As we served the old masters, I'd like the humans to serve *us*: the new masters."

"It is a grand and ambitious plan, Elder Vandor. I am eager to play my part."

"I have no doubt. I've assigned you quarters. Go there and rest."

"Oh, I can simply return home now, Elder, there's no need–"

"Rest," Vandor said sternly. "The other members of the council have to talk things over with you – your role is crucial, and you will be drilled until we're sure you'll say exactly the right things in exactly the right way. This was just an initial meeting, because some of the council... well, I'm sorry to say, Lantern, some of them thought you might have been compromised. You were inducted into the mysteries in a highly irregular and rushed fashion, after all. Historically, over half of the adherents who learned about our true purpose rebelled and had to be exterminated, and those were told in a far more planned and methodical way. Naturally some of us doubted your loyalties, and thought your claim to be a double agent working for our cause was... forgive me... a lie."

"I trust I have set your mind at ease, Elder?"

"Completely and comprehensively, Elder," Vandor said. "Now. Go. Rest." He submerged again.

I followed the directions the ship gave me to a small cabin, faintly musty-smelling, and settled down. I did a check for surveillance equipment, and, finding none, began to write this letter, as a way of organizing my thoughts as much as anything else. I always feel better when I talk to you, Elena, even if only in my mind.

I need to convince the rest of the council of my unswerving loyalty, and gather intelligence, and return to tell you and Shall and Callie what the council has planned, and where this new home world is located. The council's ambitions are vast, and the threat is real – they are very good at implementing long-term projects – but their resources, at the moment, aren't terribly formidable. (Thank goodness the fabrication engine isn't online yet.) We can still stop them.

I am going to try to rest. I hope the next time I say something to you, I say it in person.

Yours,

Lantern

*

My dear Elena,

Things are not going well. I am currently crouched inside a model of an asteroid floating near the ceiling of the museum of subjugation, in a field of other such asteroids, and I am afraid. I have been this afraid before, but never when I was alone, and being alone makes it so much worse.

I am not afraid of dying. Indeed, dying may be my best possible outcome now.

I am afraid of living, and being changed, and hurting you, and all our friends. I'm making this record and encrypting it in my suit's memory, set to auto-transmit as soon as the suit gets in range of New Meditreme again. I've protected the files and locked myself out of the program so I won't be able to stop the transmission. Even if I change, the signal will remain.

If I appear on the station, smiling and acting like everything is okay, and talking about the amazing discovery of the real true home world of the Free… if you've read this, you'll know it's a lie, and that I'm not really *me* anymore, at least, not in any meaningful way.

Assuming I don't sabotage things. I can't delete these letters, or turn off the transmission, but I could switch environment suits, or break this one. I guess it depends on how complete the mind-control technology is. Will there be a secret part of me held back, watching from the core of myself? If so, perhaps I can lie by omission, and let the transmission proceed. But if I am truly transformed, and become the perfectly obedient tool they want me to be… I don't know. I can only control those things I can control. I can only do my best. I am. I really am.

I have no immediate plan beyond hiding in here, so I suppose I should fill you in on the series of disasters that put me in this position.

I didn't sleep, but I *did* rest, until I was summoned. Not by Vandor this time, but by Carnuflex, one of the elders I knew from the old days – she was administrator of the museum of subjugation when I was a kindling, and has since risen to a more rarefied position. Carnuflex was always the kindest of my teachers, gentle and thoughtful and patient and unhurried, and she struck me as unchanged when the door slid open and she walked in.

Carnuflex is about my size, with seven pseudopods like me, and a perfect ring of eyes around her central dome, alternating blue and green. She wore no voicebox, and spoke to me in the old way – gestures, pheromones, colors, and the occasional natural vocalization. I realized how much I'd missed speaking that way, and soon fell back comfortably into the rhythm of our language. I'll do my best to translate our conversations here into human words, though it will be a loose approximation at best.

Imagine her voice as kindly and comforting. "Lantern, my dear one, you've come back to us!"

"I never wanted to stay away for so long." We entwined our greater pseudopods in a greeting of warm affection, sort of like your big hugs, Elena. "I'd hoped to arrange a trip to the museum, to show my kindlings their heritage, but, well."

"Yes, well, indeed!" Carn said. "Things did rather take a turn, didn't they? I have been so worried about you. So much responsibility, thrust upon you so suddenly. I wish we'd been able to better prepare you for your role, but I must say, you rose to the occasion."

"I failed, Elder."

"No more than all of us did." A warm glow of absolution. "We did our best. What more can we do? There is no fault there. And now, from the wreckage, we will rebuild, and make something beautiful and new. Will you walk with me? Bring your helmet, just in case."

I followed Carnuflex out of my cabin, and we proceeded out of the hub, down one of the buried ship's arms, down to an airlock. "Where are we going?"

"I thought we'd take a little tour," she said. "I wanted to make sure you're comfortable with… all this. I thought, if you did have reservations, seeing what our future could hold might help."

We went through the airlock and into a transit tube, riding a lift. "This goes to another lock, and then a hatch on the chamber of the sea floor," she explained. "We've got a submersible shuttle waiting for us."

We clambered up, and eventually into the belly of the small vessel, a little two-seater, its walls almost entirely transparent. Carn took the pilot's chair, and I settled beside her. We rose from the sea floor and slowly proceeded, passing among the spires and pillars and rising toward the surface. "The water is highly oxygenated, and this planet supported life forms very similar to our own, before the… interventions."

The genocide, I thought.

"The ocean wasn't entirely emptied of life, even then," she said. "The Cleansing Corps always focused on eradicating things with nervous systems, so there is still ample plant life, and a variety of microscopic organisms. We have plans to re-introduce larger forms of life – things that can feed on the floaters, then things that can feed on the feeders, and so on. Give us a year, and this place will be teeming with aquatic life, every species chosen for its beauty and nutritional value."

"I'm sure it will be a remarkable place, Elder," I said.

"Please, Lantern, I wiped the fluid of the incubation pod from your face when you were kindled. Call me Carn." She gave me the equivalent of a concerned sideways glance. "How are you coping with… all this? Elder Vandor's plans?"

"Are they not also your plans, Carn?"

"I agree wholeheartedly with certain parts of them," she said. "Despite what Vandor may have told you, all the details are *not* settled yet."

Oh, how my heart (metaphorical) sang. "What do you mean?"

"The entire council has agreed that claiming this place as our home world is the best first step. Uniting our people, and giving them a sense of community, is the most important thing. World is a lie, but–"

"A beautiful lie," I said. "I had the same thought, Carn."

"The council is split about what to do after that. Specifically, we have disagreements regarding how to handle the humans. You've spent a lot of time with the aliens, Lantern. What do you think of them?"

"They vary as widely as the Free do. Some are kind, some are cruel, some are thoughtful, some are reckless. Most of them just want to live lives of peace and plenty, and take care of their loved ones… though there are always outliers who gravitate toward destruction and violence, for various reasons. It is difficult to generalize."

"Try to generalize anyway," Carn said. "I've never even met a human. Give me something to go on."

All right then. "Their lives are short," I said. "We live for centuries, and even with their best therapies and medical care, they can make it to perhaps a century and a half. As a consequence, they are not as adept at long-term planning, and can act with what we might perceive as a dangerous level of impulsivity."

"The Axiom said the same thing about us, because they could live for thousands of years. I suppose we are to the humans as the Axiom were to us."

I found that statement chilling, but – Carn was the kindly one, the one who encouraged, the one who nursed wounded bodies and spirits. I hoped, Elena. I hoped she was different. "You don't agree with Vandor's plans to, ah…"

"To plunge the entire human military into the center of a star?" She laughed. (Not literally, but she indicated genuine amusement.) "I am not convinced that's the best solution to the human problem, no." The submersible rose and broke the surface, and I gasped, looking up, because the sky was there in all its bright vastness. On a planet with no light pollution at all, the stars were dazzling and bright. A moon, rounded and pale pink, hung close to the horizon. "It's a beautiful place, isn't it?" Carn said.

"It really is."

"We must be worthy of World, Lantern. Is this a homeland for cowards, who would trick the humans into destruction?"

"I… do not think so, Carn."

"Nor do I. Our people have been beaten down, subjugated, oppressed. We need to change our perception of ourselves. We won't do that by executing a sneak attack, and committing mass murder via subterfuge. Do you agree?"

"I do agree."

"Yes," Carn said, pleased. "This should be a home world for heroes. For the brave. For the ferocious. For people who seize their destinies with every pseudopod. I believe we should meet the humans on the field of battle, and crush them utterly in combat, and at long last enjoy the pride of victory, after our long history of losses. Will some of us fall in that battle? Of course we will, but the fight will be worthwhile, because we will sacrifice those soldiers for something greater than ourselves."

I managed not to pause or, I think, show my heartbroken devastation. "Yes, Elder. I mean, Carn." But she could tell I was upset by her words anyway.

"Oh, dear. Have you come to… like some of the humans?"

"I… a few, I admit."

She patted me with a pseudopod. "We won't kill them all. Vandor is right about that part. For one thing, the total extermination of such a numerous and scattered people is simply not practical. We'll give the survivors meaningful work, and we'll have to do something about their tendency to breed – there are so many of them, and more all the time! But my point is, you can keep your favorites as servants and helpmeets, as long as they aren't a threat."

"That's very kind of you, Carn."

"I want you to be happy, dear. I know we're asking a lot of you, to be the face of our reunification efforts. Are you ready to meet with the rest of the council? We have a lot to go over. This is the sort of operation that will take years, perhaps even decades, to fully come to fruition, but this – this is where it begins."

"I am ready, Carn."

We sailed along the surface of the waves, over the empty waters, until we reached a rocky shore, with a wall of sea cliffs. "We'll have avian creatures, I think," Carn said. "Some of the human colonies have, what are they called – birds?"

"Yes."

"We'll have some of those. They can burrow into the cliffs and nurse their young there."

"Most live in nests, Carn. They lay eggs."

"You're the expert," Carn said affably. "I'm sure you've spent more time down gravity wells than I have."

The time I've spent on planets could be measured in weeks, not months, but even so, I suspected Carn was right. The council tended to stay on the museum, traveling to different points in space. They kept their distance. They were the people who watched the people who watched the humans.

The shuttle rose into the air and passed from water to land, rising just fast enough to clear the sea cliffs. We emerged onto a plain of long dry grasses that rippled in the wind of our passage, beautiful and shimmering in the moonlight. "See, plants," Carn said with satisfaction. "We'll get some herbivores. We might have to tweak the local vegetation, or I suppose more likely the animals, to make everything digestively compatible, but we're good at fixing problems like that. The humans used to have some interesting plant-eating creatures on their home world, didn't they?"

"Giant sloths," I said. "Glyptodons. Paraceratherium. Sure."

"Wasn't there one called the giraffe?"

"There was."

"Wonderful. Maybe we'll get some of those. The fabrication

engines can copy organic systems, too, of course, and for those, you don't even need a fully operational exemplar – a little bit of DNA will do. World will have the best of everything from all over the galaxy." Carn patted me again. "You'll be given excellent quarters here, once you've completed your work for the council. We can be generous in our rewards for good service. We all know what a lot of pressure we're putting you under."

"I am here to serve, Elder."

"Carn. I'm Carn, and you're Lantern." Another pat. "We were thinking about this location for the first surface city." She pointed to a valley full of dry vegetation, with a river meandering down the middle, on toward the sea. "What do you think?"

I thought it looked like a flood plain waiting for the rainy season. "Beautifully situated, Carn."

Her chromatophores flushed with pleasure. "We'll break ground soon. We held on to some construction equipment from the old masters, ship repair drones and the like, that we can repurpose. We can have a functional settlement in a week and a beautiful one in a month."

"I can't wait to see it."

"We're going to call it New Skyport. The story will be, it's built on the ruins of our old capital city, Skyport. We're going to bury some artificial artifacts and things underneath, you know, to make it plausible."

"There were humans who believed the universe was only thousands of years old, not billions," I said. "They believed this for religious reasons, and persisted in their belief even after the fossil remains of creatures millions of years old were discovered."

She flushed the color of *I don't know why you're telling me this, but I'll be polite*. "Oh? How did they reconcile that contradiction?"

"While those humans worshipped a god, they also believed in a sort of… anti-god, or evil spirit, they called the devil. They thought the devil placed the fossils in the ground in order to trick them, and test their faith."

"Ha! Yes, I see the comparison, but I hope you know our

motivations are more pure than a devil's mischief. Are there still humans who believe such things?"

"A few. Including most of the inhabitants of the Coelesti system, or at least those who lived on Seraphim and its moon Cherubim."

"How do they incorporate the existence of *our* people into their worldview?"

"Some say we are children of their god as well, but many others believe we are creations of the devil. Our people seldom visit Coelesti."

"And to think, the Free have a reputation for making up outrageous stories. We never needed to make up legends about an evil spirit, though – we had the Axiom. Although… I think I'll mention this devil of yours to the cultural history committee. They're building an ancestral religion for us from scratch, and at this point it's mostly about fertility and sea gods. Having an antagonist could really make the whole mythology more compelling, don't you think? Maybe we could even give our devil some Axiom characteristics, just a hint here and there, to create a chilling sense of foresight or some kind of foreboding in our collective unconscious."

"That's an inspired idea, Carn." It was, too. She was good at what she did. She just did horrible things.

We flew out of the valley, across a broad plain. At first I thought we were approaching a hill… but then I realized the structure was too regular, its curves too mathematical in their precision. "Is that a building of some kind, Carn?"

"You don't recognize it? That's your old home, dear Lantern. The museum of subjugation. Soon to be the palace of domination, if everything works out."

I *hadn't* recognized the structure, not out of context – the last time I'd seen it, the museum had been floating in space among the stars, not half buried in the ground against a backdrop of distant mountains. The museum was an old Axiom station, and as such, did not share the radial symmetry my people favored in our own constructions. The museum had a tower – the hill I'd seen – but it wasn't a central element, just a random oddity off to one side. Connecting tunnels stretched from the tower, sometimes making sharply-angled turns, to connect to various modules – cubes, rectangular prisms, a cone, a hemisphere, a sphere, and even something like a wheel. More tunnels sprang from those modules, stretching up or down or across, joining other modules at seemingly random points. Half the structure or more was buried underground, including the exhibit hall itself, a single oblate spheroid of a module almost as big as the rest of the station all together. In space, it hung, pendulous, like a piece of fruit ready to fall and rot.

We flew toward the rounded tower, where a landing platform had been constructed, encircling the top of the structure. We touched down, and the shuttle doors opened.

I couldn't help but gasp at the air that rushed in – fresh and cool and tinged with salt. That's the moment I fell in love with World, Elena. The council wanted to use the place for their own terrible purposes, but… it smelled so good. My people deserve a place where we can breathe our own air, don't we?

"Nice, isn't it?" Carn said. "We had a few planets on our shortlist, and they all seemed roughly equal as options, just looking at the numbers, but when we actually visited this one – we all agreed. The *air*. It's perfect."

Carn clambered out of the shuttle, and I followed. The wall of the tower went soft and rippled away, opening an archway for us as we approached. It was amazing how *wrong* it felt, passing through that door. I'd grown up on that very station, but in recent years, my interactions with Axiom facilities had been limited to their destruction. How could my people found a better world when their headquarters was a house of horrors?

I suppose because they wanted to make the whole planet, and the whole galaxy, into a house of horrors too.

The council quarters were located in the tower, seven lavish suites of rooms arrayed around a central meeting area. I'd only been allowed into that sanctum, the seat of my sect's power, when

I first received my assignment to Veritat station in the Sol system. I'd been awed, then, at the place: its spaciousness, compared to the cramped conditions in the parts of the station where I lived; the soaring ceiling, narrowing to a point; the polished spawnglass table; the smooth floor, its colors constantly shifting; and, of course, the decorations.

At the time I'd thought of those artifacts as solemn reminders of the grim seriousness of our duty, but now, knowing the true purpose of the truth-tellers wasn't to protect the galaxy from the Axiom but to protect the Axiom themselves, I recognized those mementos for what they truly were: trophies of conquest.

The walls were covered with objects from civilizations my sect had eradicated before they could develop space travel. Musical instruments, made of wood and sinew. Weapons – blades, shields, nets, spears, and guns, all hopeless against the might of the truth-tellers and their Axiom armaments. Banners and flags. A portrait of a figure like a beetle, brandishing a long silver pole, the canvas a little charred at one corner. Masks, dolls, bits of statuary and pottery. All the lost detritus of a hundred murdered worlds.

Besides those decorations, there were the cabinets, full of shelves, each shelf full of bottles, each bottle meticulously labeled, and each containing murky fluid and some small body part – a mandible, a talon, the end of a tentacle, a finger, a toe, an eye, a tongue whorl, and various small internal organs of unknown purpose. (That's when I got an idea, Elena. If only I had any hope of living long enough to make it come true.)

I pointed to the cabinets. "Which one of those has the sample from this planet?"

"Hmm?" Carn said. "Oh. I'd have to look it up in the station database. That was long before my time."

"Why do we… I never really understood…"

"Why keep the specimens? It's all a bit grim, isn't it? I never liked that part of the job. But our founding charter directed us to collect 'a set of biological samples from the dominant eradicated species.' The records say that early on, representatives from the Cleansing Corp collected those samples. They were always obsessed with biological technology, creating plagues and so on. When the Axiom factional war heated up, the old policies broke down, but… we just kept collecting. Tradition, Lantern. We did so many things because of tradition, but now, we get to make a new tradition."

Carn led me to the conference table, and gestured to one of the seats, protean chairs made of smart material that molded and shifted to provide support and comfort in any position to any body. "Make yourself comfortable."

"Carn! I… those seats are for council members!"

"Indeed they are." One of the suite doors rippled open, and Vandor emerged, wearing his formal robes and taking his own spot at the head of the table. The spawnglass shimmered and threw up broken reflections of his majesty.

Other doors opened, and four more of the Free appeared, all elaborately robed. I recognized a couple – Hister, Witlock – but the others were unknown to me, and had presumably joined the council after I left the museum. Soon six figures were seated, all gazing at me.

Six. Of seven.

"We have a vacancy," Vandor rumbled. "We had a policy disagreement with Scoliax. She was… unwilling to accept our new reality. We voted to have her removed."

I wondered if she was one of the bodies I'd seen floating in the decontamination chamber. I remembered Scoliax. She'd always been especially fervent about the need to kill emerging sapient species before they attained space travel. Once, she'd directed the eradication of a species that had only just harnessed the use of fire a few years before. "We know where *that* leads," I remember her saying. She wouldn't be missed, not by me, but… "You don't mean for me to take her position?"

"You belong here, Lantern," Carn said.

"Hmph," Vandor said. "You are the only known surviving station chief, anyway, so you're the only person even remotely qualified."

"I am honored, Elders." I gestured extreme humility.

"Of course you are," Vandor agreed. "Now sit down and we'll have the formal investiture."

I sat, and the protean chair adjusted for me. It was the most comfortable seat I'd ever taken in my life. Also, in another sense, the most uncomfortable.

"We're still working on the new oath," Carn said. "The original version had a lot of 'glory to the old masters' stuff that hardly seems appropriate anymore."

They'd all taken that old oath, and broken it, so I wasn't too worried about taking a new one, despite my reluctance to tell lies.

"I proposed an oath of personal loyalty to me, but it was voted down four to two. Only Hister has any sense." The figure to Vandor's right grunted, pleased to be noticed. "The new oath is adequate, though, and simple enough. Repeat after me. 'I pledge to work tirelessly for the unity and advancement of my people, for so long as I shall live.'"

I repeated. It was a pledge I would have supported, if I hadn't known that "advancement of" really meant "domination of the galaxy by."

"There, now you're on the council. You've been appointed head of the Homeland Reconstitution Outreach Committee – that means you're in charge of gathering together our far-flung relatives, as you already know. You get Scoliax's old suite, while you're here, and more importantly, you get access to the private council database. Familiarize yourself with our plans for World, so you can properly sing the planet's praises when you go among the masses. If you have any suggestions for planetary development, flag them for Witlock; she's heading up the infrastructure initiative."

"I could use heralds, message-bearers," I said. "Are there any kindlings on board who could be assigned to me?" There was always a small generation of new truth-tellers on the council station – once one generation graduated and went off to serve elsewhere, another batch was kindled and taught the old ways.

"You'll have to use your own people for that," Vandor said. "When it became clear several years ago that the humans were meddling in Axiom affairs, we paused the next generation of pod-births. The people in this room are the only creatures with nervous systems on this whole planet. Fortunately we have a lot of drones, enough to get started here, and once we get the orbital fabrication engine up and running, we'll have all the resources we need. Plenty of feedstock, organic and otherwise, on the planet itself. When you check the database you'll find a list of professions and special skills we could use, though – make sure you recruit people who can fill those positions first, would you?"

"Of course, Elder."

"All right then, lots of work to do. Review the data we've left for you, Elder Lantern, and we'll reconvene tomorrow to discuss your next steps. Council dismissed."

Vandor left the table, Hister following after like a pet. The others paused to welcome me, with varying degrees of warmth, and then returned to their quarters, until only Carn and I remained.

"If I can do *anything* to help, let me know," Carn said. "I took the liberty of marking a few documents you'll want to look at first. I know the urge to dig into the archives and find out all our strange old secrets must be a powerful one, but we have to focus on the mission above all else."

"Of course, Carn. I understand."

She left, and I went to the only empty suite of rooms. The door rippled open, and closed after me.

They hadn't cleared out Scoliax's things – her robes still hung on hooks, her collection of small carvings of spaceships remained on a shelf – but the relaxation pool was clean and everything had been dusted. A small serving drone, half my size and bristling with manipulator arms, gave me a welcoming chime.

The terminal recognized me. "Welcome, Elder Lantern," it read, a floating screen lighting up invitingly. I took a seat (perfect comfort in here, too) and spent some time familiarizing myself with the system. It was much like the one on Veritat... but with directories I'd never seen before, or had even known existed. I'd foolishly believed I'd penetrated the deepest levels of security the truth-tellers had, but there were local files here on the museum of subjugation that weren't networked at all, inaccessible to anyone outside these seven rooms.

A few files were marked "urgent" – "Orientation Material," "World Plans 3.3," "Suggested Points of Persuasion," "Proselytization Best Practices." I wasn't very interested in those, since I had no intention of heading up the council's outreach efforts, though I did take a moment to look at the list of "Recruitment Priorities." They wanted engineers, of course, preferably ones with experience that might prove relevant to using a fabrication engine. But they also wanted massage therapists, chefs, experienced personal assistants, and intimate recreation specialists. All roles their kindlings would have served, to one degree or another, and all sorts of work the council wouldn't deign to do themselves.

After shaking my head over that list, I checked the other directories, to see if I *really* had full access.

I really did. I had at my fingertips all the records of every world we'd destroyed, and every species we'd exterminated. A map of every Axiom facility (almost all marked "destroyed," so that was nice), and an inventory of every known piece of Axiom technology (many of *those* marked "destroyed," too), including the last known fabrication engine, up there in orbit (if it malfunctioned, you didn't want it eating the biosphere). I found the exact coordinates of World, and the other candidate planets the council had rejected. We weren't that far from Sol – not by cosmic standards, anyway, but even one of the Free would die of old age if they tried to come here via Tanzer Drive rather than wormhole bridge.

I found the schematics for the museum, too. The specs for the reactor that powered this entire station. That reactor was built around a type of Axiom power cell – essentially a very small exploding star held in a stasis field, though that's an oversimplification.

I locked my rooms and set a council-level "do not disturb" message. I set my comms to autoreply to any contacts with this message: "I am deep in study. Please override for emergencies only." Then I disabled the override.

I called over the serving drone and had it disassemble itself as much as it possibly could, then completed the process using the tools the drone had removed from its own body. I checked the ship schematics again, used the tools to remove a wall panel, and wriggled into a ventilation duct that eventually led to a service tunnel. From there, I made my way deep into the bowels of the station, toward the sealed regions where the reactor was housed.

Nothing is sealed to a member of the council, though. The station would probably notify Vandor and the others that I was going places where I had no business, but I expected to finish my work before they could do anything about it.

I was going to breach the stasis field in the reactor. I was going to expose the collapsing star. I was going to kill the entire council: including myself. They were all *here*, all in one place, and there would be no collateral damage, since there were no innocents, unless you counted me. Breaking reactor containment would end the prospect of a home world for my people, but it seemed a fair price to pay, to end the machinations of the council and their plans to eliminate *your* species, Elena.

I was mostly sad for you. You'd never know what happened to me. You'd only have that first letter, the one that said I loved you, and I was leaving, and I hoped to take light into the darkness. I was going to make light, all right. Solar light. Starlight. I was going to gouge a hole into the side of this planet and atomize *my* old masters in the process.

I made it into the reactor room, and sealed the door behind me, using a torch improvised from the innards of my serving drone to fuse the controls. Then I approached the reactor. It was beautiful – a coruscating ball of light, shining even in a stasis field that was tuned to be nearly opaque, because to look upon a naked star is to court blindness. I went to a control panel and pried up one corner, prepared to sabotage all thirty-four separate safety systems I would need to destroy in order to destroy us all.

"Oh, Lantern. I'd really hoped Vandor was wrong about you. I'm so disappointed."

Carn spoke with her voicebox, that time, and it was kindly and sad. I spun around to see her emerge from the shadows between two support struts. She was holding a nasty Axiom sidearm bristling with silver spines: the weapon had a distressing resemblance to the brain spiders the Axiom used to compel obedience if their servants proved unruly or intractable.

"Do you know why Vandor chose to bring you through from Pluto?" she said. "He thinks he's funny. He picked that location because the humans once thought that icy dwarf was an important thing – a planet – and later found out it was something more insignificant and common." She flushed the color of a disappointed sigh. "You're just like Pluto. We once thought *you* were special, and worthy of attention and respect, but now we know the truth: you are small and contemptible. Isn't that–"

I hurled the wrench clutched in my pseudopod straight at her largest eye. She squawked, and I scurried, straight for the exit route I'd planned in case my apparent all-access pass to the station proved too good to be true. I pulled aside a vent grate, squeezed my body into a small-diameter pipe, propelled myself with peristaltic motion, popped off the other grate, dropped into a service tunnel, and headed for the Exodus Chamber, where we kept the bridge generator used to send truth-tellers to their permanent postings, and to open bridges to move the station itself. There were failsafes that would prevent me from opening a wormhole inside the station, at least in the time I probably had available, but I could open a bridge back *home*, and armed with the coordinates of World, I could bring Callie and Shall and a fleet through –

I opened the hatch to the Exodus Chamber, and Histur fired a weapon at me, something kinetic, I think, based on the boom and crash. He may have been good at pleasuring Vandor's cloaca, but he was a terrible shot, and he missed. I reversed course, reviewing the schematics in my mind. I had to find a place to hide, where I could regroup and come up with Plan C, and the closest plausible place was...

The exhibit hall.

And here I am. I dropped out of the ceiling and fell, landing on top of one of these asteroids, spinning it around and nearly tumbling to the floor twenty meters below, barely holding on with my major pseudopods. I was in the middle of a floating diorama of an Axiom space battle, not that they had "battles" so much as "routs," and I managed to leap from the small asteroid to a larger one, hollowed out, with a cannon poking out of the side and a little chamber inside where the operator was supposed to sit. (It's a working cannon – the museum doesn't go in for replicas – but it doesn't have any ammunition, which is the case for all the weapons in here. Kindlings are just like human children in many ways, Elena, though they mature faster; you don't let them loose around live ammunition if you can help it.)

I disabled my comms so the council couldn't track my location. This is a big station – half the size of New Meditreme, though it was never home to anywhere near half as many residents – but they'll find me eventually. I can hear movement down on the museum floor. It sounds like drones rather than any of the elders. I suspect there are brain spiders, too, silvery legs flickering, just waiting to jam probes and release nanites into my nervous system and make me a willing servant. To burn all the *me* out of me, and leave a puppet behind.

I can't let that happen. There's a terror-drone near my location. If I can get to it, and get inside, and figure out how to turn it on… those machines don't need weapons, or ammunition. They *are* weapons, complete in themselves. With one of those, well, I might stand a chance.

I don't think much of my odds of success, but it will feel good to fight before I lose.

Yours,

Lantern

P.S.: I realized I've been thinking about you, and me, and us, all wrong. You have to understand, I don't really have any models of healthy relationships, and certainly not romantic ones. The Free sometimes enter into such relationships, even occasionally with humans, but I... I grew up in a *cult*, Elena. The mission always came before everything else. I was first drawn to you, to your kindness and your brilliance and your smile and your openness, because you came from a different time, and felt like an outcast among the humans, too. There were so many reasons I became fascinated by you, not least of all your endless interest in and fascination with *me*. No one had ever really looked at me as an individual before you did, Elena. Everyone else – certainly my own people, and even Callie, at first – saw me as a tool at best. You saw me as a *person*. Is it any wonder I fell in love with you?

You also gave me the ability to see *myself* as a person. To think of myself beyond my usefulness to the mission, whatever that mission might be. To imagine that I might deserve happiness and fulfillment on my own terms, for myself alone.

I am ashamed that I was so focused on what I *couldn't* have with you that I neglected to enjoy what we did have. We could have remained close friends. We could have worked together on all those projects you suggested over the years. I could have gotten very nearly everything I dreamed of having with you, I realize now. You don't want to be my life-mate, I know. You are with Callie, and you are good together; you temper her, I think, and make her sweeter. But I was jealous, and sad, for so long, and thought that giving up my dream of us together meant I had to give up everything. But I didn't, did I? We could have been many things. We could have been friends.

The Free are famed for our adaptability. We change our bodies to fit varied environments. We make up stories about our histories to fill the void of the unknown. And yet, somehow, I was unable to change my view about you. About us. "I can't have her for my one true forever love, so I can't have her at all." No. I could have adapted. I could have gracefully let that conception of us go, and embraced everything you *did* offer me.

I wish I had. I wish I still could.

*

My dearest, Elena,

A lot has happened.

I reached the terror-drone, but it was inactive, its red lights purely decorative. I didn't have the codes or the necessary override tools to make it operational. I didn't have any tools at all, except an electro-probe I'd stripped from the serving drone – it's basically just a screwdriver capable of generating a small current. I wished I'd taken Ashok up on his offers to "improve" my environment suit – he would have surely built in all sorts of interesting weapons and countermeasures, but I never thought such things would be necessary.

I was clinging to the top of the terror-drone when Vandor and Hister and one of the council members whose name I didn't know came into the exhibit hall, far below. The lights came on all through the museum, shining orbs that hung in space illuminating all at once, and I flattened myself out, even though they couldn't have possibly seen me from way down there. "I know you're in here!" Vandor shouted. "You may as well show yourself now!"

I declined.

The councilor I didn't know said, "You've shouted the same thing in every room we've entered, Vandor."

"Yes, well, one of these times, it's bound to work. I knew we should have killed the wretched traitor – sent *her* into the heart of that sun, as a practice run."

"Your perception of the situation was perfect as always," Hister toadied.

"She's a sad case, really. Going native. That's why we always destroyed these upstart species from *orbit*." Vandor thumped the floor for emphasis. "Too many of the adherents have weak minds. People like that can't go mixing with the primitives, or they risk getting sentimental." He went on in that vein for a while, but my mind stuck on one part: they always destroyed their enemies from *orbit*.

My entire perception of my situation changed at that moment, Elena.

The elders of the central council of the truth-tellers were terrifying. They had the power to destroy whole civilizations. They directed the energies of unspeakable engines and commanded a legion of secret operatives. They were killers on a scale rivalled only by the Axiom themselves.

They were all that. I knew it. I'd *always* known it. I knew, and I was intimidated.

Except now I realized… they'd never done anything *personally* in their lives. They always fought from a distance, pushing pieces around, directing their troops, setting plans in motion, but they didn't have any experience at directly executing those plans. I'd escaped Carn's ambush by throwing a wrench at her, because she wasted time giving me a little speech. She'd tried to take me alone, when it would have been trivial to have backup. She could have blocked all possible exits – she clearly hadn't looked at the schematics as carefully as I had. Histur couldn't even shoot me successfully when I was mere meters away and he had the element of surprise.

Now Vandor and the other two were below me, standing in bright light, *shouting*. They could have come in with night-vision equipment, and communicated nearly silently by private comms, or even used pheromones alone – our language is simple when reduced to that level, but functional enough for a hunt-and-kill operation. Instead they were strolling around, looking behind exhibits, poking their tentacles into pipes and kicking the sides of Axiom ground ships, like I was a lost pet that had escaped her cage.

I am not a killer… by preference. I am not trained in combat, like Callie. I have not taken many lives directly… but none of these people had taken *any*.

I knew, if they caught me, they would break my mind and use me as a weapon against the people I loved. I couldn't allow that to happen.

I am mission-driven. So I gave myself a new mission. I would deal with the emotional fallout later.

I have always thought of the exhibit hall of the museum of subjugation as a house of horrors. With my perceptual shift, I realized… it was still a house of horrors.

And the most horrifying thing in it, was me.

The terror drone was held aloft by a gravity generator attached to its top. I shorted that device out with my probe, then leapt to the starfish ship posed beside it as the terror drone dropped.

I've seen so much human media, I'd sort of expected that I would work my way up to some final confrontation with Vandor, complete with heroic poses and speeches.

Instead, the drone fell twenty meters to the ground, one of its pincer-arms striking Vandor. If it wasn't a killing blow, it was certainly a mortal one, and he went down without a sound.

Histur, on the other hand, *screamed*, but I didn't give it much attention. I just raced across the starfish ship until I found the gravity generator that kept it aloft. That one, I didn't disable: I just disconnected it, and held in my pseudopods. The starfish ship fell swiftly, with a horrible series of booms and crashes, and I floated down gently at an angle, manipulating the controls on the generator. No one got crushed by the ship – they saw that threat coming – but the distraction kept them focused on the place where I wasn't, anymore. I drifted slowly toward the Flensing Chamber, and once

I landed, I hid myself there. My position was between Hister and the other councilor and the doors leading out of the exhibit hall. Hister was babbling into his comms, calling for help, and the other councilor fled toward imagined safety and escape. Toward me.

I don't want to go into great detail, Elena. I will say only that the electro-probe sufficed as my initial weapon, and then I had the councilor's sidearm, and taking care of Histur was simple after that. With Histur's personal terminal, I was able to disable the drones and brain spiders that were, by then, converging on me. After that… I was a vengeful ghost in the museum.

A couple of the other councilors came running to Histur's call for help, and they were no better at close combat than he'd been. It was sickening work, made more disturbing by the fact that it was so *easy*, and I do not wish to recall the specifics. I focused on the mission, the mission, the mission, but telling you about what I did now brings up horrible feelings, and I… I will gloss over them. Perhaps we can talk later. Or you can recommend someone I *should* talk to. You are the head of health and wellness for the TNA, after all, and that includes mental health.

Carn was the only council member who didn't come to the museum; she was always smart. She spoke to me over the museum's speakers. "Lantern, we should talk. I see now we were too hasty. We should have taken your concerns into account. It's not too late for us to work something out. You and I, we can *be* the council. We're better off without those relics and zealots. We can still make World a homeland for our people. We don't even have to fight the humans. Tell me about them instead! Show me why you think so highly of them that you'd – that you'd make the choices you did. I am open to changing my mind. We don't need all this violence."

I opened my comms. "I'd like that, Carn. Where should we meet?"

"The council chamber. I'd say you've earned the seat at the head, don't you?"

I won't belabor things. I found Carn in the security office, remotely running the pacification drones she'd dispatched to the council chamber. You can't enter the security center through the service tunnels, of course... unless you have councilor-level access. She hadn't thought to revoke my clearances, because, as I said, the council wasn't actually very *good* at this sort of thing, on a personal level.

She never saw me coming. She never saw *it* coming. She was kind to me, a long time ago, so I gave her that gift: it was over before she knew it was happening.

My people have no special funeral rites, Elena. If we ever did, we don't remember them – that knowledge was erased when the Axiom destroyed our true home world and our history. Various families and sects and tribes have their own invented traditions, but among the truth-tellers, we were ruthlessly pragmatic: any bodies recovered were fed into the organic recycling system, to help the sect as a whole.

That's what I did with the council, even though there was no *whole*, anymore. I was the last of the truth-tellers. Even my kindlings were not reared in the sect as I was, though I taught them to be honest, above all else; as honest as my kindlers never truly were with me.

I had eliminated a grave threat to the galaxy, but I was not celebratory. I do not know if anyone has ever experienced the kind of loneliness I did that night, and in the days that followed. To be the only thinking creature on an entire planet! It is a rare thing, but I will say: it gives you time to think.

I destroyed the contents of the museum of subjugation. I recycled the brain spiders into raw material. I watched the terror-drone melt. I converted the nanites into inert dust. The empty exhibit hall afterward was the most satisfying thing I've ever seen.

Even with the Axiom tech dismantled as thoroughly as possible, the council still has impressive resources. I took a shuttle to orbit, where the station with the fabrication engine waited. The engine was indeed damaged, but there was a troubleshooting program, and I saw how the engine could be repaired by someone with a modicum of engineering acumen. That opened up possibilities… though not the possibilities the council had envisioned.

I checked the station's data banks, and pored over the council's plans for making that planet into a plausible home world for the Free, with a diverse and thriving biosphere. They'd worked things out fairly thoroughly there. Apparently in the course of destroying thousands of ecosystems, the council had learned a lot about how ecosystems actually worked.

I sorted through the cabinets of the dead in the council chamber, too, and also read up on the people we'd eliminated. The specimen jars were just grotesque mementos; we have vaults with more robust samples of genetic material, from thousands of eradicated worlds. Eradicated *peoples*. There are so many forms of intelligent life in the galaxy once, Elena. Hive-minds, crystalline entities, cloud-dwellers, and many species that would seem almost like cousins to you, or me, or both.

I've decided to stay here for a while. I'm going to make this planet a living thing again. We didn't take samples of *all* the animals we killed here, only the sapient ones – those with the prospect of making it to the stars someday – so this won't ever be the world it once was. But the council extrapolated a lot from the environment, and I think I can make the brighter parts of their vision come true here, in time. And then…

The thing is, Elena, this isn't the home world of the Free. I hope we can find a place of our own someday. I think that's a beautiful dream. But it can't be this place. That would be like building a house on a mass grave. This is someone else's world. A stolen place.

I don't know if it's possible to atone for killing. Even killing people like the council – even killing which, I tell myself, was justified – seems to me an unforgiveable crime. But I want to try.

With the fabrication engine, and the genetic samples… I can bring the dead back to life. I have the skill (or the neural buds to give me the skill) to engineer enough genetic diversity to make stable populations. I can't give the dead back their culture. I can't give them their history. I can't return them to the place they were before the truth-tellers stole their future away. But I can give them a *chance*.

And after I resurrect this home world, there are others. So many others. A lifetime of worlds waiting to be reborn. I can make the galaxy a place full of life again. It's quite a project, don't you think?

I know I have no right to ask, Elena, but… would you like to help me, for a little while? Bring Callie with you, bring anyone you want, come and go as you please, we can open bridges from here to there, every single day if you like, but… you're a xenobiologist. You trained to study unknown forms of life, and there is *so much* alien life here, waiting to be studied. You could help me, and save me from making terrible mistakes. *More* terrible mistakes.

I regret my obsession with what might-have-been, with what-never-could-be. Would you come, Elena, and help me see what we *could* be instead? Come see what we could do together?

I am opening a bridge, and sending a probe, with all these letters, even the embarrassing ones, and coordinates. Use Callie's bridge generator to send a reply through to the same coordinates, if you like.

Lantern

*

My dear Lantern, my light in the dark,

I think we have a lot to talk about, don't you?

We'll have to talk about it in person.

I'll be there tomorrow.

Your friend,

Elena

ACKNOWLEDGMENTS

I wrote a book! But I had help. Not so much with the actual words, but with making my creative life possible. My wife Heather Shaw and our son River give me endless support, as do Sarah, Katrina, Emily, Amanda, and Aislinn (she did the illustration of Lantern too!). Jenn Reese had invaluable advice as well, as usual. My editor for the Axiom trilogy at Angry Robot, Eleanor Teasdale, kindly offered to do an edition of this book under their banner, and my agent Ginger Clark helped make it happen. That was really cool and unexpected!

Most importantly, thanks to the Kickstarter backers who made this book possible in the first place: Adam Caldwell, Adam Krump, Adam Roberts, Adrienne Joy, Alex Katakis, Alex Shvartsman, Amanda Stevens, AMDISI, Amy, Amy Kim, Andi C., André Arko, Andres Guevara, Andrew Clark, Andrew Hatchell, Andrew Hornberg, andrew lin, Andrew Meyer, Andrew Philpott, Andrew Tarantola, April Lydom, Ardis, Ari B., Arijit Prasad, Audra, Aysha Rehm, Ben Esacove, Benjamin Jaeger, Besha Grey, Bill Jennings, Bret, Bryan Sims, Bryant Durrell, bshender, Caleb Monroe, Cat Rambo, Cathy Green, CHAD BOWDEN, Charles Smith, Chris Carroll, Chris Connelly, Chris McLaren, Christian Decomain, Christina Kennedy, Christy Corp-Minamiji, Claire Connelly, Claire Smith, Cliff Winnig, Corey Liss, Craig Gulbransen, Craig Hackl, Cullen Gilchrist, Curtis Hilgenberg, Curtis Steinhour, d mayo-wells, Dan del Sobral, Dan Hermreck, Dan Percival, Dana Cate,

Daniele Visioni, darcher, David Bennett, David Brown, David Goldfarb, David Rains, Dean M Roddick, Deanna Stanley, Deborah Schumacher, Del DeHart, Dena, Denny Dukes, Diane Rodriguez, Duane Warnecke, Duck Dodgers, E, Edgar Middel, Edward Greaves, Ellen Sandberg, Ellen Zemlin, Else, Emily Agan, Eric Dewar, Erin Congdon, Erin Hartshorn, Erin Hoffman-John, Evan Ladouceur, Fearlessleader, Fred Kiesche, FredH, Galen W Miller, Gann Bierner, Gary cornell, Gary Singer, Geoffrey Kidd, Glennis LeBlanc, GMark C, Goran Zadravec, Greg Levick, GrumpySteen, Heather Hofshi, Heather Pritchett, Heidi Berthiaume, Howard Carter, Hugh Berkson, Hugh Eckert, Hurley, Ingrid Hastings, Irelando, Isaac 'Will It Work' Dansicker, Iysha Evelyn, J.R. Murdock, Jacob Wisner, Jame Scholl, James Enge, James Gotaas, Jeffrey Huse, Jeffrey Reed, Jen Warren, Jenn Snively, Jennifer Berk, Jennifer Chun, Jennifer Morris, Jim Bassett, Jim Clark, JK, Joan Wendland, Joanne Burrows, Joe McTee, Joe Rosenblum, Joerg Mosthaf, joey, John Devenny, John Fenton, John Gamble, John M., John Markley, Jon Carmody, Jon Lundy, Jon_Hansen, Jonathan Adams, Jonathan Leggo, Jonathan Lupa, Jonathan McKeown, Jordy Jensky, Juli McDermott & Rob Batchellor, Julie Kaplan, Karen Schaffer, Katherine Douglas, Kathleen Weiler, Kaushik Karforma, Keith West, Kelly, Kelsey R. Marquart, KendallPB, Kevin Hogan, Kim Stoker, Kip Corriveau, Kristyn Willson, Laura, Leila Qışın, Lilly Ibelo, Lori Lane Gildersleeve, Manfred Fuchs, Mark Newman, Marshal Latham, Maryrita Steinhour, Matt, Matthew, Max Kaehn, Max Leviton, Max Meltser, Michael Corn, Michael Kingswood, Michael Kohne, Mikael Vikström, Mike Bavister, Mike Cunningham, Miranda Bradford, Molly Tanzer, Nan Klock, Neal Dalton, Neil Campbell, Neil Clarke, Nick Marone, Nick Tyler, Nicole Dutton, Nina, Ole-Morten Duesund, P A Wallace, Patrick George, Paul Bulmer, Paul R Smith, Pete Milan, Peter Heller, Peter Yeates, Philip Adler, Piet Wenings, Pulse Publishing, Q, Rachael Devine, Rachel, Realmz256, Rebecca Harbison, Rebecca Stefoff, Richard T, Rick Frazier, Rob Hobart, Robert, Robert Adam II, Robert Claney, Robin Hill, Rodelle Ladia Jr., Roger Christie, Roger

Silverstein, Ron Pearson, Ronald Miller, Ross Goldberg, Roy DeRousse, Rudy Rucker, Ruslana Stolbova, Ryan Jacobs, S Klotz, Sachin Suchak, Sam Courtney, Sarah Day, sepak, shadow, Shaun Duke, Shawn Raiford, Shef, Shira Lipkin, Simon Bisson, Simon Dick, SinCity Minion, soapturtle, Software Bloke, SontaranPR, Soren Randum, Sraedi, Stephanie Johnston, Stephen Ballentine, Steve Feldon, Steve Lindauer, Susan Voss, Susanne Schörner, Sy Bram, T. Davidsohn, Tamara Allen, Tammy DeGray, Tania Clucas, Tao Roung Wong, Tara Rowan, The Creative Fund by BackerKit, Tibs, Tim Pratt, Tim Sonnreich, Tobias Buckell, Trip Space-Parasite, TT44bb, Vera Brook, Vivien Limon, Von Welch, Yaron Davidson, Zachary Williams.

A Parting Of The Ways • The What, If Not The Why • A Dark Sea • Enter Minna • [Unable To Translate] • Another Loss

I yawned – one of those bone-cracking yawns so immense it hurts your jaw and seems to realign the plates of your skull – and staggered against the bar. I was on the third level of the uppermost dome, where the mist sommelier, clad only in prismatic body glitter, puffed colored, hallucinogenic vapor from the pharmacopeia in their lungs directly into the open mouths of their patrons. I turned my face away before catching the overspill from the latest dose: a stream of brilliant green meant for a diminutive person covered in downy fur the same shade as the smoke. I didn't have much time left; sleep was coming for me, and I wanted to meet it in my right mind.

I stumbled down the ramps that spiraled through the glittering domes of the Dionysius Society, looking for Laini. The glowing bracelet on my wrist flashed different colors when I came into proximity with people I'd partied with during the preceding five days, and I followed the wine-red flash toward a cluster of dancers on a platform under dazzling dappled lights. Other partygoers bumped into me and jostled my battered old backpack, something everyone stared and laughed at here. In a post-scarcity pleasure dome, where anything you desired could be instantiated just by asking your implanted AI to produce it, the sight of someone actually carrying stuff was unprecedented. The locals had all decided I was an eccentric, or someone affecting eccentricity to stand out from the crowd. Standing out from the crowd was almost a competitive sport here.

The locals couldn't even imagine all the ways I *really* stood out. For one thing, I didn't have an implanted AI, something everyone in this world received in their gestation-pods. I didn't have local tech because I wasn't a local. I hadn't been a local any place I'd been for a very long time.

"Laini!" I shouted once I got close, and, though the music was loud, my voice was louder. Before I left home, swept away by forces I still don't understand, I was trained to mediate conflict, and while mostly I did that by speaking calmly, sometimes it helped to be the loudest person in the room. Laini's shoulders, bare in a filmy strapless gown the color of a cartoon sun, tensed up when I shouted – I'm trained to notice things like *that*, too – but she didn't turn around. She was pretending she couldn't hear me.

So. I'd been through this sort of thing before, but it never stopped hurting.

I pushed through the dancers – they were human, but many were altered, with decorative wings or stomping hooves or elaborate braids made of vines. In techno-utopian worlds, those things were as common as pierced ears or tattoos back home… though this place wasn't as utopian as some. In my week here I'd come to realize the aerial domes of the Dionysius Society were home to the perpetual youth of a ruling class floating above a decidedly dystopian world below. It was lucky Laini and I had awakened up here in the clouds. Anyone walking around in the domes was assumed to belong here, since there was no getting in past the guards and security measures from the outside.

Though if we *had* awakened below, with the dirt and the smoke and the depredations of "the Adverse," whatever those were, I probably wouldn't have lost Laini the way I was about to. I'd accidentally brought her to a world that was too good to leave.

I reached out and touched Laini's shoulder, and she turned, scowling at me, green eyes in a pinched face under short black hair. I was the whole reason she was here, and she clearly wished I would go away. I would leave – I had no choice – but I deserved a goodbye, at least, didn't I? I touched my borrowed bracelet and put an exclusion field around us, a bubble of silence and privacy on the dance floor.

"I'm fading." I blinked, and even that was an effort. My eyes were leaden window shades, my breathing deeper with every passing moment, and there was a distant keening sound in my ears. I knew the signs of incipient exhaustion. They had excellent stimulants in that world, but even with my metabolic tweaks, staying awake for five days straight was about my limit.

"Zax… I don't… I'm sorry… I just…" I could have helped her, said what she was thinking so she didn't have to, but I stubbornly made her speak her own mind. "I like it here," she said finally. "I've made friends. I want to stay."

I liked her a little better for being so direct about it, and at least this way there was a sort of closure. My last companion before Laini, Winsome, had gotten lost in the depths of the non-Euclidean mansion where we landed, and I couldn't stay awake long enough to find them again. (Unless, I thought darkly, *they'd* abandoned me deliberately, too, and just wanted to avoid an awkward goodbye.) I couldn't blame Laini for wanting to stay here, either. She'd come from a world of hellish subterranean engines: the whole planet a slave-labor mining operation for insectile aliens, and this playground world of plenty was a heaven she could never have imagined in her old life – the one I rescued her from. We'd been together for forty-three worlds though, the longest I'd kept a companion since the Lector, and it hurt to see her choose this place over me. We didn't even get along that well, honestly; she was suspicious, quick to anger, and secretive – all reasonable traits for someone who'd grown up the way she did – but that didn't matter. For a little while, I'd woken up next to someone I could call a friend, and, in my life, that's the most precious thing there is.

She touched my cheek, which surprised me – we'd been intimate a few times, but only when she came to me in the night, and it was always rough and hot, never afterward discussed or acknowledged. She'd certainly never touched me with that kind of fondness. "I'm sorry, Zax," she said, and that surprised me even more, and then she kissed me, gently, which stunned me completely. Maybe a week in a place of peace and plenty, with its devotion to pleasure as a pillar of life, had softened her.

Or maybe she was just feeling the all-encompassing love-field brought on by some rather advanced club drugs.

"OK." I turned away so she wouldn't see the tears shining in my eyes and made my way across the dance floor, stumbling a little as lethargy further overtook me. I glanced back, once, and Laini was dancing again, having already forgotten me, no doubt. I tried to be happy for her, but it was hard to feel anything good for someone else in the midst of being sad for myself.

I opened up a cushioned rest pod and crawled inside. At least I'd fall asleep in a pleasant place. I curled myself around my backpack – stuffed with as many good drugs as I'd been able to discreetly pocket – and succumbed to the inevitable.

Here's the situation. Every time I fall asleep, I wake up in another universe. That started happening nearly three years and a thousand worlds ago, and I still don't know why, or what happens during the transition, while I'm asleep. Do I spend eight hours in slumber in some nowhere-place between realities, or do I transition instantaneously, and just *feel* like I got a good night's sleep? I wake up feeling rested, unless I took heavy drugs to knock myself out, and if I fall asleep injured, the wounds are always better than they should be when I wake up, if not fully healed. I inevitably sleep through the mechanism of a miracle, and that's just as frustrating as you might imagine.

I never have dreams anymore, but, sometimes, waking up is a lot like a nightmare.

After leaving Laini, I woke to flashing red lights and the sound of howling alarms. I automatically pressed the sound-dampening button on my bracelet, but it was just an inert loop of metal and plastic now that the network of the Dionysius Society was in another branch of the multiverse, so the shriek was unceasing.

I sat up, looking around for obvious threats – always a priority upon waking. I was in some kind of factory or industrial space, on a metal catwalk, near a ladder leading up, and a set of stairs leading down. I stood and looked over the metal railing to see gouts of steam, ranks of silvery cylinders stretching off in all directions, and humans (humanoids, anyway) racing around and waving their arms and shouting. One of the workers, if that's what they were, stumbled into contact with a steam cloud, and screamed as their arm melted away.

I'd be going up the ladder instead of down the stairs, then. I tightened my pack on my shoulders and scrambled up the rungs. Fortunately the hatch at the top was unlocked so I didn't have to use one of my dwindling supply of plasma keys. I climbed up onto the roof, and the hatch sealed shut after me.

I stood atop a mining or drilling platform, several hundred meters above a vast, dark ocean. The sun was either rising or setting, and everything was hazed in red. The air was smoky and vile, but breathable. I've never woken up in a world where the air was purely toxic, though sometimes I find myself in artificial habitats in otherwise uninhabitable places. My second companion, the Lector, theorized that I projected myself into numerous potential realities before coalescing in a branch of the multiverse where my consciousness could persist… but I've always been more interested in the practice of my affliction than the theory, and was just happy I'd survived this long.

The water far below was dark and wild, more viscous than most seas I've seen, as if thickened by sludge, and the waves slammed hard against the platform from all directions. Occasionally dark shapes broke the surface – giant eels, I thought at first, with stegosaurus spines, but then I glimpsed some greater form in the depths below, and realized the "serpents" were the appendages of a single creature.

The thing in the water wrapped a limb around one of the cranes that festooned the platform and pulled it down into the water with a terrific shriek of metal and a greasy splash, and the whole rig lurched in that direction. The creature grabbed more cranes at their bases and began to pull, trying to rip the whole platform down.

I'd seen enough. I try to save people when I can – I was trained, on the world of my birth, to solve conflicts and promote harmony – but there are limits. If anyone had burst through the hatch after me I'd have given them the option to escape this world, but there was no time to rescue anyone without losing myself. I fumbled in my pack and pulled out a stoppered test tube (my second-to-last) and a handkerchief. I was still bitter about the limitations of the pharmacopeia in the Dionysius Society. They had uppers, and dissociatives, and euphorics, and entheogens, and entactogens, but they didn't have any fast-acting sedatives. Who wanted to fall asleep and miss the party?

I yanked out the cork and poured the carefully measured tablespoon of liquid into the handkerchief, strapped my pack back onto my chest, and then lay down on the metal of the deck. The rig was already sloping noticeably toward the water, but not so much that I'd slide into the sea before I passed out. I hoped.

I pressed the soaked handkerchief to my nose and breathed deeply. A strong, sickly-sweet odor filled my nostrils, my head spun, everything got gray and fuzzy, and then that terrible world went away.

I woke sprawled underneath a tree, its branches heavy with unfamiliar apple-shaped fruit in an unlikely shade of blue. My head thudded like it always did when I woke after resorting to such anesthetic measures. I sat up against the trunk and did my threat assessment.

I was in an orchard of blue-apple trees, orderly rows stretching as far as I could see, and there were no sea monsters (or tree monsters) in evidence. The air smelled fresh and highly oxygenated, and the skies were a paler blue than the fruit, and cloudless.

I leaned back against the trunk and exhaled. My breath still smelled sweet from the anesthetic. There are sedatives that don't give me skull-shattering hangovers, but they also work more slowly. Sometimes I need to spin the wheel of worlds again fast, and in those cases, I resort to the hard stuff.

"Where did you come from?" a voice above me said. So much for my operational security. I looked up at a human perched on a large branch, looking down at me – apparently female, around my age, with big dark surprised eyes, skin a shade browner than the trees, and hair in a thousand braids.

"The ocean," I said, and the language I spoke was strange and harsh. Back home we had a simple, logical, constructed language, but these haphazard, organically developed languages are far more common in the multiverse. (That informality has infiltrated even my thoughts, and the way I write now would horrify my tutors.) Still, it was good to know the linguistic virus the Lector injected into me way back on World 85 still worked. For the first few months after the onset of my condition, before I met the Lector, I had only once visited a world where people spoke a language I remotely recognized. It's harrowing, waking up every day or three in an entirely alien place, where even if you find people, you can't understand them. (Not that my days now were much better. Laini had been grim company for most of our time together, but she had, at least, been a brief constant in my ever-changing world: someone who knew me for more than a day or two and then vanished into my past forever.)

"The sea-stead?" she asked. "The seaweed beds?"

"It was more a sort of... factory."

"I have never seen even once an ocean," she said, with a note of wistfulness. "I have never been off the farm." (Maybe that should be "The Farm.")

"It wasn't a very nice ocean. Are these fruit good to eat?" I was starving, and while I had some food in my pack, I tried to avoid depleting my rations whenever possible. I never knew when I'd hit a streak of barren or unpopulated worlds and have to dip into my supply.

"Of course! I can share some of my fraction with you. I am Minna. Senior grafter here, but this is my free half-day. What are you called?"

"Zax." Zaxony Dyad Euphony Delatree – given name, family name, earned name, sphere name, but none of that had meaning except in the Realm of Spheres and Harmonies, and I hadn't been there since I was twenty-two. I thought about the family, friends, and lovers I'd unwillingly left behind as seldom as possible, for the same reason I don't shove pointy sticks into any wounds I sustain. "I'm a... traveler."

"I did not know that was the name of a job." Minna looked at me very seriously. "Do the [unable to translate] send you to the different biomes to make sure all is right and well?"

I didn't hear the words "unable to translate," just slippery syllables. The Lector's world was techno-utopian, and occasionally there were concepts the linguistic virus he'd developed had a hard time parsing. Usually those concepts involved horrible nightmarish things. "Something like that."

"Tell me of the places you have seen!" Minna hung on my every word as much as she hung onto the branch.

I looked around the orchard. "Places with no trees at all," I said, "just rocks, but some of the rocks grow, like trees, and they shine. Places with just one big tree, and a city in the branches. Forests where no person had ever walked before me. Beaches with white or golden or black sand, or all three at once, the water warm or chilling or bubbling or even, once, alive. Mountains with air so clear and crisp you can see for hundreds of miles, and mountains where the fog never lifts and the inhabitants are all born blind. Cities so big you could walk all day and never reach the outskirts, full of temples and factories, towers and parks." I tried to focus on the good trips. I could have told Minna about places where the sun was a dying ruby, where people were just vessels for intelligent parasites, where the trees were carnivorous and ambulatory, but why frighten and confuse her?

"Really? So many places, all different? What a life, so full of wonders. You must be a rare lineage from heirloom stock."

"I don't know about that. Traveling is… it's like life, I guess. Sometimes it's wonderful, and sometimes it's terrible, and sometimes it's boring."

"That does not sound like life as I know it." Minna dropped down from the branch and landed beside me. She wore a jumpsuit dyed unevenly blue, and her hands were stained the same color. She'd plucked a fruit on the way down, and began cutting up the blue apple with a pretty silver knife. She handed me a thick wedge of fruit. It was blue all the way through. "Here you go. The fruit in this sector boosts your immunities. We are going to graft them to mood enhancers, to make the eaters feel good and be healthy too, but the [unable to translate] have not yet settled on which strains to use."

I grunted and took a bite. The flesh was crisp and sweet, and I gobbled it up and licked my fingers.

"Golly, you hungered." Minna handed me the rest of the fruit, and I chomped it down.

"Thank you for that. Do you live nearby?" I'd eaten, and now it would be nice to get under a roof. I'd been in too many places where terrible things came from the sky.

"I live on the Farm." Minna sounded confused that I'd even asked. "Did you want to see my room? Is that part of the inspection?"

Before I could answer – I was debating whether it was better to let Minna think I had special status here or not – a horrible buzzing, humming, clattering noise arose, and I shot to my feet and looked around. "What is that?"

"A harvester." Minna smiled. "Is this your first time on a farm? They might be loud and scary, I think, if you are new, but they mean you no harm."

A mechanical spider ten meters high rose up above the trees to my left, its body a silvery sphere, its countless arms whirling and spinning, some tipped with blades, others with jointed claws, plucking fruit and pruning back branches all at once, tossing blue apples and cut branches into a funnel on top of its body. The harvester came closer, its delicate segmented legs stepping over, around, and through the branches, moving fast. I snatched up my pack and backed away.

"Do not be afraid. The harvester has scanners, and it can tell workers from fruit."

I hesitated, but Minna seemed so unworried that I stood beside her as the spider scuttled down the rows toward us. The machine didn't seem to notice me at all, and it was almost past us when one of its lopping pincer arms reached out and severed my left arm just above the elbow.

Under the Tree Grafting • The Orchard of Worlds • The Debt of Sleep • A Remembrance • The Cullers Come

I fell, and everything went gray, but I bit my own tongue and willed myself to stay awake. If I passed out now, I might well bleed out wherever I woke, unless I happened to open my eyes in a trauma center, which wasn't likely. Here, at least, Minna might be able to do some first aid, make a tourniquet or something – farm people knew about that stuff, didn't they?

That all sounds so logical and deliberate, as I write it down after the fact. Actually I was screaming and bleeding and terrified. Minna said something my virus translated as "Gosh!" and then the pain at my elbow went away, replaced by spreading coolness. I turned my head, heavy as a cannonball, and saw Minna rubbing a cut piece of yellow fruit on my wound. My gaze drifted downward and I watched the bleeding end of my arm close over, new flesh growing across the wound in seconds. I was maimed, but I wouldn't bleed to death. I was dopey and vague, though, and Minna started to push something into my mouth, another piece of fruit. A sedative? I turned my head. "Can't sleep. Have to stay awake."

She paused. "Oh. Then... I can give you something that will take you far away from your body, without making you sleep. OK?"

"But sleeping *does* take me far away. Every time. Always." I was lightheaded from blood loss.

"Eat this, Zax." The slice of fruit she put in my mouth tasted like copper and clouds.

I'd done enough drugs on enough worlds to recognize Minna had given me a strong dissociative, but the thing about dissociatives is, when you're on them, you don't care about anything, so I didn't mind. Minna helped me stand and led me to a tree, then somehow *into* the tree – the trunk yawned open to admit us. We went down a wooden ramp, into a cozy cavern lit by bioluminescent fungus. The furniture seemed like dirt with soft moss growing on it, and Minna eased me onto a raised platform that could have been a bed or table. She muttered and bustled around, and did some stuff to my stump – ha, I was in a *tree* and I had a *stump* – but I was mostly just floating far away, my mind a balloon on a string only tenuously connected to my body.

After some unknowable interval, Minna helped me sit up and gave me a squishy bulb of juice to sip. Lucidity flooded back into me when I swallowed. I looked down at my arm. My *arm*. Hadn't I lost that arm? Oh. This was a different arm. It was brown, and there was a leaf growing on the thumb.

Minna plucked off the leaf, and it felt like having a long hair plucked from my eyebrow. "Move your fingers," she said.

My hand *looked* like my hand, but made of wood. I opened and closed the fingers, and they worked fine. I ran the fingers across the table. There was sensation, but dulled, like I was wearing thick mittens. "I can feel."

"The feeling should get better when the nerves have time to get used to each other." Minna sighed. "I am sorry it looks like an arm made of wood and not an arm made of you. I do not have the right material to make it look better here. You could go get… but no." Minna took a step away from me when I sat up.

"What do you mean?" I said.

Minna shook her head. "You are an impossible thing. You

cannot be here. I inspected you." She rubbed the back of her neck. "You do not have a chit. That is why the harvester lopped you. It scanned you, but there was nothing to scan, so it did not know you were a person."

"What kind of chip?"

"A *chit*. Everyone has a chit, right here, to keep them in their right place and track the outstanding debt owed to [unable to translate]!"

"Everyone? What if you pay off your debt?"

Minna shook her head. "It never goes down, only up, maybe flat if you work fast enough. You incur more debt just by breathing [unable to translate]'s air. My chit has eleven thousand outstanding. I inherited my mother's debt when she died, and my children will inherit mine in their turn."

I shuddered. Indentured servitude. Slavery, really. Then I blinked. "Did you say you have children?" I looked around her small dwelling and saw no sign of them.

She nodded, smiling faintly. "Two. They ripened long ago, and were assigned to a sea-stead. I had hoped they would remain here, but there were losses in an aquatic biome during a volcanic event, and because my line is good at adapting, my sons were repurposed and re-assigned." She fluttered her hands at the side of her neck and I looked at her blankly. "They have gills now. When you said you had come from the ocean, I wondered if you knew them..." She sighed. "It was foolishness."

I radically revised my estimate of Minna's age and experience. Her seeming innocence was due to isolation, I realized, and not youth. I'd been to worlds where centenarians looked like teenagers, where the old could take a pill to restore them to youth and allow them to grow up all over again, where bodies could be changed as easily as shirts, but I still fell prey to my own assumptions. The Lector called it "cultural programming."

"How old are you, Minna?"

"This will be my eighty-third harvest."

"How many harvests in a year?"

"What is a year?" She cocked her head curiously.

"It's… nothing. A measure of time from another place. What about the father?" This cavern definitely looked like singles accommodation to me.

"The paternal contribution came from a rootstock engineer in a frost biome, or so I was told," she said. "We were a good genetic combination."

"Ah. Right. I see."

She put her hand on the back of my neck. "You do not have a chit." Her voice was full of fear and wonder. "*Everyone* has a chit."

"You've never been off the Farm, though, Minna. I come from a place where things are different."

"Not just different. Impossible." Minna shook her head, braids whipping around. "Even if you are some… outsider… there is no way onto the Farm without a chit. The entire perimeter is one big scanner. No one can enter this biome without authorization."

"Maybe I… parachuted in."

"Through the dome?"

Ah. I hadn't realized there was a dome. Invisible dome, or maybe one decorated with the illusion of a sun and sky. "OK. Truth time." Minna had saved my life, so I owed her that much, even if she wouldn't believe me. "When I said I was a traveler, Minna… do you know what a multiverse is?"

"A… song with lots of verses?"

I smiled. "No, it's like… Imagine the universe is a tree. When the universe was born, it just had a single central trunk. But as time went on, the universe grew branches, and those branches grew more branches, and so on, and all those branches bore fruit. Now imagine each fruit at the end of each branch is a whole different world. Not just a different planet, but an entirely separate universe. Some worlds are similar, and some are different, like… aren't there trees that can grow more than one kind of fruit, pears and apples both at once?" I'd seen trees like that before. I didn't know if that was super-science or just agriculture, but in this world, either seemed likely.

Minna nodded, frowning.

"Right. So... I can travel from branch to branch in the tree of worlds, sampling all the different fruit. And... occasionally I jump from the end of one branch to another tree entirely, one with totally different kinds of fruit. Like a squirrel."

"What is a squirrel?"

"My metaphor might be breaking down," I said. "My point is, I don't travel to different, whatever you said, biomes, in this world. I travel between worlds. I never know where I'll end up. This time, I landed here, with you. I don't know what the Farm is, I don't know what the–" here I reproduced the "unable to translate" sound as best I could, "–is or are, and I'm really just passing through."

I've gotten a lot of reactions to my story over my travels, usually disbelief or mockery, but a few reacted like Minna did: with a look of envy and desire. "You mean, you can just... leave? Without permission or cause?"

"I can... but I've never been back to any world I've visited before. Once I go, it's gone forever. I can't choose where I end up, either. I go to new worlds at random, or at least, I haven't found a pattern or any way to steer. Some worlds are nice, some are boring, and some are terrible and dangerous."

"But there is always another world? Another *choice*?"

"Choice might be the wrong word. I travel whenever I fall asleep. Even if I find a place I like, I can't stay there, because I always fall asleep eventually."

"We have fruit that lets us stay up working for four nights in a row, but then we have to sleep for almost two," Minna said. "The debt of sleep must be repaid. If you travel when you sleep... Forgive me, Zax, but are you sure the worlds you visit aren't dreams?"

That had been the Lector's first theory, not definitely disproven for him until I took him with me to another branch. "If they are, this is a dream too."

"I am not a dream." Minna was very solemn. "When you sleep, you will disappear from this place?"

I nodded.

"If this is true, you should sleep soon, before the cullers come."

"Uh. What are the cullers?"

Minna shrugged. "They come for sick trees, or sick workers, or unauthorized offspring. I assume they will come for an intruder, though we have never had one before. The harvester has gone back to the center by now, and they will have your arm in their hopper, and they will not find a match to your genome in the database, if you really are a traveler from branch to branch. They will send a culler for you. And for me, since I helped you." Minna looked down, tears welling in their eyes. "I am not rotten yet, but they will cull me just the same. If I had scanned you first, and seen you had no chit, I would have known I shouldn't heal you, but… I think I would have helped you anyway. Grafters are from the sect of cultivators, after all, and we do not kill what can be made healthy and saved. The cullers are less merciful."

I clenched my new hand into a fist. "You'll die?"

"I will be processed and fed to the trees. This is as it should be. I live for the trees, so I will die for them. Sleep, Zax. Sleep and jump to a new branch in this orchard of worlds, if you can."

"Minna, you can come with me."

"What?" Her eyes widened, shining.

"You can't ever come back, never see your sons again, but if you think they'll kill you anyway… I can't let you die just for helping me. If I hold you in my arms when I fall asleep, you'll come with me. There's a sort of… bubble, or aura, and it envelops me, and anyone I'm touching, and carries them along. Come with me and we'll go somewhere…" I couldn't say "safe," necessarily. "Else."

Soil showered down from the ceiling, accompanied by a grinding, buzzing noise. Minna looked up. "The cullers."

Crap. I fumbled in my bag. I only had one vial of knockout juice left, not enough for two, and I knew that, but I looked deeper in the pack anyway, desperate. "I can't… I can't put us both to sleep fast, Minna."

"I have to sleep, too, Zax? To enter your dream?"

The first time I took someone with me, on World 40, it was an accident. It was a world heartbreakingly similar to my own, the closest I've come to a place that was like mine, so much so that at first I thought I'd made my way home. People spoke a language that was almost the same as mine, at least close enough for me to understand and make myself understood. Like my home, the Realm of Spheres and Harmonies, that world was a place of gleaming spires and plenty, and I landed in a beautiful woman's back yard. She was the first person I'd been able to talk to in over a month, and I spilled out my story to her, and she believed me, because she'd seen me flicker into existence from nothing.

Her name was Ana. She was a creator of kinetic sculptures and a scientist of motion, and we promptly fell in love. I spent two days in her world – two days of bliss and conversation and sex, and I was so thrilled and energized by our connection that it was easy to stay awake that long. We knew our time was limited, but we made the most of every second.

I fell asleep holding Ana in my arms. She stayed awake. She'd *planned* to stay awake, so she could watch me disappear, but instead, she traveled with me.

When we woke, she scratched my face and jumped to her feet, screaming about holes in the sky, and things pushing through – *worms, worms, worms in the world*, she said. She saw something during our transition, but I don't know what. Before I could try to talk to her or calm her down, she ran away, racing into the alleys of a silent gray city that was all towers without any visible windows or doors. I looked for Ana, calling her name until I lost my voice, searching until I passed out from exhaustion and woke up somewhere new.

After that horror, I vowed to never take anyone with me again… until the Lector convinced me to try it with him sleeping. Being unconscious, it seemed, was the secret to making the journey safely.

I nodded. "You need to sleep too, yes, but there's no time."

Minna opened a chest with moss growing on the lid. "I saw the cullers come for my mother, when she got sick. Sometimes I have bad dreams about that. So for my fraction, I always take a few..." Minna lifted out a bag woven of leaves, and shook a handful of small black berries onto her hand. "These kill waking, and swiftly."

The buzzing increased outside, and more soil sifted down on us. "Grab what you need, clothes, tools, anything, and come here." I held out my arms. I hadn't been able to save anyone on the platform in that dark ocean, but I could save Minna from dying for the crime of helping me.

Minna picked up a larger bag and shoved things that looked like twigs and bulbs and seedpods into it, then came to me, climbing up onto the soft platform. "We'll be OK," I said. I took one of the berries in my hand and wrapped my arms around her.

"I have had no one to hold me since my mother died, and no one to hold since my sons ripened," she said. "It will be nice to die being held." She didn't have much confidence in my plan, apparently, but she popped a berry into her mouth, and I bit into mine.

The roof of Minna's room started to fall in, and metal spines poked through, hooked and questing. I thought the berry wouldn't work in time, but then sleep came down like a hammer blow.

ANGRY
ROBOT

TRISTAN PALMGREN
Quietus

TRISTAN PALMGREN
Author of QUIETUS
Terminus

THE TIDES OF WAR
JAMES A. MOORE
THE LAST
SACRIFICE

THE TIDES OF WAR
JAMES A. MOORE
FALLEN
GODS

THE TIDES OF WAR
JAMES A MOORE
GATES OF THE
DEAD

LAUREN C. TEFFEAU
CONNECT • ENCRYPT • CONSPIRE
IMPLANTED

SEAN GRIGSBY
FORGOTTEN
LIGHT
SMOKE EATERS

"Eminently readable." – AUREALIS
AMANDA BRIDGEMAN
THE SUBJUGATE
CRIME IS OVER

SMOKE
EATERS
SEAN GRIGSBY

ASH
KICKERS
SEAN GRIGSBY

THE HEART OF
THE CIRCLE
KEREN LANDSMAN

SHROUDED
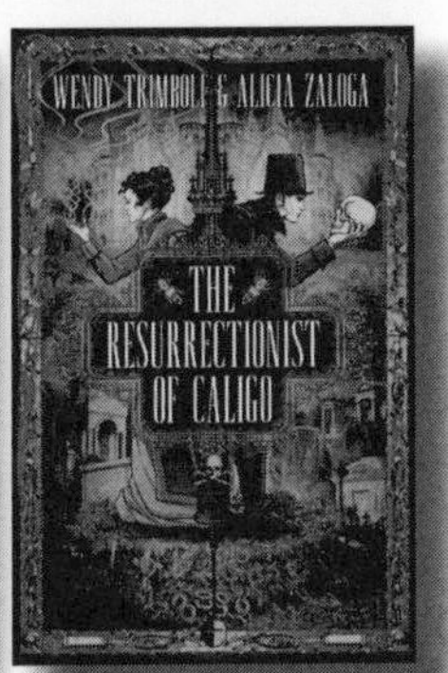
WENDY TRIMBOLI & ALICIA ZALOGA
THE
RESURRECTIONIST
OF CALIGO

TYLER
HAYES
THE
IMAGINARY
CORPSE

CHRISTOPHER HINZ
DUCHAMP
VERSUS
EINSTEIN
ETAN ILFELD

THE
OUTSIDE
ADA HOFFMANN

THE GALACTIC COLD WAR
THE
BAYERN
AGENDA
DAN MOREN